Time Torn

by

Jeanie R. Davis

The Somerset Series, Book 3

Time Torn

Cover Art by *Kim Mendoza*

The Wild Rose Press, Inc.
PO Box 708
Adams Basin, NY 14410-0708
Visit us at www.thewildrosepress.com

Publishing History
First Edition, 2021
Trade Paperback ISBN 978-1-5092-3576-6
Digital ISBN 978-1-5092-3577-3

The Somerset Series, Book 3
Published in the United States of America

Hudson blinked, raising a hand to shield his eyes. London hadn't been so bright, especially indoors. He *was* inside, was he not? The faint aroma of tea hung in the air, but nothing else felt familiar in the least. "Where—where am I?" And who had said his name? Still squinting, his eyes darted from one odd contraption to the next. Warm air hit his neck, coming from somewhere above. He glanced up to discover the cause of it, but only saw a metal grate on the ceiling.

"Hudson! It is I, Sarah."

He jolted in response to the woman's voice. It couldn't be Sarah. Not here in London. Eyes fully adjusted now, he stared hard into the girl's face. A frisson of electricity shot through his veins at the sight of her. "Sarah…is it truly you?" He reached out to touch her, then jerked his hand back, fearing something unearthly was happening to him—for without doubt she was not of this world. "Are you a ghost, a specter, sent to reprimand me for my misdeeds?" He stared intensely into her face. "Or perhaps I am dreaming. Surely, you cannot be real. I have searched for seven long years."

Her eyes teared up. "I am real, Hudson. You are no longer in London—or even in the nineteenth century." She stepped toward him, lifting her arms, then halted, dropping them to her sides. Her brow lowered and her lips—her beautiful, rosy lips—turned down.

"What is it? Why did you pause? If I am no longer in London, where am I?" If she were truly real, Hudson longed for Sarah to not only reach for him, but take him in her arms, prove she existed in the flesh, not just his dreams.

Dedication

In memory of our good friend Carter. I ended this book
with the bang he has wanted since book one of the
series. Wish he were here to read it.

Chapter One

Present day Colorado

Sarah Somerset emptied a bottle of sleeping pills into her hand, then placed the vacant container on her nightstand. If she *could not* travel back in time, she *would not* travel forward.

Father's haunting words still reverberated through her. "You act like a trollop, throwing yourself at that boy. You are no longer his equal. When my status fell, yours did, as well. Hudson will soon become Earl of Alleyne and have his pick of young debutantes."

Not her first attempt to end her life, but it would be her last. Soon she'd be with Hudson in immortality. Her attempt to plunge a dagger into her heart years before pierced through her brain. *And because I am weak, the blade left little more than an ugly pink scar.* Self-loathing enshrouded her like a tomb. Perhaps Father had been correct; her childhood sweetheart would reject her even if she had remained in the nineteenth century. However, in Hudson's letters, she found hope—*a fruitless hope since we live centuries apart.*

She'd refused to believe Father's venomous barbs. Hudson had assured her he could never love another. *But Father destroyed all hope when he irreversibly severed our connection, forcing our family onto that ungodly time-traveling device, propelling us forward*

1

two hundred years into an uncertain future in America.
All to satisfy his greed. Her heart spasmed at the
memory. But in the back of her mind, she suspected
Father had derived a perverse satisfaction from her
unhappiness. Resentment erupted like a volcano in her
gut, and she squeezed the tiny pills in her hand.

Her journal lay open beside her on the bed. She
perused it once more, ensuring her sentiments rang
clear.

Dearest Family,

*After heeding your well-intentioned counsel—
attending university, working at the market, and such—
I still find I can no longer abide in this futuristic world
into which Father has thrust us. Interacting with people
and their unanswerable questions overwhelms me. 'Tis
difficult to play the part of a twenty-first century
maiden. For she I am not, and I fear all whom I
encounter ascertain my pretense. I long to be with
Hudson. And because we are now living two centuries
in the future, he is without doubt dwelling in paradise. I
love you, but I cannot love this life I did not choose.
Please forgive me. I go to abide with Hudson now in the
heavens above.*

Sarah's hopeless circumstances were nobody's
fault but Father's. His cruelty toward her, coupled with
his actions, had caused irreparable damage.

"Cease your incessant brooding, Sarah." Father had
sneered. "You are just a chit. Females will never
amount to anything beyond bearing offspring in any
century."

His words had stung worse than his lashings.
Before becoming a drunk and a failure to his peers, had
Sarah not been his little bluebell, nicknamed for her

intense eye color? And once dubbed his raven-haired princess? Memories of such compliments falling from Father's lips had become faint—out of her reach.

Tears gathered in her eyes.

This ends now! With too much force, she grabbed a glass of water from her nightstand, causing it to drip onto a bundle of letters nestled in her lap. Letters from Hudson. "No!" She set the cup and pills down and sprang to her feet. Locating a cloth to dry her precious epistles, she dabbed at the paper, then breathed a sigh of relief—only one letter was marred. It was illogical to care about the running ink on a missive she'd not see after tonight, yet her heart could not bear any ruin to the last vestiges of her lost love.

Perhaps I will read them one final time. She took meticulous care ordering the jumble of papers. Each night before bed since her brother Joshua had delivered them to her, she'd read them, savoring Hudson's words. "It has been months, and I am no closer to finding my way back to you now than I was then. I am sorry I left, Hudson. We will meet again soon in the world beyond." She kissed the note in her hand, then began to read.

Dearest Sarah,

I found no letter from you in the tree hollow today. Then I heard reports of your father committing a jewelry heist—even murder. Oh, my dear Sarah, how I long to console you. Wherever your father has carried you, I will find and rescue you. We are destined to be together forever.

All my love,
Hudson

She read several more letters, Hudson's concern for her increasing in each. His determination to find and protect her intensified, as well. *Little did he know I was far beyond his reach—anyone's reach but Father's.* She fought back a sob.

Hudson's final missive, dated the third of August 1814, gave her pause, springing ideas into her mind she had never before considered.

Sarah, if you do not hear from me in the coming months, it is because I have hired a Bow Street Runner to help locate you. This will require my absence from London for what may become an extended period. I shall begin my search in the country, at Somerset Manor—the home of your youth. Although the runner assures me the area has been thoroughly scoured, I shan't leave any stone unturned. If my search takes me off to the continent, it will be months before I am able to write again. However, that your brother has not collected my letters for several fortnights tells me that, rather than fearing you shall miss my letters, I should fear for your safety. I'll stop at nothing, Sarah. I will find you.

He said he'd stop at nothing, yet Sarah had *done* nothing except pine for him. *I haven't even attempted to go to him when the traveling machine sits in my basement.* Glancing at the handful of pills she'd dropped onto her nightstand, she shook her head, eyes burning with unshed tears. *Not yet. I haven't tried everything.* Both of her brothers had commandeered the time-traveling device. She'd pleaded with Christopher to take her back to nineteenth century London to be with Hudson, but he had adamantly refused, claiming it was far too dangerous to return to the place Father had committed his original heist and murder.

She paced the room, needing focus. Her hands fluttered at her sides. The idea of surprising Hudson in life, rather than searching for him in death, held more appeal.

Still, if anyone understood the peril of being recognized in London, it was Christopher. He'd risked his life attempting to return Father's purloined jewels. *But I had spent so little time mingling with society when I lived there, surely I'd not be known.*

She stopped pacing, squared her shoulders, and peered down at a miniature of Hudson propped on her nightstand. *If my brothers refuse to take me to you, I shall puzzle out the mystifying device myself.* She smiled and suppressed a shout that rose from her heart to her throat.

Retrieving a satchel from her closet, she packed it with a few necessary items and crept down the stairs. Peering into the darkness, she fumbled her way to the bookroom, where the trapdoor to Father's secret lab hid under the rug. A surge of excitement pulsed through her body as she descended the ladder. Hudson was mere hours away.

Although it had been months since the machine had been employed, a chemical odor still hung in the air. Chemicals…she knew nothing about them. Music and art were her strengths, not science and mathematics. But both Christopher and Josh had deciphered Father's notes, and if she wished to be with Hudson, she must, too.

She made her way past the original machine, which had brought her family in a terrifying rush through time in 1814. The large, disc-shaped piece of crude metal still made her skin crawl. Next, she came to the modern version of the disc—much more sleek and smaller in size. It shone like something bright and good, betraying its creator's evil intentions. Pausing for a moment, she deliberated. With her satchel, this might be the right option for her journey through time, as it had been fitted with a storage compartment. She lifted it and staggered. Though constructed of a light metal alloy, the disc was still too heavy for her. The third option, a time-traveling vest would be less cumbersome, especially traveling solo, and she could carry her bag.

She freed the vest from its hanger and analyzed the vials and control panel inside the large front pocket, wishing it came with instructions. After turning on the desk lamp, she located Father's book of chemical compound mixtures. She let out a deep sigh. The words and numbers looked like a foreign language. She stared at the formulas until they began to swim on the page. *This will not do.* Standing, she took a turn about the room to clear her head, then reclaimed her seat and the book. Three chemicals appeared repeatedly in the notes. She could do this. However, pairing the labeled beakers to the chemicals in the book proved to be more difficult than she'd imagined, as Father must have had his own abbreviated labeling system. *I wish I'd taken a chemistry class,* she thought for the tenth time tonight.

Five minutes turned to fifteen before she determined she had the correct substances. Now for the amounts of each. Fractions and arithmetic had her wracking her brain.

An hour later, she was no closer to knowing the answer. She rubbed her tired eyes and slammed her fist on the table. Out of desperation, she poured equal parts of each until the vial was full.

She turned one knob back two hundred and seven years and the other to LE, which she assumed meant London, England.

"Hudson, I am coming."

Chapter Two

London 1821

Hudson Drake stumbled through the door of his London townhouse, heart pounding in his ears. He'd cut it too close at the tables tonight, nearly losing everything. A series of heavy breaths huffed out in quick succession. After having been accused of cheating, he'd landed in a skirmish, setting the room in commotion. Most of the men, too foxed to know what they were fighting for, had made it easy for Hudson to slip out when an opening presented itself. He wiped beads of perspiration from his forehead.

"She is not coming back."

Hudson jumped at his mother's voice. "Mum? You startled me. It is nearly dawn. Why are you awake?"

"I should ask you the same question."

He groped through the black room until locating his mother. "Why are you sitting in the dark?" He lit the nearest lamp, pulled up a chair, then glanced at her. Her drooping, bloodshot eyes told him more than he wished to hear. Had she waited up just to reprimand him? "You do realize I am a grown man. I no longer need my mum's permission to leave the house." Saying such a thing was risky. Mother often spoke of moving into the dower house. "That's where dowagers live," she'd reasoned. But he wasn't married and had no desire to occupy the large manor alone.

"I only wish to talk, Hudson, not reprimand. You sleep all morning, leave before I know you've risen, then return long after I have retired for the night. We have always been close, especially since your father's passing." Her voice hitched. She paused, closing her eyes for a moment. After letting out a long sigh, she motioned to a teapot on the table between them. "Cook brewed us tea." She filled a cup and set it before him. "It has cooled considerably but might help you relax."

Hudson gulped the soothing tea, hoping it would mask the smell of liquor on his breath. "What did you say before"—he shrugged—"about someone not coming back?"

"I have been waiting up for you, which has given me ample time to think." She angled her head, her gaze deep and penetrating. "I do believe I have discovered the reason you are living life so recklessly. 'Tis Sarah."

A powerful jolt brought Hudson to his senses. "S—Sarah?" He glanced toward the door. Sarah was not up for discussion—even with Mother.

"I know you think she will return, but it has been over seven years. Son, your father has been gone for nearly two years now. His upstanding reputation as the Earl of Alleyne is beginning"—her voice softened—"to fade."

"With me at the helm." Hudson knew the truth of the matter. Mother's sad eyes reflected disappointment each time she looked at him.

"I did not say that."

"You didn't have to." He expelled a long breath. "I know I have not met Parliament's expectations."

Worse, he hadn't met Mother's expectations. Now that Sarah had disappeared from his life, she was the only person he cared to please.

"But you could. Your potential did not leave with Sarah."

He winced at the word "leave." Sarah hadn't left him—her father had spirited her away. He was certain of it. "Sarah will be back once she extracts herself from her ogre of a father."

"Back from where? She's not left you any indication or clues. You spent six months searching the continent for her and seven years pining. She's likely de—"

"No!" Hudson shot to his feet. "Sarah is not dead!" His fingers trembled. He curled them into balls, then paced the dark room, forcing the image of Sarah suffering or dying from his mind. He reclaimed his seat. "Forgive me." Tilting his head, he peered into Mother's troubled eyes. "May I ask you a question?"

She let out a humph. "Have I ever kept secrets from you, son?"

He shook his head. She had been his confidante for as long as he could recall. Other men stopped confiding in their mums soon after outgrowing their short pants. Not Hudson. On occasion his friends would jibe him for it, then turn around and plead for Mother's navigation through their own rocky journeys where women were concerned.

"What is your question?"

She pulled him from his musings. "I have wondered why, over the years, you have never expressed disapproval of Sarah. Everyone else, including Father—before he died—warned me away from her, saying she is no longer my equal and I would do well to forget her, find a more appropriate lady to wed. I am not blind to what became of her family, but that doesn't change my sentiments toward her." He sipped his tea before raising his gaze to meet Mother's.

"Son, you know I have always adored Sarah. I'd not have loved her more had she been my own. Watching the two of you grow up…" Mother smiled and closed her eyes. "'Twas as if together you two made a whole person—you completed each other. Time has cruelly torn her away from you, leaving gaping wounds in its path. I fear you have not only lost the woman you love, you have lost part of yourself." A tear slipped down her cheek.

A painful lump formed in Hudson's throat. It had been a mistake to tread down this path.

Mother wiped her eyes. "Sarah was one of the most generous, loving people I have ever known—much like her mother, Beatrice, my dearest friend. I do so miss Bea." Her voice turned wistful. "How I longed for her when your father died." She sniffed.

Hudson's own heart quivered as he recalled Father's drawn-out disease and eventual death. He had prayed most earnestly for Sarah's return through such a dark and lonely time.

"And her elder brother, Christopher. What a man of fine character. Opposite in the extreme to Benjamin Somerset." She shook her head. "Perhaps the entire family has fled to a distant place—India, or more likely, America." She sipped her tea, a faraway look in her eyes. "I hope Christopher finds someone worthy of his affection. His father has not made it easy for his children to form suitable matches, were they ever to return to London." Her voice had taken on a bitter edge. She huffed out a breath. "But, Hudson, I could never find fault with Sarah. Her father's sins belong to him alone. Nothing would please me more than to see her walk through that door right now." She tilted her head toward the parlor's entry. "Perhaps I am alone in my way of thinking, but no one has ever made your brown eyes sparkle as did Sarah Somerset."

Hudson swallowed down the rising emotion. Why didn't all of society see things as he and Mother did?

She put her hand on his shoulder. "That is one reason you need to spend less time in public houses and at gaming tables. What would Sarah think of you, were she ever to find out how you spend your days?"

A punch to his gut would have hurt less than his mother's searing words. He shoved the delicate teacup onto the saucer, causing liquid to slurp over the edge. "I suppose we shall never know, because, as you said, Sarah is not coming back."

Standing abruptly, he straightened his cravat, then aimed for the front door. "I need a drink."

Chapter Three

"Sarah!" A strong arm yanked the vest from Sarah's shuddering frame. "What are you doing?"

She whipped around. "Josh! Why are you down here?" She stomped her foot, angry she hadn't yet pushed the transport button.

"Why am *I* here? Why are *you* here? You don't even know how to operate this machine." He held the vest aloft. "What chemicals did you put in the vial? Where do you think you are going?"

Joshua's questions struck like hurling daggers, ripping through her already fragile spirit. Hot tears burned her eyes. Josh didn't need to know her destination. He didn't need to know anything. He was her younger brother, not her parent. She grabbed at the vest, but he held it away.

Sniffing the contents of the vial, he frowned. "This isn't right—there is far too much methanol in here." He looked up at her, his face pale. "If you had pressed the transport button, you would have blown up! And possibly taken down the house, as well."

The firm tone of his voice told her he wasn't exaggerating—she'd made a brash judgment that could have destroyed her innocent family.

She had been jittery from nervous anxiety before Josh had found her, and now the blood drained from her head and the room spun. Her knees buckled, but she was able to stumble to the desk chair before losing her balance. She'd been reckless. *And I am too old to be falling into a swoon like a spoiled debutante.* Chemical odors wafting through the air were not helping her lack of focus. Pinching the bridge of her nose, she willed the turbulence in her head to calm.

Josh knelt beside her. "Please, Sarah, can we talk about this? I know you have put forth a great effort to adjust to the changes Father put us through, but you really didn't give your job at the market long before giving it up. Granted, Pueblo is small, and I know so many curious customers and their questions—especially about Father—were overwhelming. And school…" He shrugged. "You must admit you have caught the eye of several men, but you have rebuffed them all."

"Josh, courting doesn't even exist in this day and age!" Her emotions had risen so near the surface, she worried she'd either fall apart or rip Josh apart, which he didn't deserve. After all, he'd just saved her from making a deadly mistake. She swallowed. "There is nothing I can tell you that I haven't said before. I have asked you and Christopher—pleaded and begged—for your help with Hudson, only to be pushed aside. Ignored." She had taken everyone's advice and suggestions. Everyone's.

She was weak. She didn't need to be told that by her younger brother.

In London things had been different—*she* had been different. Friends had called on her daily. And her future—being at Hudson's side with their children to rear—was steady and secure. She loathed the person she'd become. As for possible suitors in this era, she had no hope of finding a man who wished to know her before pressing for physical affection. Her old-fashioned ideals were a thing of the past. *At twenty-two I would be considered a spinster where I came from.* She missed her life in the nineteenth century. She sorely missed Hudson.

"You think Chris and I have ignored you?" Josh's voice echoed through her senses. His question sounded more like an accusation.

"Yes!" Her voice rose as sparks flamed in her chest. "And I won't stand for it any longer." The resolve she had lost earlier returned as she found energy strengthening her limbs. "I must be with Hudson. I do not belong in this time. You have said I will eventually adjust, but it has been seven years, Josh. Seven years! And I am no closer to adjusting now than I was when we first arrived in the twenty-first century."

As she spoke, Joshua's face contorted, displaying a range of emotions. Anger? Confusion? Surprise? She didn't know, but she wouldn't be pushed aside one more time. He opened his mouth to speak, but now tilted his head. As he expelled a breath, his expression changed to condescending. "Sarah, we've all made sacrifices—"

"Wrong answer, Josh!" A mix of determination and anger ignited her. She stood strong and tugged the vest out of his hands as she jabbed her finger in the air. "Now either help me get the chemicals right, or risk getting blown up beside me."

Josh plucked the controls pouch from the vest pocket before she could stop him and held it away, then read the settings on the dials. His lips moved silently as his eyebrows lowered. "Sarah, do you realize that returning to London at the same time we disappeared would put your life in danger? Did you learn nothing from Christopher's experience?"

Gritting her teeth while she let Joshua's logic sink in, she reflected on the events of the previous year. Christopher had nearly died in a nineteenth century prison. He, Josh, and her sister-in-law Arianna had barely escaped with their lives. Why did she think she would fare any better than they had? Even Hudson couldn't shield her from Father's crimes, should she be recognized.

Her arm dropped to her side as her determination crumbled into bits. Tears splashed down her cheeks, and she gulped to keep from wailing.

She couldn't stay, and she couldn't go.

Despair closed around her like a heavy cloak, and she sank to the ground under the weight of it. "I just want to die."

"What?"

"Go away, Josh." Her voice—devoid of hope, devoid of life—was just above a whisper. Darkness filled her empty soul. Loneliness consumed her—and she embraced it. *Take me away from here. Let me disappear into nothingness.* Exhausted from the fight for love—the fight for Hudson—she closed her eyes and tried to let go of her existence.

"Sarah. Sarah." Moisture hit her face.

She opened her eyes to see Joshua kneeling down beside her, tears streaming down his cheeks.

"Please, Sarah, do not say such things—even though you are distraught." His voice hitched.

Her fractured heart cracked further to see the pain she was causing her brother. "You cannot force me to stay where I have no purpose, no love." The words came out in a sob.

"What do you mean no love? We all love you."

She grasped Joshua's wrists and looked into his bloodshot eyes. "My love for Hudson is real. My pain is real. My loss is real. But no one understands. I am utterly alone in this world." All air left her lungs, and she released his arms and let her head drop.

"Let me help you, Sarah."

Josh's warm hand rested on her shoulder. His offer to help was sincere—she knew it. She and Josh had formed an unbreakable bond since they'd been living in the future. Being held hostage by Father in their own home, centuries apart from anything familiar, had linked them together. They had endured unimaginable cruelty at the hands of their father. *And dear Mother suffered, too. I cannot hurt her.*

Another tear slipped down her cheek. Thank goodness for Christopher. He and his wife Arianna had literally freed them from Benjamin Somerset's cruel dominion…Yet Sarah's purpose for living still evaded her, and short of giving her the power to travel through time, she did not see how Josh could help.

"Please, Sarah," Joshua's voice was infused with emotion, "give me a week. I vow I will form a solution, or at least a compromise. Promise me you won't do anything rash."

"My desire was never to harm anyone, Josh. Not even myself." She sniffed. "I only thought to find Hudson—either in the past or in the great hereafter."

"But, Sarah, do you believe Hudson never married in all his years?"

A shock pulsed through her body. When she had determined to transport back to 1814, she imagined she'd find Hudson right where she'd left him, but the gap in time changed everything. A scenario she hadn't considered. Throughout their childhood, until the day she had vanished from existence, she and Hudson had pledged themselves to each other—their love was eternal. However, having been gone for seven years, Hudson might have assumed the worst and wed another. He, after all, as heir to an earldom, was bound by duty to marry and father a son to inherit his title.

Pain pierced through her already tattered heart. In such a case, Hudson would not be searching for her in the afterlife; rather, he'd be spending it with his earthly wife—someone else. She gasped. "Not me," escaped her trembling lips.

"What?" Josh reached out to her again.

"I must get to him before it's too late." Her breath came out in pants. "It might be too late now, but I must know, and so must he! Hudson needs to learn I am alive and have not forgotten him. Help me, Josh, please. I need you to deliver a note to the tree hollow for me." A frenzy of emotions caused her an adrenaline rush. She rose to her feet and began to pace, twisting her fingers together. She bit down on her lip to stop it from quivering.

"Calm yourself, Sarah." He placed the chemical-filled vial on a shelf away from her. "Your energy alone might cause an explosion." He half smirked, but worry settled in his eyes.

"One trip to the past. It doesn't have to be to 1814—like you said, that time is too dangerous. Just make it two centuries—straight there and back. Leave him a letter."

"And how will you know if he receives your letter?"

She tapped her chin. "Perhaps you should find a courier instead of using our tree. We cannot leave anything to chance. Hudson *must* receive the letter. Please, Josh. It would afford me so much comfort if you'd do that for me. If he has moved on with his life, I promise to improve my efforts to adjust to this wretched century." Tears welled in her eyes again. She needed Hudson to know she hadn't disappeared without so much as a thought about him. She loved him.

Josh ran his fingers through his hair and exhaled a heavy breath. "Very well. Write your note, and I shall deliver it tomorrow. However, I must travel by night. I'll not risk being seen, even by a courier. After my experience traveling back to the past, I am not ashamed to admit my fear of being caught and trapped there again. I shall leave your letter in the tree hollow, then return a night or two later to see if it has been retrieved."

Chapter Four

"Oomph!" Hudson rolled onto a gravel trail into weeds. Dust sprayed up from wagon wheels, stinging his eyes. In the dark, he had no idea where he was—purgatory, if Charlie and his thugs had had their way.

"And stay away from the tables!" a man yelled from the landau.

Instinctively, Hudson groped his coat pocket. Yes, it still bulged with coins, along with the deed to Charlie's country manor. Lord Charles Finley, Earl of Rovenal—a grand title for a poor card player—what a sore loser. Not much of a gentleman at all, dumping him in the middle of nowhere. "If you are going to bet big, be prepared to lose big!" he hollered as he pulled himself to a sitting position. *It isn't my fault Lady Luck is on my side.* Standing and dusting off his clothes, he shook his head to clear it, wondering if he'd be this lucky if he ever played cards sober.

A horse nickered nearby. Where there was livestock, there was water. A good dunking would sharpen his thinking. Without it, he had little hope of discovering where he'd been discarded, nor find his way home.

After plunging his head in the water trough, he slicked his hair back and replaced his hat. The cold night air aided in repairing his focus, as well. A church bell tolled—sort of. The chimes began with clear tones only to end in a wretched clanging sound. Hudson smiled. "Ahh…Charlie did not count on my familiarity with London's east end. Sarah once lived here. She attended that church. For once I am grateful those bells were never fixed."

He began the long trek home. Once he drew nearer the city proper, he could hail a hackney cab.

An hour later, he stumbled up the drive to his London townhouse. Out of habit he thrust his hand into the hollow of the huge plane tree, expecting disappointment. He should chop the thing down—rid himself of memories of the enchanting Sarah Somerset. She probably never existed at all.

As always, his fingers found nothing but air…Wait…there was something. But…it couldn't be. He drew out a finely crafted paper carrier and held it up to read with the help of a moonbeam. His name, scrawled on the front in Sarah's distinctive handwriting, gave him a shiver of excitement. His heart thudded out the beat of a Russian march song. Sarah had written him a letter. He held it aloft, then pulled it to his lips and planted a kiss on it. Had the sun been out, he would have ripped it open and read the note immediately. Instead, he tucked it into his vest pocket and aimed for the front door.

"Sarah's alive!" he couldn't help singing out.

Sarah's alive and has not made contact with me in seven years. The sudden realization jarred him to a halt. His fast-beating heart constricted in his chest. Possible scenarios of where she was and what might have kept her away buzzed through his partly-sober mind.

Benjamin Somerset had held a tight rein on her. Perhaps she'd somehow escaped. Come to think of it,

Benjamin had been captured and held at Newgate for a time—until he mysteriously disappeared. Sarah clearly hadn't been under his dominion while he'd been imprisoned. *So, why not come to me then?* He shook his wet head to rid himself of the chill setting in.

Another thought gnawed at him—had she been nearby this whole time but witnessed his reckless behavior and kept still about her whereabouts? The notion made him shudder.

Ridiculous. *Sarah wouldn't deceive me by hiding.*

The dark house didn't fool him. Of late, Mother waited up for him. He'd take his questions to her.

He padded through the parlor. "Mum, are you awake?"

No answer.

After lighting a lamp, he made his way to Mother's bedchamber. He shouldn't wake her, but this was an emergency. Lud, why did he seek Mum's advice? He was a grown man. Yet he did. Perhaps because she was the only other human who understood his despair at losing Sarah.

Under the moon's soft glow through her window, Mother looked peaceful. Hudson paced her room. He should wake her because, of anyone, she would give him the wisest counsel. He reached down to touch her arm. No. Waking her would be inconsiderate. Not to mention, she would likely deliver him a lecture after taking in his wet hair and dirty clothes. He continued to pace.

"I had that carpet imported from France. I do hope you plan to replace it after you are finished wearing holes through it."

Hudson startled. "Sorry, Mum. I did not mean to wake you."

She sat up and narrowed her eyes. "Hmm. No? Then perhaps you could continue your pacing in another room. *Any* other room. The home is enormous—if you hadn't wished to wake me, why pace in the only room where another human being existed? Honestly, Hudson, I do not know why you insist I reside in the manor instead of the dower house." A hint of amusement tinged her tone. "And your clothing! Son, have you been wrestling with the dogs again? I thought you were over that phase—about ten years ago." A wicked smile stole across her face. She was enjoying this.

"Yes...well..." He stumbled over his words, his tongue in knots.

She patted the chair next to her bed. "What is it, Hudson? You know I always have time for you, day or night. And since you choose to spend your daylight hours elsewhere, I will take what I can get."

"This!" He threw the letter into Mother's lap. "I—I just don't know what to make of it."

Mother held the note up, squinting to read the name. Then she flipped it over and glanced up at Hudson, her forehead wrinkled. "How much have you had to drink tonight?"

"Mum?"

"You must be foxed. The boy I raised is intelligent enough to open a letter before questioning its contents."

"Bu—"

"Hudson, read the letter. Then we shall address your concerns."

He stood to leave.

"Oh, no. Sit back down and read it aloud. You do not wake me just to listen to you worry over what that fancy letter may or may not contain."

Embarrassment mingling with relief put him at odds with himself. Reading Sarah's private letter could expose his soul's secrets, which he'd worked hard to bury. Yet Mother knew his despair over losing Sarah as no other person did, so to have her input on the matter—whatever the matter may be—could be a great relief.

"Very well." He reclaimed his seat, then pulled the lamp near. "What sort of ink is this? 'Tis blue."

"That answers everything then. Sarah has become a witch." A sparkle lit Mother's eye.

Hudson blew out a puff of air. "Mum, please be serious. You know how vexed I've been without Sarah."

His mother gave his hand a squeeze. "Read, son."

"Hudson,

If you are reading this letter, you must still be residing in London. If you have found another to take my place, I cannot fault you, after the way I disappeared so long ago. My father has done unspeakable things to gain power and wealth. And to keep his secrets, he imprisoned Mother, Joshua, and me in a different place for several years."

Hudson pounded the nightstand. "I knew it. Benjamin Somerset is behind Sarah's disappearance. I must find her!" He wished to begin a search this instant.

"Perhaps"—Mother shrugged—"but will you finish the letter first?"

Hudson took a deep breath and continued.

"Do not think I am speaking of our home in London; we are a great distance from there."

He slowly expelled the breath.

"So far away that the entire British army could not find us.

Because I do not know if you now have a wife and family, I will spare you the particulars of my life. And I will not ask the details of yours. Only know that I never wished to be separated from you and would do anything to restore the stolen years from us.

I fear this shall be my only missive to you. However, if you are quick to respond, there is a slight chance I will be able to receive your reply. I cannot explain further.

Yours, and only yours,

Sarah"

"I do not understand. If your Sarah was able to deliver the letter, she cannot be far," said Mother.

Hudson leaned forward and kissed her cheek, then stood to leave.

"Where are you going, son? I thought you wished to talk about it."

"You heard the letter, Mum. I must hurry if I wish for her to receive a reply. We can discuss the fine points of the note in the morning." He fairly ran to the bookroom where he kept his paper and ink.

How long had the letter been in the tree hollow? It might be too late. He closed his eyes to conjure up the last time he had checked. His brain, still unfocused from the spirits, refused to call up the last time he'd passed by the tree. Surely it hadn't been more than a day or two. In any event, a reply would never reach his sweet Sarah if he did not write one.

My Dearest Sarah,

No, no, no! I've not moved on without you. How could I when you are the very air I breathe?

He thought of telling her how his life had spun out of control since her departure but decided against it. If even a remote chance of getting Sarah back existed, she couldn't learn of his drinking, gaming, and such—especially the "and such." He sank deep into his leather seat, his guilty conscience adding weight to his soul.

I have so many questions for you. But you made it sound as if I shall be left forever wondering, since you say you shan't be answering my letter. This troubles me, Sarah. And why can you not disclose your location? It must be somewhere exotic to have blue ink. India, perhaps?

A sudden urgency to get his affairs in order and journey to India had his heart pounding again.

The color is fitting, as your eyes are blue. However, your eyes are a much more vibrant hue than is the ink. It reminds me of my favorite poem, you remember—

"And all that's best of dark and bright
Meet in her aspect and her eyes…"

He was quizzing her now. If it truly was his Sarah, she would instantly know Lord Byron's poem, "She Walks in Beauty." Just published months before Sarah's disappearance, Hudson had said the words had been penned with her in mind.

My darling, how did you get this letter to me—in our special, secret repository? Are you in truth nearby and not in some faraway place? Or do you have a friend to help you? How can I find you? Who will help me? I cannot live without you now that I know you love me still!

Tears burned his eyes. He wiped them, then finished the letter, pouring his heart out to her in words he'd never before conveyed. She must know his truest feelings, if he was to get only one opportunity to express them.

After the ink dried, he folded the paper and sealed it with wax. He stared at her name written on the front. *Childish. I am acting childish to write such things to a grown woman. Sarah is no longer fifteen.* A sudden fear of rejection seized him, and he spied the trash bin. *If she learns the truth of my fallen character, she'll likely not have me—no matter how much I beg.*

Chapter Five

Sarah heard the vibrations of the time-traveling device, although they weren't as loud and bothersome as usual. Her heart pounded in anticipation of what Josh might bring back with him. Hopefully a letter. At the very least news—bad news if her note had remained in the tree hollow. Uncertainty if it had been retrieved but not replaced with a note in response.

She bit her lip and held her breath, waiting for Josh to ascend the ladder.

The trapdoor burst open. Sarah jumped, then giggled. *'Tis like one of those toys with a popping clown*—the clown never failed to startle, no matter the first or the tenth time it sprang from the box.

"Well?" She looked him over. Nothing in his hands. A pocket, perhaps. She willed herself not to fall apart if he had not returned with a letter.

"Sarah, I cannot believe you waited up for me. It's late."

"But…the letter?"

Josh frowned. "It was gone, but the tree hollow was empty. No note filled its place. I'm sorry, Sarah."

Uncertainty, then. Her insides writhed. "Perhaps he did not find my letter right away. If you wait a day or two, then return…"

"Sarah, you promised you wouldn't ask more of me."

She dropped her head. Her heart ached so badly; she needed to know if Hudson had moved on with his life. "But the letter was gone. That must mean something." Her words came out as a low mumble. Her eyes burned with tears. She blinked them back. *I promised not to fall apart.* Gritting her teeth, she released a breath and faced Josh again. "Will you please try one more time in a day or two? Hudson may have just found my note today." Her voice had risen from a mumble to a panic-induced shriek as she realized how easily Josh was giving up on Hudson. Yes, she'd only asked him to make the one delivery, but she'd desperately hoped to glean some information—any information—as a result.

Josh let out a huff. "I'll do it…on one condition."

"What? Anything!"

"Do you know who Henry Carver is?"

Not another blind date. Sarah's shoulders slumped. Josh had lined her up with some of his coworkers before. They'd been pleasant enough but had moved too fast with their physical advances for her nineteenth century upbringing. "I have never heard of Henry Carver. Is he another coworker you wish me to go on an outing with?"

"No." A gleam lit Joshua's eye. "Henry Carver *owns* Wireless World."

"Where you work?"

"Yes."

"You want me to date an old guy who employs you?" Josh had sunk to a new low.

He wrinkled his forehead and scowled. "He's not that old, and I don't want you to date him. Just listen to me, Sarah."

"Can we at least have this conversation over a cup of tea? I have been pacing the bookroom for hours, and I'd like to sit while you recite your latest scheme." And figure out a way out of it, if possible. She pivoted and headed toward the kitchen.

"Very well, but it isn't a scheme. It is a job—"

Sarah stopped abruptly and sucked in a breath. She turned on Josh. "You know I don't do well in public." Her attempt at working in the market hadn't lasted long. The people of Pueblo were friendly and inquisitive—too inquisitive for Sarah. Her British accent had them asking all sorts of questions—things she couldn't divulge, such as, why did she move to Colorado from London? Who were her parents? Josh had told her to make up a narrative, but Sarah struggled with lying.

"It isn't that sort of job." Josh proceeded to pour the tea. "Just hear me out."

Sarah scooted a chair up to the table and sipped the warm liquid, the soothing herbs calming her nerves.

Josh took a seat across from her. "Henry Carver is the founder and owner of *all* the Wireless Worlds in the country." He drew out the word "all" as if it would impress her. It didn't.

"He's rich. Our father is rich, but that doesn't mean anything to me, Josh."

"He is also ill and has recently moved back to Pueblo from Chicago to semi-retire and run his businesses remotely. I don't know why he doesn't just sell—he'd make a bundle. Nonetheless, he is looking for a companion—someone to keep him company. You know, read to him, and such."

She lowered her brows, wondering precisely what Mr. Carver would wrap into the meaning of "companion." She had trust issues, and being tossed into the home of a stranger raised a multitude of red flags.

"Seriously, Sarah. It's nothing more than being a friend. He's too ill to try anything inappropriate. He said he expends all his energy running the business. A housekeeper comes in each day, but she doesn't speak English. He just gets lonely rattling around in that big house of his. The pay is good, and you can pretty much choose your hours."

"I know nothing of nursing."

"He has a nurse on call at all times. He's a billionaire, he has everything he needs—except a friend. Now that you are more confident in your ability to drive, I think this would be the perfect job for you."

The work did sound intriguing. Interacting with only one man instead of a store full of curious shoppers seemed much less intimidating. And she was an excellent reader, having made books her escape since her family's exodus from London. "How do I apply for the job? It sounds like something many people will be interested in."

Josh shrugged. "I might have told him you'd do it." His cheeks turned pink.

"Josh! You should have asked me first!"

"I know, but he's so kind, Sarah. I really believe you are the perfect person for the job. He wants to meet you tomorrow."

"So soon?" Her stomach flipped—and not in a good way. Nervous energy pulsed through her.

"You're shaking. I'll go with you, Sarah. If it is too much, I promise not to push."

"But will you still check Hudson's tree for a letter?"

"If you give this job an honest effort, I shall."

****

"Mr. Carver, this is my sister, Sarah Somerset...er...Somers." Sarah wished Father hadn't dropped the "et" from their name. Now all their legal documents in this new century were inaccurate.

The man appeared younger than Sarah had imagined—close to Mother's age, but his thin body and pale face were proof of his illness. "It is nice to meet you, Mr. Carver." She dipped in a graceful curtsy.

Josh cleared his throat and pointedly looked at Mr. Carver's outstretched hand.

Of course. Hot shards of embarrassment shot through her. How could she have been so forgetful of the era in which she now lived? "I—I apologize." She shook his extended hand.

"Not to worry, Sarah. You are a foreigner. Do they still bow and curtsy in England? I confess, as busy as I have been here in the U.S., I have not made it to your native country since I was in college."

"In some regions they do," Josh was quick to answer.

"Charming. You made me feel like royalty." Mr. Carver chuckled.

Sarah breathed out a sigh of relief and followed Mr. Carver and Josh into a parlor. She noticed his uneven gait and wondered what illness ailed him. A cane leaned against a large recliner. And a wheelchair sat a few paces from the cane. He must be feeling well today. Josh had mentioned that some of his days were better than others.

"Please, take a seat." Mr. Carver collapsed into the recliner and let out a few pants. The short walk from the foyer winded him.

Sarah's heart ached for the man. Josh had described him as full of vitality, bursting with ideas, and unwilling to work for anyone but himself. Now disease was his master.

The house, large for one person, didn't compare to the mansion in which she lived. And while the décor looked professional, her sister-in-law Arianna, an interior decorator, had made the Somers' home—though she hesitated to admit it—beautiful and comfortable. Mr. Carver's house, cold and masculine, had the ambiance of a museum rather than a home. No wonder he was lonely.

"Your house is very nice," she said.

"It's much too big for me, but I haven't the strength to do anything about it. I'm afraid I've come to realize—too late—that throughout the years, I should have worried less about getting ahead and more about people. I should have married, had children. What good is all of this"—he motioned to the art on the walls—"without someone to share it with?"

A portly woman in a blue dress brought in a silver coffee service, reminding Sarah of England. Perhaps it was because of his wealth, or maybe his weak limbs required this type of service. Either way, Sarah couldn't keep a smile from her face. Mr. Carver could have been from her century.

"You have a beautiful smile, Sarah." Mr. Carver's deep voice pulled her back to the present.

Flattered and embarrassed, she dipped her head. "Thank you. I've not seen a coffee service like this in the United States. It is lovely."

He said nothing in reply.

She peered up to see his gray eyes appraising her. Ordinarily this sort of scrutiny would make her squirm, but there was something different in his gaze—a gentle kindness, sincerity. Instead of causing her discomfort, a surge of confidence sparked in her chest. Squaring her shoulders, she looked straight at Mr. Carver. "May I ask you some questions regarding the position you are hoping to fill?" She wondered what had possessed her to be so direct.

"By all means. Fire away."

Thirty minutes later, she and Josh said goodbye to Mr. Carver and headed back to the mansion. Sarah was now employed.

"Josh, you were absolutely right, the man is a gem. I look forward to working for him."

Josh shook his head. "I've not seen you so happy since leaving London. I think this job will be as good for you as it will be for Mr. Carver. You'll make a wonderful companion."

She smiled. Her life would finally have purpose. "So, you'll check the tree?"

"I said I would."

When they had parked in the garage, she pulled him in for a hug. "Thank you." She was excited to share the news with Mother.

As they walked past the bookroom, Sarah paused. "Josh, I've been wondering something. The night I tried to use the traveling device to find Hudson, why did you come down to the lab? Does it have anything to do with how quiet the machine is now?"

Josh gulped. "Uh…"

Sarah narrowed her eyes at her brother as he walked two paces ahead of her. "Josh, what have you been doing down there?" The sudden realization that he could be doing exactly what Father had designed the machine to do—travel through time, collecting valuable art, jewels, and rare artifacts—halted her in her forward motion through the house—the very mansion built from Father's ill-gotten gains. Her breath caught, making her dizzy. She leaned against the wall to steady herself. "Josh?"

He stopped and faced her. "I've been working on something in the lab. 'Tis nothing for you to worry over." She might have taken his words at face-value if one eye hadn't twitched—a telltale sign he wasn't speaking the whole truth.

She knew Josh far too well to let it go. After all, he'd inherited Father's intellectual genius. His interest in the traveling machine would be natural. Still…it terrified her to think Josh could be involved in anything nefarious. "Be specific, Josh. If it really isn't anything for me to worry over, you have nothing to hide."

"You are home!" Mother rushed toward Josh and Sarah before he had a chance to defend himself. "How did the interview go? Did you like Mr. Carver, Sarah? Do you think you'd like to work for him?"

Sarah speared Josh with a quick glance that meant "this isn't over" before smiling at Mother. "I am officially Mr. Carver's companion. I begin next week."

Chapter Six

Hudson awoke to the smell of sausage and bacon. His stomach reacted with a loud grumble as he stretched his neck to work out a nasty kink. Questions bombarded his hazy mind. Why was he sleeping at his desk in the bookroom? What had happened to make every bone in his body ache?

As he stood, a paper crunched beneath his foot. He looked down to see Sarah's name scrawled across it. *My letter to her.* The memory floodgates opened, and he recalled everything. Lord Charlie the not-so-great card player had tossed him from his landau—thus the bruised bones. And, much more remarkable, Sarah had written him a letter. He bent down to retrieve his own note, which had fallen to the ground near the trash— that, or he'd aimed for the trash and missed. Still hazy. Memories of his regret for exposing his heart to Sarah then surfaced. "Lud! Why did I not deposit the letter in the tree hollow last night? I've likely missed my chance." Though spilling his honest feelings onto the parchment made him vulnerable, she needed to know he still loved and longed for her. If it wasn't too late.

Without waiting another second, he sprinted from the room—shoeless, no less—out the door and stuffed his letter into the hollow. How could he have regretted writing his personal feelings when this was his only opportunity? He mentally pummeled himself all the way to his bedchamber.

Tempted to collapse and get a few more hours of sleep, he eyed the large bed and felt lonesome. He should be married by now. To Sarah. Oh, how he ached for her.

His stomach growled again, and he gave up the desire for more sleep. If he had his days right, Parliament would be in session in a few hours. He could sleep then.

His mother's displeasure at his conduct of late tripped through his mind. He should really take his position as Earl of Alleyne more seriously. He fingered Sarah's letter tucked away in his pocket. Beginning today, he would limit his drinking, only frequent gaming tables two or three days a week—White's, Brook's, Almack's, all of them—and he'd stay awake at Parliament meetings. For Mother…and Sarah. An irrational part of him hoped making these adjustments to his lifestyle would somehow bring her back to him. "It's worth a try."

An hour into the meeting at the House of Lords, Hudson's eyes drooped. Perhaps he should start his new and improved way of living tomorrow—after a good night's rest.

****

"Nobody wins every game," growled Lord Burke, the card player who'd just lost his third round to Hudson. "Not without cheating." He pounded the table and cards scattered everywhere.

Hudson threw his hands in the air. "I do not cheat! Perhaps you should not gamble away your assets so freely, Burke. Know when to stop, man." He shouldn't speak after vowing that very morning not to gamble or drink so often. But did it really matter when he was on a winning streak?

Ed Falwell, his friend since they'd been chums at Eton, then Oxford, nudged him. "Hud, perhaps we should return to the dancing—let the action in here simmer down a bit." Ed—Eddie to Hudson—always had his back—when he was around. Lately he'd been spending more and more time with his father, learning the responsibilities of a duke, his impending title— should His Grace ever relinquish it. He'd been sick for years, but the stubborn man had an unrelenting clutch on both his title and his son. Hudson missed their carefree days at Oxford, when Eddie's main concern was where to get his next drink.

Hudson and Eddie pushed through the crush of people on the dance floor and located a refreshment table. Hudson's eyes roved over thinly-sliced bread and dry, crumbly cake, then landed on lemonade. A refreshing drink for a warm ballroom. He gave Eddie a cup of ratafia, knowing his dislike of "sour lemon water," as he referred to it.

"I do not know why you let Burke get under your skin, Eddie." Hudson gulped his drink, imagining how much better it would be if it were cold such as the lemon ices served at Gunter's.

Eddie kept his voice low. "It is not just him, Hud, I've heard talk of a money reward for anyone able to remove you from the games—permanently. You are taking everything they own, and they are not having it."

Hudson winced. "What are you talking about? A bounty on my head? I've heard nothing of the sort. And as far as my winning goes, you know I never cheat. I win by using my wits and a bit of luck."

Eddie let out an exasperated breath. "Don't be daft." He downed his drink in three swallows and shoved his cup back onto the table. "Do you really think anyone would share this information with *you*?"

"Good point. Who is after me?" Hudson threw back the last of the lemonade and licked his lips.

"The better question is, who *isn't* after you? This winning streak you have been having has ruffled a lot of aristocratic feathers. But really, could you not throw a game now and then? What will you do with four country estates—besides the two your family owns—anyway?"

Hudson chuckled. "Did you forget about the one I picked up last night from good ole Charlie Finley?"

Eddie scoffed and raised his eyes to the ceiling. "How do you do it? You say it is luck, but I believe you've a talent for it."

Hudson tapped his temple. "I remember everything."

"You remember everything?" Eddie's brows lowered, and he tilted his head in question. "I know your marks were always the highest in school, but—"

"Yes. I remember *everything*." Hudson shrugged. "I can tell you during any given game which cards have been played and what threats are yet to be unveiled." His keen memory was both a blessing and a curse. Not only did it aid him in cardplaying, Hudson also remembered the intense blue of Sarah Somerset's eyes, the ruby red of her soft lips, the rose scent of her skin, and the feel of her silky hair when it glided through his fingers. In seven years, no other woman held a candle to Sarah's beauty.

"You have that faraway look in your eyes." Eddie waved a hand in front of Hudson's face, pulling him from his trance. "Must be dreaming of a woman."

Before Hudson could respond, the music ended, and debutantes were being escorted back to their guardians. Several eyes landed on Eddie and him—two of the most eligible bachelors in London. However, with his ever-intensifying rakish reputation, fewer mammas were eyeing Hudson than usual. It didn't bother him. The only debutante's mother he cared to impress was somewhere far away from this stuffy ballroom.

"Drake."

Hudson turned to see three hulking men standing behind him. How did such goons get into the dancehall? Did they not have anyone guarding the door, watching for unsavory individuals such as these? The thought then occurred to him that these possibly *were* the guards. He couldn't help a smirk escaping his lips.

One man moved toward him, a sneer marring his face. "You think 'tis funny, do ye now?" He had a nasally Irish accent and sour breath. "Well, ye shan't be laughing for long."

Chapter Seven

Sarah shoved the cupboard door shut, then jumped back at the unexpected bang. "Oh!" she yelped, hoping she hadn't disturbed anyone in the quiet house.

She'd not seen Josh for a day and a half, and she knew he wasn't at work because his car hadn't left the garage. Likely, he was dodging her and her questions about the time-traveling device. Perhaps he'd been hiding out in the lab. Pondering the possibilities—reasons to use the machine—turned her stomach. She loved Josh and would be heartbroken if he chose to follow in Father's footsteps.

Her sister-in-law Arianna had asked Christopher to destroy the devices years ago but had eased up ever since her family had returned from the dead via the miraculous machines. Sarah, too, had loathed them until recently. If time travel could reunite her with Hudson, she'd never want the devices destroyed. How could something that produced so much evil also deliver an equal amount of good?

The Colorado mansion, so big and mostly empty, echoed with loneliness. Sarah peeked out the window. Mother waved to her from the garden, where she spent endless hours. Josh had suggested they hire a groundskeeper, since he didn't have time to do more than mow the grass, but Mother protested. "I shan't have strangers wandering the property," she'd argued.

Then, once she tried her hand at gardening, she found it so therapeutic, she began spending more time outdoors than inside.

Sarah waved back and smiled. Mum was happy. But that left Sarah alone in the house most of the time. She read many books and took it upon herself to prepare meals and do the banking and grocery shopping, but she'd be glad for Monday to arrive—the first day of her new job.

She stirred the carrot and ginger soup she'd prepared for lunch, breathing in the aroma.

"Lunchtime?"

Startled, Sarah dropped the spoon. It clattered against the side of the pan. "Josh! You scared me! Where have you been?"

He shrugged. "I have been…around."

She narrowed her eyes at him. "I've not seen you since my interview with Mr. Carver." She turned her attention back to the bubbling soup. "If you have been here, where is it you've been taking your meals? Certainly not at our table."

"If you must know, I have absconded with some of your leftovers and eaten them elsewhere."

"Have you been spending your days down in the lab?" She knew it. If Mother found out, she'd be so hurt.

"I took the food on an excursion." He held out a letter. "I had to travel there a couple of times, but Hudson finally answered your missive." His impish smile betrayed his excitement.

She blanched. Shame tugged at her heart for suspecting the worst. "He wrote me back? I am so sorry for my accusations, Josh." Her heart began beating double-time, and she clapped her hands together. "Hudson—"

She reached for it, but he held it away.

"Mother must not learn about this," he said, his voice low. "You know she wishes me to destroy the machine."

"I won't tell her. But, Josh, if you have been time traveling, why can't I hear or feel the vibrations?"

"You must have slept through them."

"Not likely. I distinctly recall they once shook the entire house."

He grinned that quirky grin he'd teased her with since childhood.

The back door opened, and Mother stepped into the kitchen. "I smell soup. And since today has turned chilly, it is just the thing to warm me. Fickle spring weather." She sniffed the air and smiled.

Josh slipped the letter into his back pocket.

Sarah's spirits plummeted. She needed to read that letter—now. But she swallowed her disappointment and smiled at Mother. "Yes, Mum. I made your favorite: carrot and ginger." She would have to bide her time until lunch was finished. But she still wasn't convinced Josh hadn't been doing something else in the lab. Uneasiness crept over her once more.

After an awkwardly silent meal, Mother thanked Sarah and returned to the garden.

Sarah folded her arms and huffed out a breath at Josh. "Is there a reason you are holding my letter hostage?" His actions were so suspicious.

"Oh, yeah." He chuckled, but it sounded forced. "I nearly forgot." He tossed the note across the table to her.

She shook her head. "I don't know what is going on with you, little brother, but because you are helping me, I'll not pester you about it."

His shoulders relaxed, and his features softened.

She took the letter and dashed to her room.

After reading it for the third time, she blinked away tears. Hudson's words, especially the last paragraph, yanked so hard at her heart, she thought it might burst.

Sarah, I am opening my soul as I never have before—to you and only you. I am here, should you decide I am still worthy of your love. Please, darling Sarah, reveal your hiding place, and I will come to you.

Forever Yours,

Hudson

He hadn't moved on. Relief washed over her, and she closed her eyes to ponder each passage from his letter. He'd always loved the color of her eyes— hopefully the vibrant hue he'd spoken of hadn't faded. And he'd quoted the poem he once loved and dedicated to her not so long ago—yet, in reality, centuries ago. She ached when she'd read his plea to disclose her whereabouts. How she longed to tell him everything.

Without so much as a thought about how she would convince Josh to deliver it, she began penning a response.

Dear Hudson,

Words cannot express how happy you have made me. Your letter was a godsend. Like you, I have not moved on with my life. You are the only man I desire to share my future with. However, my current circumstances prevent it. Please do not think I am hiding from you willingly. I am not. If I could come to you, I would. Thoughts of you rise with the sun each

44

day and frequent my dreams at night. I love you, Hudson. I will continue writing as long as possible.

She thought of telling him about the job she would begin on Monday, then realized how odd that would sound. In fact, anything she might say about her current living conditions would make little sense. Such as why her ink was blue. She smiled, enjoying the bit of mystery the ballpoint pen had created.

She continued writing.

Of course I remember your favorite poem. It is mine, as well.

"Thus mellowed to that tender light
Which heaven to gaudy day denies..."

She would never forget their shared loved for Lord Byron's tender poetry.

Do not think my love for you has ever waned. It has not. My love for you waxes strong still. Please be patient for just a little while more.

Always yours,

Sarah

Now, how would she talk Joshua into delivering yet another note to the nineteenth century? The question was easily answered. She knew he was doing something in the lab he didn't wish Mother to know about. Though Sarah worried he was experimenting with the time-traveling device for his own reasons—good or bad—she lay ready to hold that over him.

****

Monday morning brought on the jitters. "I can do this," she repeated on her drive into the city. Mr. Carver had given her his security alarm code so she wouldn't have to roust him to answer the door. After letting herself in, she headed for the parlor, where she thought she'd find him in his recliner.

She was correct. Opening her mouth to announce herself, she stopped before making a sound, realizing he was asleep. His head faced the window, so she couldn't see his eyes, but there was no mistaking his soft snoring. *I'll just find something else to do and let him sleep.*

As she slipped into the kitchen, she saw a few dishes in the sink. Thinking the housekeeper must be cleaning elsewhere or shopping for groceries, Sarah shrugged and washed and dried each dish. Then, after checking in on the still sleeping Mr. Carver, she wandered the house, looking for other rooms to tidy.

"Ahh." Her eyes widened when she stumbled into what must be a music room. "A grand piano." The black finish polished to a high shine could have been a mirror. She peered around, making certain she was alone, then sat on the bench and began to play softly. Her heart soared. How she adored music. Father hadn't thought it important to purchase a piano in the twenty-first century. Not surprising. It seemed he hadn't valued anything Sarah loved. She hummed along to the piece as her fingers danced across the keys. Before long, she was singing and loving every minute of it.

When the piece ended, someone clapped. *Oh no.* She sucked in a breath, knowing she shouldn't have been playing without gaining consent to do so. She stood to see Mr. Carver propped against the doorframe.

"I am terribly sorry, sir. I didn't mean to wake you. And I should have asked your permission before playing your piano. It's—it's a beautiful instrument."

With his head tilted, his expression was hard to read. "Your voice. I've heard nothing like it—so clear and rich. Beautiful, just beautiful."

She looked down, trying to hide the blush warming her cheeks.

"And you didn't wake me. This room isn't close enough to my den for that."

Relief spread through Sarah like butter melting on a hot roll. "Still, I should have asked your permission."

He scoffed. "Don't be ridiculous. You are welcome to play and sing any time you'd like. You have a gift, dear girl. I played…once upon a time." He held his hand up and wiggled his fingers. "But now my hands are numb and clumsy." He wobbled, looking as if he might fall.

Sarah sprang to her feet to help, but he righted himself before she reached him.

"What can I do for you, Mr. Carver?"

"You can lend me your arm to help me maneuver toward that chair over there." He motioned to a padded seat. "Then you can sing a few more songs for me. And since you and I are going to be spending time together, call me Henry."

She smiled, delight bubbling over in her heart. "I'm happy to lend you my arm, Henry." She rushed to his side and assisted him to the cozy chair nearby.

By the end of her workday, Sarah had played and sung nearly all the songs she'd ever learned, read several chapters of a surprisingly interesting, modern espionage book to Henry, and listened in rapt attention to him regale her with stories of his exciting life. Her job wasn't work at all—it was pure joy.

****

A few days passed. Sarah relished the time spent with Henry Carver. He filled a hole in her heart left by her abusive father. Each day brimmed with laughter and learning.

She drove home remembering how peaceful he'd looked when she'd left him, dozing in his recliner. Hopefully this job was helping Henry as much as it was helping her. She hadn't been this happy and fulfilled since leaving the nineteenth century. The only thing that could make it better would be to have Hudson by her side.

"How did it go?" Josh seemed to be waiting for her when she entered the mansion.

She jumped, startled, then giggled. "Josh, stop that! You must derive some sort of pleasure from scaring me. But I am glad you are here. Work has gone well. Very well, in fact. Henry is a dear man. I am grateful I can help him."

"You're welcome." Josh smirked.

She gave him a playful shove. "Thank you for recommending me for the job." She narrowed her eyes. "Where have you been spending your time? I've not seen you since I began working for Henry."

"Henry, is it?" He lifted his lips into a lopsided grin. "Things must be going very well if one of the richest men in the world allows you to call him by his Christian name."

Sarah smiled. *Christian name*—first name—the phrase was obsolete in this modern world in which they now resided. "Times have changed. Most people call each other by their first names nowadays. I admit it took a while to grow accustomed to the idea—it felt too presumptuous—but he has already become a dear friend."

The house began to vibrate. Sarah clutched Joshua's arm, a cloud of dread replacing the sunshine in her heart. "If you are here, then who is arriving on the time-traveling device?"

Josh steadied himself on a nearby table. "That sounds and feels like an old machine."

"An old machine?" Sarah cocked her head and tightened her grip on his arm. "What do you mean?" Her voice cracked with fear.

"Not precisely the machine itself, but the inner workings of the machine."

"And?"

"And I figured out—" His eyes shone with growing panic.

The floor jolted again. "Josh, is it him?"

Chapter Eight

Hudson rubbed the bulging lump on his now uncovered head. How long he'd been out, he couldn't say. Nor did he know where he was—again. *I really must stop winning at the gaming tables. That, or hire bodyguards.* The thought of traipsing around London with armed men made him smile. A slash of excruciating pain shot from ear to ear. *Ahh…I mustn't move my head.*

His stomach lurched as he slowly pushed himself to a sitting position. The motion made him dizzy, and his muscles burned from the effort. As he massaged a crick in his neck, he realized his hand was wet and sticky. The room, cloaked in darkness, made it difficult to see much, but by the pain shooting up his arm, he knew the moisture on his hand was blood. He must have gone down swinging. Good.

The floor was firm. He ran his good hand along the wood—*ow! A splinter.* He put a finger in his mouth to coax the wood out. The wall he leaned against felt bumpy, stone-like. An indoor chamber, then. Probably an outbuilding. The distant sound of a lowing cow caught his attention. *An outbuilding in the country. That explains the smell of dung. Finley has upped his game.* But Charlie Finley hadn't even been at the gaming tables. Burke had been the evening's sore loser. He wondered who then had nabbed him.

He'd been conversing with Eddie in a ballroom when three Irishmen approached. Stale-tobacco breath had soured his stomach just before someone shoved a hard object into his ribs—no doubt a pistol. From there his memory shorted, giving him only snippets of conversation he'd heard between the thugs during a jarring carriage ride. He strained to recall what the goons had said.

"Why not kill the bloke now, collect the reward, and disappear?" asked a deep, raspy voice on his right. Another Irishman, but his tone differed from the nasally thug from the ballroom.

A long huff of whiskey-laden breath had assailed him from his left. "Seamus, ye are daft, ye are. This man holds the deeds to properties we must recover before disposing of 'im. We'll be gettin' no reward money without them deeds."

And there's the nasally buffoon. Hudson had continued to sit still—his head lolled to the side—and listened. The carriage lurched onward.

"So, we are taking 'im to—"

"Hush, his head's covered; there's no tellin' if he's woked up. Keep the particulars of where we are goin' quiet."

Then a jab to Hudson's ribs had nearly made him yelp, but he'd gritted his teeth and remained slumped over.

"He's still sleepin'. You knocked 'im a good one, you did." The scoundrels had laughed like apes in the jungle.

Hudson remembered nothing more of the ride to hades.

Evidently Seamus had been right. He'd been knocked a good one. Hudson rubbed his sore head again. Another faint memory unfolded of waking a few times to find a tin plate of scraps and a saucer of bitter ale. They'd been left in front of him as one would a dog to lap up. Fuzzy-brained and hungry, he'd devoured the offering. *I must have been dosed.* And now he sat in the dark, wondering his location—and what day it was. Someone must be searching for him by now. Mother? No, she was accustomed to his erratic comings and goings from the townhouse. She'd think nothing of his absence. Members of Parliament? He shook his head, bringing on more searing pain. Those stuffy men cared little for Hudson unless they needed his vote. Eddie. Yes, Eddie had been there, had witnessed the whole rotten deal go down. He'd surely be looking for him. Perhaps he'd even followed the thugs to this dungeon. A spark of hope surged in his chest.

He attempted to stand but realized his feet were lashed together. How were his hands free but not his feet? Another memory flashed through his hazy brain. Eddie—*he untied my hands.*

They'd taken him, as well. His gut wrenched.

"Eddie, are you here?"

Silence.

With little effort, he freed his feet from the ropes, then groped along the stone wall, feeling for a door, a window—Eddie.

Thud. His foot rammed into something besides the ground. A soft moan came from the lump.

"Is that you, Eddie? Say something." Hudson knelt down to pull the man to a sitting position, ignoring the intense pain in his hand. The earthy smell of Bay Rum told him he'd indeed found his friend. Eddie's hands were still bound behind him. *I must have blacked out before I could untie him.* "Eddie, wake up." He made swift work of loosing the bindings.

Another groan. "Hud…is that you?"

"Yes." He let out a breath of relief. "How do you feel? Are you injured badly?" Hudson kept his voice low.

"Ow. My head"—he paused—"and my right leg. But I do not think it is broken."

"Do you know where they've taken us off to?"

"I would say the underworld, but it is far too cold." He chuckled. "Oh—that hurts!"

"What are your last recollections?"

"*You* trying to untie my bindings but passing out instead." Eddie sounded none too happy about his predicament. "I must have gone down soon after. Then the odor of rotten food woke me, and the taste of tainted ale. I think it was poison. I remember nothing more."

"Eddie, I'm sorry you are here. This is my fault. I shall make it up to you. Drinks are on me for the next year."

"I'll take you up on that, if we get out of here." He let out a low moan. "The men said they will pummel you until you give them what they want, then kill you for the reward money." He exhaled a heavy breath. "I've no clue why I am here, nor why I'm still alive. I've got nothing they want."

Witnesses. Hudson closed his eyes and shook his head. "They dragged you along so there'd be no witnesses. The way those Irishmen surrounded me must have concealed their act from everyone but you." The air deflated from his lungs. Eddie was right—there was no reason to keep him alive. *My dissipated lifestyle has affected someone other than myself. Now I need to make this right.* His stomach tightened at the thought of having put his friend in danger.

"Hmph. Seems your winning streak has come to an end, my friend," Eddie whispered.

Hudson cared little about his winning streak, the country estates he'd amassed, or, until his recent news from Sarah, his own life. But he did care about the people close to him. And Eddie topped the list just after Sarah and Mother. *But right now, Eddie is my main concern.* He shook thoughts of Sarah from his head. "Forgive me for getting you involved. We must flee from here. I vowed only this morning, or yesterday, or…do you know how long we've been away?"

"No. Feels like weeks."

"It makes no difference, I suppose. I vowed to change my behavior. If I had followed my own counsel, we wouldn't be trapped here in this"—he shrugged—"whatever it is. We have escaped sticky situations before; we can find our way out of this one." They had to. Now that Sarah had begun communicating with him, he'd do anything to remain alive.

Eddie grunted.

"If I'd only been conscious during the entire carriage ride, I would have a map in my head and know where we have been imprisoned."

"You and that incredible memory of yours."

"But first, we must get out of this room. Are you strong enough to walk?"

Eddie heaved, pushing against Hudson's shoulder until he was up. "I might require some help. My leg—"

"I've got you. Let's walk the perimeter of the room in search of a door or a window. Also, if you stumble over anything light enough to carry, yet hard enough to whack a man…I owe someone a knock on the head."

He clutched Eddie around the waist. "Perhaps I should do this alone."

"Oh no you won't. My leg will improve; it just needs stretching is all."

He kept a firm grip on Eddie with one arm, using his other hand to run along the wall as they took slow steps around the chamber. Eddie's labored breathing and heavy limp worried him. *I need to get his mind off the pain.*

"We'll get out of this fix, Eddie." Hudson panted. "Remember His Grace old man Dumfery and his beautiful young bride? The lady only had eyes for His Grace's money…and for you. And"—he paused to catch his breath—"your appreciation for auburn tresses"—more puffing—"made her dreams come true."

Eddie emitted a guffaw, then did some panting of his own.

Hudson slowed the pace a bit, but the urgency to get out of this cage clawed at him. Did this dungeon have no entry? The space was much larger than he'd imagined. Cavernous and cold.

"What"—Eddie spat out words between heavy breaths—"is your point"—more pants—"about Dumfrey?" Another pause to catch his breath. "Or are you just…rambling on about my past indiscretions? As you recall, I too have changed my ways."

"No, no." Hudson inhaled a lungful of dank air before continuing. "After Dumfery caught wind of his wife's…diversion"—he chuckled, then instantly regretted it and closed his eyes to squelch the pain—"he sicced his hounds on you." He gulped more air. "Who was there to head the old man off and convince him Finley was the culprit?" Yet another possible reason he and Eddie had been nabbed. *I need to change my ways. And if we ever break out of this dungeon, I will.*

"You. You were there." Eddie stopped and bent over for a rest. "And Charles Finley deserved it after the all the larks he's pulled on us through the years." He stood upright again. "I just hope we can find our way out of this mess."

They continued their slow journey around the room. The short break had given them added strength.

"Hud, you said you vowed to change. Why now?"

Hudson hadn't planned on telling anyone besides Mother about Sarah's note. Since her disappearance, he'd earned the reputation of a rogue. If word leaked that he still had a soft spot for his childhood sweetheart, the scoffing would have no end.

"Hud?"

"'Tis nothing, really. I have realized I should take my responsibilities seriously—be more like my father."

"Ha!"

"Shh. Keep it down, Eddie."

Eddie continued in a whisper. "You do know you are talking to me and not old man Dumfery, right? What *really* prompted the change of—" Eddie stopped. "You've found Sarah, haven't you?" He took a deep breath. "She's the only person I know who could persuade you to change your ways. After all, you didn't acquire the title Drake the Rake by following your *mother's* advice."

Hudson swallowed hard. His friend knew him too well. Even though Eddie had never met Sarah in the flesh, Hudson had described her in fine detail and had even talked him into helping him search her out when she'd vanished. "Eddie, you must tell no one about her. I haven't precisely found Sarah, but I have received a missive from her. Yes, she is the reason I must change. I hope she hasn't learned of my behavior. If so, it may be too late for me to reclaim her good grace, but if not, I cannot be found in gaming halls or public houses so often."

"So, the elusive Sarah Somerset has risen from the dead." Eddie blew out a soft whistle. "I wonder where her father dragged her off to. What has it been, six, seven years now?"

"Yes, seven and—"

Hinges creaked like an old man's bones, freezing Hudson in his tracks. Both men sank to the ground. Hudson put his hands behind him, bending his legs back to hide his unshackled ankles. Hopefully the goons wouldn't remember where they'd dropped them in the first place, since they'd stepped several paces from that spot.

One of the thugs entered the room with a lantern. He located Hudson, then kicked him in the side. Hudson winced, but didn't let out a noise or open his eyes.

The man hollered to someone outside, "Looks like they're still out." It sounded like Seamus.

The man must be dimwitted—thank the stars above, thought Hudson.

The nasally voice of the foul-breathed goon whined a response, though Hudson couldn't say what.

"Kill 'em now, then? What about obtaining them deeds?"

A pause and more yelling from outside.

"If the boss says so."

The whisk of metal against leather sliced through the air. A dagger or sword?

The goons must have found a way around obtaining the actual deeds. Hudson tensed every muscle in his body.

Forgive me, Sarah.

Chapter Nine

Sarah stood frozen with Josh in the hallway while the vibrations in the floor increased, then eased up. *Didn't Father die at Newgate Prison?* Sarah's stomach soured. In reality, she could not even think of Benjamin Somerset as her father. No one so cruel to their own flesh and blood deserved such a title.

Beatrice emerged from the kitchen, a dishtowel over her shoulder and a ladle in her hand. "What was all that racket?" One glance at Sarah and the spoon dropped, clanking on the wooden floor. "It cannot be." She wobbled.

Sarah and Joshua clutched her arms, steadying her.

"Why would Father come here? He's a wanted man. We must get out of here and contact Christopher immediately!" said Sarah.

"If only we had cell service." Josh jerked around, his eyes wild. "We need to leave or hide!"

"Take me to the parlor," said Mother. "'Tis time I settled things once and for all."

"But he's a madman!" Sarah shrieked. "We must leave!"

Mother shrugged out of their grips and aimed for the parlor. Sarah and Josh rushed to catch up. Josh hollering, "He's come for his safe full of treasures. Let's pray he takes what he needs and leaves quickly."

Mother had seated herself in a chair. Why wasn't she running from this monster—the man who had brutalized every member of the family?

Sarah's stomach twisted like a tornado touching down, ready to shred her apart. "The safe is empty! Christopher returned all of Father's purloined goods." Cold dread spread through her limbs. Father would not be happy when he discovered his jewels, art, coins, and precious metals gone. "Please, Mother. We must flee."

"Here you all are." Benjamin Somers entered the room as if he'd just returned from a day's work. "It smells delicious, Beatrice. What have you prepared for supper?"

Sarah glared at her father. How dare he barge into their lives again after everything he'd put them through?

"What, no welcome?" He arched his brows.

Josh put a protective hand on Mother's shoulder. "Why are you here, Father?" His eyes darted around the room, perhaps in search of a weapon.

"This is my home. I have come back to live with my family, the way we had always planned."

Mother cleared her throat. "You are not welcome here, Benjamin."

Father's body jerked as if he'd been punched.

Sarah wondered if he could really be surprised at his family's displeasure of his return. He'd hurt them all. At the time, she'd thought he'd singled her out because she was weak in body and spirit. But looking back, she was certain Mother had ached for the loss of her once-upstanding husband. Josh took his share of abuse, mostly physical. She glanced at him. Now, nearly three years later, his height exceeded Father's by inches.

"I built this house. I've more right to reside in it than any one of you." Angry sparks lit Benjamin's coal-black eyes.

Sarah wanted to run, to hide. *Not this time. I must stand my ground—protect Mother.* "Why come back now?" She tried to sound confident, unafraid, though she felt neither.

"I see you are still the insolent chit you've always been, Sarah. I had hoped to find you had matured."

Tears burned the backs of her eyes, but she willed them away. "I have matured enough to see you for what you truly are: a manipulative, greedy, abus—"

Father lunged toward her and swung at her face.

Josh grabbed his hand before it could reach its target. "I think you'll find we have all changed since you have been gone—and for the better." Josh spoke firmly, not even a quiver in his voice. Gone was the frightened little boy who had hidden from Father's wrath in the past.

Sarah's heart warmed, but she had no time to react to Joshua's gallant action.

Benjamin stomped his foot, piercing Josh with threatening glares. "How dare you, boy?" He sneered. "This is my house, and I will come and go as I please. You are my family. You will treat me with respect and obedience."

Josh stared at Father with the gleam of equal threat.

Mother stood up in the middle of Sarah and Josh. "Respect must be earned, Benjamin. You have done nothing but snuff the life from this family." Unlike Josh, Mother's voice shook.

Sarah wrapped a reassuring arm around her. Josh did the same from the opposite side. His other hand closed into a hard fist. As a threesome they were strong—hopefully strong enough to stand up to the monster before them.

Benjamin's brows lowered as a guttural growl rose from his throat. His face enflaming.

Sarah stiffened, despite her resolve to remain steadfast. She'd never seen Father so angry. Her grip on Mother tightened.

He erupted with a string of curse words Sarah hadn't heard in years. He grabbed Mother by the shoulders, yanking her from their grasps as he spat words into her face. "I brought you here! Built this house! Gave you everything you could wish for!"

Sarah thought Mother would crumble, melt into tears, and submit to whatever Father demanded. But when she glanced at her mother's face, she didn't see tears, though hurt was in her eyes.

Beatrice straightened and looked directly at Benjamin. "You forced us here! Built this house to use and protect your evil time-traveling machine! And provided everything but what we needed most in our oppressed and dire state—love. Now unhand me." Her words were strong, but the quiver in her voice betrayed her fear.

Father, fiery red, threw Mother to the ground. Her head hit the wooden floor with such force she lay motionless. Taking advantage of the shock which had immobilized Sarah, he slapped her face with stinging ferocity. Then without hesitation, he pivoted and punched Josh in the stomach, doubling him over. "I am the master of this house and this family! I demand respect!" he roared, then stomped from the room. Seconds later, they heard the door of the bookroom slam shut.

Sarah dropped to her knees. "Mother, Mother." Tears spilled down her cheeks, burning her own fresh wounds. "Wake up." She looked up at Josh, who still appeared dazed from the pain in his gut. "Do something, Josh!"

He knelt down and felt Mother's neck for a pulse. "She is still alive." Relief was evident in his voice. "Do you have any smelling salts, Sarah?"

"I don't, but Mother once did. I'll search her room. Keep trying to wake her." Sarah's voice broke into a sob.

She raced up the stairs and into Mother's bedroom, barely aware of her stinging face, then rifled through her belongings. *This cannot be happening* cycled through her mind. *Father died at Newgate.* Finally, she found an old reticule Mother once carried. In it were treasures from over two centuries ago—including a small bottle of smelling salts. Sarah wasted no time returning to the parlor, salts in hand.

Josh snatched the jar from her and waved it under Mother's nose. No reaction. Her skin was ashen and cold. "The ammonia has surely lost its potency over the years. We must get her to a hospital. I wish we could call an ambulance. One day I'll earn enough to buy a satellite phone for this place."

Together Sarah and Josh lifted their unconscious Mother, supporting her on both sides. With some effort, they managed to get her into Joshua's car and sped to the hospital.

What Father was doing while they fought to save Mother's life, Sarah didn't know. A darkness fell upon her she'd thought she'd been freed from—the cruel dominion of Benjamin Somers.

"Call Christopher. Tell him to meet us there," Josh said, motioning to Sarah's phone.

As soon as they were within range, she called Chris with the news.

"Father is back?" Christopher's voice registered shock. "I'm on my way." The phone went dead without further question.

Just knowing her older brother would be there gave Sarah some degree of comfort. Christopher had watched over and protected their family for years—sometimes from a distance, but always there.

She sat in the back seat with Mother's head cradled in her lap.

"Sarah." Mother's eyes fluttered open. "Stop him." Her eyes closed and her head rolled to the side.

"Mother!"

No response.

Sarah put her ear near Mother's face. "Josh, I don't think she is breathing." Sobs shook her body.

Chapter Ten

Hudson squinted his eyes open just enough to see Seamus circling him, his large cloak flapping behind him. His eyes were narrowed, and Hudson was certain he could read his thoughts—should he stab him in the heart or through the back? The back would be the coward's way. But by aiming for the heart, Seamus would risk his prey awaking and waging a counterattack. The goon stopped outside of Hudson's view.

So, you are a coward—not surprising. Hudson readied himself for the attack. He watched the shadow on the wall cast from Seamus's small lamp, and the second the buffoon raised his dagger, he rolled over to face him, kicking the legs out from under the man in the process. Seamus fell hard on his back, and the dagger flew from his hand but was caught by Hudson. "You should have chosen my heart, bloke." He pointed the knife at Seamus, who quivered on the ground.

"Kill him already." Eddie had risen and now stood beside Hudson.

"Patience, my friend. I'd had the same thought, but look at him cowering. It doesn't seem very sporting. No, I have a better idea. But first we need information." He flicked the thug's chin with the end of the dagger. "How long have we been confined?"

"I—I dunno. A few days," Seamus stuttered.

"Days—as in plural? You've been dosing us for multiple days? Why prolong our lives if your end goal is to kill us?"

Seamus's teeth chattered. "Boss said to wait…'til now. That's all I know."

"Hmm." Hudson walked a slow circle around Seamus, keeping the blade near his throat. "Eddie, you were just saying you were cold, were you not?"

Eddie tilted his head and lowered his brows, then gave Hudson a lopsided grin. "Why yes, yes I did say that." He mock-shivered.

"Seamus, Eddie here is chilled after being in this"—he shrugged—"cellar, of sorts, for so dreadfully long."

He flicked Seamus again. "Take off your coat."

Seamus wasted no time shedding his long, woolen cloak, careful to avoid the sharp end of the blade. "Whatever you want. Just donna kill me."

Eddie pulled the cloak over his shoulders. "Ahh. Hud, you need to get one of these."

"In good time." Hudson still had the dagger pointed at Seamus. "Where are we?"

"I—I think it be called Brixton. Yes, that's it."

"We're in Lambeth, then," said Hudson, never taking his eyes or the knife off Seamus. "Who hired you to bring us here?"

Seamus grunted.

Hudson lowered himself to his haunches and held the knife over the thug's heart. "*Who hired you?*" He emphasized each word.

"*Stad! Stad*! I dunno names, but what ye should be askin' is who didn't hire us? Loch and me, we got ourselves three diff'rent agreements to kill ye, we do.

They dunno it, but after yer gone, weel be rich, we weel."

The man had to be daft. Hudson ignored a snort coming from Eddie's direction and continued his interrogation. "Where will you be collecting this coinage for disposing of me, pray tell?"

Seamus's lips quivered and he kept his gaze focused on the blade. "Down at the dock at dawn."

"Dock, which dock?"

"White Hart. We've a partner meetin' us there wif da coins. Heel be collectin' it now, I 'magine."

"In that case, Eddie is going to need the rest of your clothes."

Seamus flinched. "Wha for? I gave 'im my cloak. I'm near freezed to death, I am."

Hudson stood and flicked the thug's chin again. A drop of blood appeared. "Not to worry, Eddie will give you his fine clothing in return. Now stand up and disrobe. If you holler or make any sudden moves, I will run you through."

Seamus obediently stripped down to his small clothes and made the exchange with Eddie. "Thank ye for lettin' me stand to change m'clothes."

Finley, Burke, or whoever hired the thugs had picked some real winners for their dirty work. Hudson shook his head at Seamus' gratitude.

"One more question, Seamus." Hudson tapped his chin, looking into the goon's dull eyes. "Your friend Loch, is it? What sort of weaponry does he have?"

"Loch's got a dagger, like me. He said pistols is too loud."

"You have been very helpful. Thank you, Seamus." He turned to face his friend, now dressed in the thug's clothing. "Eddie, do you have something for Seamus?"

During the interchange between Hudson and Seamus, Eddie had pried up a wide floorboard. He thwacked Seamus over the head with it, toppling him to the ground. "Use the dagger. Finish the job, Hud."

"I don't believe shedding his blood is necessary. We've got what we need. Let's go get Loch."

The two crept outside, leaving the lamp in the outbuilding. Better to remain in the dark when sneaking up on an armed guard. Hudson shivered, and sweat beaded on his brow. As cold as it had been in the cellar, the night air was even more chilly.

"There he is," whispered Eddie.

"Seamus, what's taking ye so long?" the man hollered.

Hudson stole up behind him, dagger in hand. "Seamus has been…detained."

Before Loch could reach for his blade, Eddie whacked him over the head.

"You couldn't wait, could you, Eddie." Hudson huffed, icy air puffing from his mouth. "Five more minutes, and I'd have had him out of his clothing. Now I'll have to do it myself."

"I bet you say that about every thug you meet." Eddie chuckled. "Let me help you." He tugged at Loch's trousers. "This guy smells rank. I thought it was his breath. Perhaps we should give him a bath. I hear a river nearby."

"No time for larks, Eddie. We must meet the third of these buffoons at the dock by dawn. If there are some horses around here, we can make it." He sniffed and scrunched his nose. "The odor makes for a good disguise."

Once Hudson had pulled on Loch's clothing, he and Eddie set out to find horses. It didn't take long to locate a stable.

"Have you any coins, Eddie?" Hudson had kept a small pouch hidden in his boot after swapping clothes with Loch.

"You did not think I would leave my money with Seamus, did you? Why?"

"These are farmers. We cannot take their horses without payment."

Eddie shook his head. "As shrewd as you are at the gaming tables, and as rakish as you have become over the years, you've a soft core. Those thugs planned to kill us, yet you let them live. And instead of fleeing like a bat out of hades on these horses, you wish to leave payment for them." He chuckled and tossed Hudson his coin pouch.

Hudson ignored Eddie's remarks. If he could go back in time, he would change many habits which had earned him his roguish reputation. If he found Sarah, she'd likely be too disappointed in him to become his wife. If only he knew where she was hiding and if she had been aware of his actions. Vices aside, he had never been dishonest—to honest people. Ruffians and buffoons did not count. He left a pile of coins on a shelf, then mounted one of the horses.

The sky turned pink just as Hudson spotted the dock. An oily smell of pitch saturated the air. He motioned to Eddie to rein in. After dismounting the horses, the two crept closer to the water. "We should have asked Seamus if they were to give a signal or password," Hudson whispered. "Seamus spoke Gaelic. I suppose I can manage a phrase or two."

"Just act as dim as a rock, and we should be fine. Look"—Eddie pointed to an outline of someone pacing the dock—"if I'm not mistaken, that will be our man."

They tugged their hats down and pulled the collars of the borrowed coats up high as they approached the man with confidence. Hudson cleared his throat. "*Dia dhuit*," he said in a nasally voice. Loch's odor, still emanating from his clothing, aided his charade.

"*Dia is Muire dhaoibh.* Did you kill the bloke, then?" asked the man.

"The deed is done."

"And his companion?"

"Also dead. Have ye the payment?" asked Hudson.

"Have ye the proof?"

Of all the luck, Hudson and Eddie had found the only smart blackguard of the three. *Think. What would the proof be?* Hudson's mind churned through every conversation he had overheard between the three goons but came up with nothing. "We were afraid for our lives, that we were. Men with pistols chased us away before we could obtain the, uh, proof."

"Without Lord Drake's eyeballs, ye cannot have a share of the payoff. That was the deal. For all I know, ye set the blokes free."

Eddie stepped closer to the man. "The deal just changed. Now give us the coins."

The man narrowed his eyes. "Yer not Seamus." Then he shoved Hudson's hat off his head. "And ye aren't Loch."

Both Hudson and Eddie pulled their daggers from their sheaths and aimed them at the man. Hudson moved toward him. "As my friend said, the deal has changed. Now give us the booty and the names of the men—"

Before he could finish his sentence, the goon drew out a pistol and pointed it at Hudson's heart. "Nothing has changed except for me fortune. I've just become a wealthy man, I have. I should thank ye for killing me partners, but I need ye both dead. Now."

Chapter Eleven

From his periphery, Hudson could see Eddie moving ever so slowly. The wooden planks beneath his feet creaked the slightest bit. Hudson narrowed his eyes at the goon with the gun to keep his focus on him and not his friend.

"Say yer prayers, laddies. Yer about to meet the Almighty hisself." The thug cocked his pistol.

Eddie thrust the dagger up through the man's ribcage. "Give him our regards."

The blackguard let out a strangled cry as he toppled to the ground. Blood gushed from his lifeless body, staining the dock and running in rivulets, spilling into the Thames.

Hudson blew out a breath. "We must get out of here."

Eddie had dropped to his knees and now dug through the dead man's pockets. "Not until I find the reward coins." He looked up at Hudson with a gleam in his eyes, then held up three pouches. "Found 'em." Peering into the bags, he sat back on his haunches. "But only one of them contains coins. The others"—he mumbled something incoherent—"these are bank notes. There's at least two thousand pounds here!" He shook his head. "Honestly, Hud, I thought you were worth more than that. You are an earl!" His mouth quirked a grin.

Hudson blew out a low whistle. "Two thousand. And we still do not know who called for my demise. If I am seen wandering about London, I'm a dead man." He rubbed the back of his neck, then scratched his shoulder and shuddered. "These clothes must be infested with fleas."

"No doubt, but they'll also keep you alive." Eddie slapped Hudson's back and chuckled.

"Perhaps you should retire to the country for a time. I will spread word of your demise. I am certain whoever put the price on your head didn't know I'd been caught in their snare as well." They climbed a rise, and Eddie panted slightly as he limped along. "I'm near done," he said with a sigh.

"As am I, but we will make it out of here. And I agree with you about disappearing for a while." But he knew he couldn't leave London while there was even a remote chance of word from Sarah. He must stay near the tree. "Or maybe I will remain in London, but out of sight." Hudson stopped at a fork in the path, then heard the whinny of their borrowed horses to the right.

Eddie grunted. "I'll believe it when I see it. You, staying away from the tables? Ha!"

"I can do it." *I must do it.*

The horses were feasting on new spring grass. Hudson mounted his with no problem but watched Eddie struggle to get his injured leg over the saddle. His conscience hurt anew. Aside from a splitting headache, he had come away from the ugly incident unscathed, while his friend's wounds were more severe. "Need a hand?" Hudson began to dismount but was too late as Eddie managed to pull his leg over the horse.

"Augh," he mumbled, wincing in pain. "No buffoon will keep me from my greatest hobbies: horses, hounds, and hunting." He grinned, but his eyes betrayed his suffering.

Hudson hoped Eddie was correct and that his leg would heal without complications.

"Cha!" He dug his heels into the sides of his steed, his trajectory set for London—Eddie close behind.

They arrived before the city was fully awake. Having come from the outskirts, the combination of sooty fog, sewage, and horse dung choked Hudson. They rehearsed their story once more before parting ways.

"I shall tell everyone I've not seen you since the ball and shall act as puzzled as all other members of the *ton*." Eddie turned toward Hudson. "Right?"

Hudson didn't like it. "Take no chances, Eddie. If you so much as see a blade or a pistol, you must disappear. We do not know who hired the blackguards, nor do we know if they will come after you. Forgive me for putting you in this position."

"If I do not mix with society, we shan't ever know who wants you dead. I'll be cautious. But let me do the poking around. It is imperative you stay inside while I smooth the feathers you have ruffled."

Hudson nodded. "But see a physician immediately about your leg." His conscience stung him again.

When Hudson arrived at his London townhouse less than an hour later, he left the borrowed horse with the stable boy and no explanation. In his haste to get indoors, he sprinted past the plane tree, but ground to a sudden halt, took a furtive glance around, and stepped back to it as he checked the hollow. A letter. He smiled as he read his name written in Sarah's mysterious blue ink.

He entered his home to see Mother pulling a shawl over her shoulders.

"Hudson! Where have you been? I haven't seen you in days." She wrinkled her nose and narrowed her eyes as she appraised him. "What is that smell? And those clothes...are you unwell?"

"I have been with Eddie. I'm well enough—just a bit of a headache, is all. And the clothes..." What explanation could he give her for wearing Loch's foul-smelling garments? He rarely hid the truth from Mother. But this time the truth seemed unnecessary and could cause her worry. "I confess having drunk myself into a stupor. I've no idea whom these belong to, but I shall be happy to rid myself of them and bathe. Where are you off to so early?"

"Drunk yourself into a stupor? Oh, not again! You worry me, son. Your father would—"

She didn't finish the sentence, but there was no need. Father had been an honorable earl. And although Hudson had lied about drinking this time, he had not followed his father's fine example. "I vow I will do better, Mother. Starting today. You have my word."

Mother furrowed her brows. "And Eddie. I thought he had changed his ways—become serious about taking over his father's dukedom." She shook her head, then pulled on a bonnet. "'Tis a beautiful spring morning. I am headed out for a walk around the gardens." Her gaze dropped to Hudson's hands. "Is that another letter from Sarah?"

"Yes." And as soon as he rid himself of Loch's clothes, he would devour her every word. "Not to worry, Mum; Eddie has become a perfectly boring gentleman. Ask any debutante's mama. We just found ourselves in bad company. Nothing more." The letter was burning a hole in his hand. "If you don't mind, I'd like to shed these horrid clothes and get some rest. It has been a long week."

"Very well." Her wary expression told Hudson he hadn't been as convincing as he'd hoped about the events or his resolve to change his ways. Hopefully, her walk would distract her from it.

Taking a seat on his bed, he opened Sarah's letter. He read it thrice, trying to make sense of it. "She hasn't moved on and wishes to share a future with me, yet she cannot because she is in hiding?" he mumbled to himself. Anger toward Benjamin Somerset set his soul ablaze. He must free her from the monster—start his search for her again. He punched his pillow. But currently, he couldn't even leave the manor. Tugging paper from his writing table, he contemplated how to respond to Sarah's perplexing words.

My Dearest Sarah,

I am puzzled. Please tell me where you are hiding. I know your father has caused your disappearance, but I do not fear him. If you are residing on the opposite side of the world, it matters not. Just give me a clue so I can free you from the chains that bind you. Please, Sarah. My heart cannot bear to beat without you near.

He cringed at how needy he sounded. Yet every word was true, and if he had but a limited opportunity to express his feelings to the woman he loved, he'd do so. He wrapped it up by including another phrase from their favorite Lord Byron poem.

"One Shade the more, one ray the less,

Had half impaired the nameless grace
Which waves in every raven tress,
Or softly lightens o'er her face…"

Tears burned in his eyes, and he couldn't finish the stanza. The poem had become too real, cut too deeply. Reflecting on her raven tresses—so silky, so soft—left him aching to run his fingers through them. He closed his eyes to remember and savor the sensation.

He ended the letter and sealed it. Now to get it into the tree hollow. If Eddie had done as he'd promised, the *ton* would be gossiping about Hudson's disappearance by now. However, there was a possibility his friend had called for a physician, then napped after their rigorous scuffle with the blackguards. Still, in broad daylight, such as it was, the goons would be hiding in their ratholes. Hopefully. For Sarah, Hudson would chance it.

When his foot hit the bottom step of the grand staircase, Mother held a hand up, stopping his forward movement.

"What is it, Mum?"

"Would you happen to know why at least three good-sized carriages are circling our property?"

Chapter Twelve

An aseptic smell of rubbing alcohol turned Sarah's stomach. She held her breath as the doctor used a machine to force air into Mother's lungs. *Please be all right. Please.* Lines on a monitor continued to zigzag up and down, making a steady beep. At least her heart was still beating.

At last, Mother gasped, coughing and gulping air, yet her eyes remained closed.

Sarah said a silent prayer of thanks, and tears of relief spilled down her cheeks.

"We'll keep an eye on her. Hopefully, she'll wake up soon and hasn't slipped into a coma." The doctor examined the fluids funneling into her body through an IV line. "It's a waiting game now." He turned to Josh. "How did you say this happened?"

A coma. *No, this cannot be.* Sarah gazed at her sleeping mother.

Josh fidgeted, tugging on his beltloops before answering. "She…uh…fell."

"Tell him the truth, Josh," Sarah sobbed out. "Father must be punished."

The doctor jerked toward Sarah. "Your *father* did this? Did he injure your face, as well?" He pointed to the broken skin on Sarah's cheek.

"Yes. He's a monster."

The door burst open, and Christopher rushed into the hospital room, Arianna following close behind.

"Christopher!" Sarah fell into her brother's arms. "Mother might be in a coma."

"We don't know that yet," said the doctor. "Right now it's only a possibility—one we hope won't happen." He adjusted his glasses and wrote something on a chart, then hung it on a hook at the foot of Mother's bed.

Christopher held Sarah as she wept. He looked at Josh. "What happened?"

Without divulging anything concerning time travel, since the doctor and nurse were still present, Josh did his best to explain Father's sudden appearance at the mansion. He turned to Christopher. "Did you bring the warrant for his arrest?"

"It is no longer valid, Josh."

Sarah jerked. "What? Why not?" She pulled away from Christopher, who stood silent. Then she glanced at Ari and realized why the warrant for Father's arrest was no longer valid. Ari's parents, who had been killed by Father, now lived—thanks to Christopher traveling back through time to save them.

Arianna's eyes filled with tears. "I'm so sorry, Sarah. Can't your father be arrested for what he did today?"

The doctor, who had been listening to the conversation, piped up. "At the very least, you need to file a restraining order. This is a matter for the police—and courts."

A collective sigh came from the siblings and Ari.

The doctor's brows pulled down. "You must! Anyone who would do this—"

Christopher cleared his throat. "I'm sorry, Doctor…?"

"Reed."

"Dr. Reed, I must apologize for our reaction. This sort of thing has happened before. I'm afraid putting a restraining order on him would do little good."

Dr. Reed's brows lowered further, and his forehead creased. "Well, I am obligated to report this abuse to the authorities."

"And we hope you do." Josh spoke with a confidence he'd lacked earlier. "And we hope our father is punished for this. He has an uncanny ability to elude capture, is all."

Sarah thought about the years she, Josh, and Mother had spent bereft of everything—society, friends, communication of any kind—all because Father demanded it. No wonder Joshua had hesitated to tell the truth. Stronger now, they must band together to stand against their monster of a father.

Something beeped in the doctor's pocket. He pulled it out and examined it. Sarah had never seen a phone so small. It must be something else.

"I need to go. Push the red button if she stirs. I'll be back to check on her shortly," he said. The nurse tugged a privacy curtain shielding the bed from the open door, and they left the room.

Sarah closed the door tight. Talk of time-travel mustn't be heard by outsiders.

"What should we do, Christopher?" She took a seat on the chair nearest her mother.

"You say Father is at the house?" Christopher asked.

"He was in the bookroom when we left. Who knows where he is now." She moved locks of Mother's light brown hair from her closed eyes. She looked peaceful. Sarah was so accustomed to Mother's hair being pulled up, she hadn't realized how long it was. Unpinned, it fell in graceful waves to her chest.

"I'm going out there." Christopher glanced at Ari.

She nodded. "I'll come with you. Do you two need anything?" She motioned to Sarah and Josh.

Sarah scribbled a few items on a note. "I plan to stay the night with Mother. If possible, will you bring me these?" She handed the list to Ari. "And if it's not too inconvenient, would one of you mind driving my car here so I'll have it if Mother's still here when I need to work?"

Christopher's brows arched. "You got a job?"

"Actually, Josh got it for me. I just started last week, but I already love it. I'll tell you all about it when you return."

Josh stood. "I'll help you find Father."

"I think you should stay here, Josh. If Mother wakes, she'll need all the support she can get. She is still unaccustomed to places like this." Christopher motioned to the IV pole, then the noisy heart monitor. "She will likely be overwhelmed by it all."

"Very well," said Josh. "Do you have your revolver, Christopher? You will need it should you find Father." He scooted another chair opposite Sarah, beside Mother's bed.

"Yes, it's in the cruiser. We'll be back." He kissed his mother's forehead lightly, took Arianna's hand, and exited the room.

"I hope they find Father and get rid of him for good this time," said Sarah. He was her father, but she had no remorse for her venomous feelings toward him.

"I don't know if that's possible." Josh slumped in his seat. "By the way, I delivered your letter to Hudson in the tree hollow while you were at work today."

Sarah brightened. "Thank you, Josh. That's the best news I've heard all day. Did you happen to see him?" She knew Josh would never risk being seen by Hudson, or pretty much anyone in London, but she had to ask. She longed for a description of the man who occupied her dreams. She'd never forget his face—the face of the eighteen-year-old boy she'd loved so much. Had it changed with time? She craved to know it, see it, touch it.

"No. However, I did program the device to land on his property so I can come and go with less chance of being noticed."

Sarah rounded Mother's bed and wrapped her arms around Josh. "Thank you so much. You don't know what that means to me." Every time she'd asked him to travel to Hudson's era, she knew his life was at risk. That he took it upon himself to make traveling safer gave her a modicum of comfort.

Josh looked at the floor while returning an awkward hug. He cleared his throat. "Before Father showed up, I believe you were about to tell me how it has been going with Mr. Carver."

Sarah sighed, then beamed at the memory of her week—before Father had ruined it. She told Josh every detail of her time with Henry Carver, from discovering his glorious music room to the books they'd read together. "He's such a kind man. It makes me sad he never had a family of his own." She stopped herself before adding that he would have made a far better father than Benjamin Somerset ever had.

"Are you supposed to work with him tomorrow?" asked Josh.

"No. We decided I'd go there on Mondays, Wednesdays, and Fridays."

"I'm happy it has gone well for you. I told you it would be a good fit." Josh yawned and glanced around the room. "Do you suppose they have extra pillows here?"

"I'm sleepy, too. I'll go inquire at the nurses' station."

Before she reached the door, Dr. Reed pushed it open. He checked Mother's vitals, then shook his head. "Seems nothing has changed."

Josh perked up. "Did you report the abuse by our father?"

"I did." The doctor looked from Josh to Sarah with a question in his eyes.

"Our brother hasn't returned yet. He's a police officer in Denver. He'll know what to do if he finds him," said Josh.

Short of killing him, Sarah doubted there was anything anyone could do to stop Father, but she kept that to herself.

"Well, I hope someone stops him. The man is a threat. I'm glad you recognize that. Many times family members refuse to step up, in an effort to shield their abusers from the law." He shook his head. "Then they land right back here again with fresh injuries." He turned to leave. "Keep me informed. Your mother doesn't deserve this sort of treatment. No one does."

"I'll go check on that pillow," said Sarah once the doctor had left the room. She walked into the hallway, the bright lights energizing her. After asking a nurse about bedding, she decided to stroll around the hospital ward—stretch her legs a bit.

After a couple of laps through the circuitous hallways, she stopped to dodge a patient on a gurney near Mother's room. She looked down at the man, away, then back again. Was it…? "Mr. Carver, is that you?"

A nurse pushed Sarah's new boss past her, then stopped and turned him around so he could see her.

As Sarah neared him, her chest constricted, and she sucked in a breath. "What happened?" Beneath his hair bulged a large bandage on his forehead. His right leg was splinted, and his arm wrapped in a sling.

His eyes widened then settled into a sheepish glint. "Hello there, Sarah. After you left, I had some trouble getting to my wine cellar. Let's just say the stairs won." His lips pulled up into a pained smile.

She rushed to his side. "Oh, you dear man. I'm so sorry. I would have happily brought up some wine before I left you tonight. Are your bones broken, or—"

"Broken. My leg in two places, my arm in one." He grimaced and moved his uninjured arm toward his wrapped leg. "Doc is waiting on x-rays of my leg to see if I need surgery." His head tipped toward his arm. "They'll cast this later tonight, after the swelling's gone down." He looked back up at her and lowered his brows. "Why are you here? And what happened to your cheek?"

"Uh…my mother was in an accident tonight. She's unconscious." Tears welled in her eyes both for Mother and for Henry. She motioned to her face. "And this is just a scratch."

"I'm very sorry to hear that. Which room is your mother in?"

She pointed to the door a few feet behind her. "And you?"

"I'm right next door. Seems we'll be neighbors for a while." His voice slurred the words.

Sarah winced. "Are you in terrible pain?"

"I was. Now I'm loaded up on medication and feeling like I did back in my young and stupid days." He chuckled.

She wasn't certain what he meant but politely smiled.

"Sarah." Christopher came up behind her.

"You're back." They hugged briefly, and she made the introductions, then wished Henry a good night.

Once in the privacy of Mother's room, Christopher explained that he had scoured the mansion. Father was nowhere to be found. "I wouldn't get too comfortable, though. He's sure to be back. I wish he didn't have possession of a vest. Perhaps it's best you're staying here with Mother. Just in case he reappears at your home."

He glanced at the beeping monitor. "Did Dr. Reed come back?"

"Yes, before Sarah went out walking. There's been no change," said Josh in a groggy voice. He laid his head back on his pillow, closed his eyes, and was soon softly snoring.

Sarah turned to Christopher. She read indecision and worry in his eyes—ever the family protector. "You and Ari have to work in the morning. I'll call you if Mother wakes."

He frowned. "I hate to leave you. Are you certain you're all right? That scratch on your cheek looks painful. A lot like Ari's once did." He glanced at his wife, and Sarah saw love and affection pass between them. The same love Sarah would show Hudson if he were with her.

A lump formed in her throat at the thought of Hudson. At least Josh had gotten her letter to him before all this happened. "I'm fine. It's not nearly as bad as Ari's was. Father punched Josh a good one, too." She motioned to her slumbering brother. "But Mother is who we need to focus on now."

Christopher looked at Mother and let out a long breath, then hugged Sarah and kissed her cheek. "We'll be back tomorrow."

"Thanks, Chris." She watched her brother and Arianna leave, then snuggled into her own chair.

Even though it reclined, the hospital seat wasn't nearly as comfortable as her bed at home. She dozed in and out of slumber, her heart beating to the rhythm of the monitor. How Josh slept so soundly in a similar chair was a mystery. The beeping of the machine didn't keep her awake—rather, the possibility of the noise stopping struck fear in Sarah's heart, allowing her only a shallow sleep.

She squeezed her eyes shut tight and thought about Hudson's letters. If Mother remained hospitalized much longer, Sarah would drive home and collect them—just a quick dash in and out of the mansion. Reading the notes had become part of her nightly routine. The most recent one especially breathed hope into her world of despair. She'd been too shy about asking Ari to bring them to the hospital, but now she regretted it. *Ari would understand.*

After a few hours of restless slumber, a sliver of light pierced through the darkness of the moonlit room as the door opened, then quickly closed. Sarah rubbed her eyes, preparing for the lights to come on and a nurse to check Mother's vitals and IV fluids. But the room remained dark.

Shuffling noises put Sarah on alert. Who would come into the room and stay in the dark? She strained to see, but the shadow remained standing behind the hospital curtain that separated the entry from the rest of the room. Then the smell of sandalwood oil hit her— Father's scent. Her heart pounded as cold dread swept over her like an ice storm. Teeth clenched together to keep them from chattering, she sent a prayer heavenward.

Chapter Thirteen

Hudson closed his eyes and let out a breath. Now would be a good time to tell Mother the truth about his whereabouts over the last few days. Disappointed, he stuffed the letter to Sarah in his pocket and led Mother into the parlor, where he spilled all he could remember—all that he was conscious for.

"There is a price on your head?" Mother moved to the edge of her seat, her brows furrowed. "All because you won at cards a few times?"

"To be fair, I *often* win, and there are members of the peerage who think I cheat. Of course, they are mistaken."

"Often win? How often?" She tugged the shawl from her shoulders and the bonnet from her head, then tossed them aside—as if they were to blame for Hudson's situation.

"Always." He leaned forward and wrinkled his brow. Winning was not a crime. Albeit, his unique intellect possibly gave him an advantage. "You know me, Mum. My brain never quits." He threw his hands in the air. "Counting, remembering, processing—anything. Thus, I know which cards the other players are holding at all times. I couldn't shut this gift—or curse—off if I tried."

Mother stood and began to pace. "You need to get out of London, son. The sooner the better."

"I can stay away from the gaming tables and the public houses, but I cannot leave London. Not now."

She stopped, faced him, and arched an eyebrow. "And why is that?"

Hudson was afraid she'd ask that question. He dropped his gaze to his fidgeting hands.

"Hudson?" She tapped her foot, and though his head was down, he knew her hands were likely on her hips.

He tugged the letter from his pocket. "Because of Sarah. If I disappear now, I will never discover where her father is hiding her. I must save her, Mum." Tipping his chin up, he hoped she could read urgency and sincerity in his expression.

"Your life is at stake, son. You will be no good to Sarah if you are dead." Angry darts leapt from her eyes. "Neither will you be any good to me." Her voice, which had risen just seconds before, now sounded hushed, sad.

A spasm of pain shot through his heart. He cared little for his own life, but Sarah and Mother—he'd protect them fiercely. His reckless actions had endangered them all. "Mother, I will make this right. I give you my word. As we speak, Eddie is spreading word of my disappearance and possible demise. I only have to stay out of sight. Perhaps you can help with the ruse by hanging the mourning banners and dressing in black."

"I despise black. I've only been out of my mourning clothes a short time. Now you wish me to drag them back out—all for a ruse? I loathe the idea, Hudson. And who will believe me? No doubt I've been spotted just this morning on my stroll. As you can see, I am not wearing black."

"That is because word of my death has not reached you yet." The wheels were spinning at a rapid pace in Hudson's brain. "You must send a message to Eddie to come here at once and deliver the sad news. When he does, the goons outside will witness it for themselves when you dissolve into a vaporous swoon in plain view."

"Hmph. I hardly think I am the swooning type."

"They don't know that. Then, in all your grief, depart for one of our country estates, where you can wear whatever color you desire. Once I locate Sarah, we will join you there." The plan could work. He just needed to get Mother on board. "Shall we pen the message to Eddie now, then?"

"And what will happen to your seat in Parliament—the earldom? Is the ruse worth it if you must throw your future away?"

"Mother, I will have no future if the blackguards outside get to me." He ran his fingers through his hair. "What do you suggest I do?"

She opened her mouth to speak—

"And do not say I must retire to the country, because I shan't do it."

Mother lowered her brows. "Then it appears we have reached an impasse. And until we come up with a compromise, we are both prisoners in our own home." She reclaimed her seat and exhaled a huff.

"I shall think of something. Perhaps I can somehow return my winnings to their former owners. Then they might call off their goons."

"You say you didn't cheat? Never, not a solitary time?"

"Never."

"Then returning the goods will only make you appear guilty. What types of winnings are we speaking of—gold, watches, horses, landaus?"

"Yes, there are those items, to be sure. But what my card-playing friends are in an uproar about is the loss of their country estates."

Mother's mouth dropped open. "Who would be foolish enough to wager an estate?"

"Someone who has nothing left to lose. Gambling is a curse. These men always think they will win the next game." Hudson could read men's tells at the tables, but right now he couldn't read Mother's expression. Her eyes looked sharp, but not hard, her brows lowered. When she was angry, one brow generally arched. "I am sorry if I have disappointed you, Mum. As I have said, I shall no longer frequent the gaming halls."

Mother kept a steady gaze fixed on him until finally speaking. "Perhaps this is for the best. Once the situation is resolved—and you *will* find a resolution—you shall never step foot in a gaming hall again, and you shall treat your responsibility as Earl of Alleyne with gravity and give it the respect it deserves—the respect your father and grandfather dedicated their lives to."

"You speak to me as if I am a child instead of a grown man of twenty-five."

"Perhaps I should have done so long before now. But you were a fine lad—dutiful and polite." Her voice cracked. "So much like your dear father, rest his soul.

Hudson, I understand your desperation to find Sarah. Truly I do. She did bring out the best in you. And I will support you in your efforts, but only on the conditions I have laid before you—no more gaming, and you must act as a proper earl."

"I vow I will do it, Mother."

She rubbed her temples. "I fear I've a spell coming on. Once you have concocted this brilliant scheme to solve your predicament, come to me in my bedchamber." She gathered her skirts and swooshed from the parlor.

Moments later, Hudson sat drumming his fingers on the windowsill. He would keep his promise, but in the meantime, he needed to get Sarah's letter into the tree hollow.

From his vantage point, he could see two sides of the Drakes' property without being seen himself. "Thirty minutes and no carriages." He closed his timepiece. "Perhaps they had been simply sending a warning—or even better, the carriages were city traffic." He continued to observe, just in case Mother had been correct. She was rarely wrong. *The tree is approximately thirty paces from the door. I can make it to the hollow and back without being seen—I'm certain of it. Then I shall put all my efforts into devising a plan that will please Mother.* He vowed once more not to disappoint her.

As quiet as the rabbits he'd watched playing in his yard all morning and into the afternoon, Hudson stepped out the door and made a dash for the tree.

A shot rang out, the ball narrowly missing Hudson's head.

He dropped to the ground and shimmied his way back up the drive and into the safety of his home, the letter still clutched in his fingers.

"Hudson!" his mother shrieked, making her way down the grand staircase in seconds. "What happened? Are you safe?" She examined him from head to toe, then front to back, before letting him speak. "You are shaking. Sit, sit. I will call for tea."

"I am all right, Mother. The carriages were gone, but I believe they left foot soldiers to do their dirty work."

"But wherever did you think to go?" She eased him onto a sofa.

Sarah's letter still in his grip, he lifted his hand. "To deposit this in the tree hollow." Hudson wished he could erase the terror he saw in Mother's eyes.

"You realize what this means, Hudson."

"Yes. It means there will be no ruse of my demise. Word will spread amongst thugs and peers alike that I live. They will never give up until my body lies worm-infested in the ground." It also meant the price for his life had been upped—as if two thousand pounds hadn't been enough.

"Not only that, but it shall be risky for anyone to enter or exit this manor—residents and servants alike. Knaves such as the men outside have no boundaries. Should our friends wish to call on us, they might be sieged upon. Messengers, too, will be fair game to those miscreants." Her face softened, but the fear in her eyes remained. She scooted next to him and placed a hand over his. "If Sarah or whoever is delivering her letters stops by to collect or leave a note, they, too, could be shot."

Hudson's chest constricted. "No!" he roared. "I won't let that happen!"

"And we cannot even send for a runner or constable."

His shoulders shuddered as desperation shook his body. "Mother, you...your walk this morning...you could have been—"

"Shh. I was not."

The butler entered the room. "Dinner is served."

"Jameson, please bring a plate in here." Hudson rose and found his previous perch by the window. "And bring my pistol, as well."

"Your pistol? No." Mother stomped her foot. "You leave this room at once and eat dinner at the table like a civilized person."

"Mother, I must keep a vigil. I have put many lives in peril."

Chapter Fourteen

A dark silhouette moved around the curtain, confirming Sarah's suspicions. She sucked in a breath—it was him.

"Father, what are you doing here?" She stood and clutched her pillow to keep her arms from quivering. The lights from the monitor caused his black eyes to glow red with a demonic glint. Dressed in dark clothing, he blended with the shadows, all but his silvering hair.

He advanced toward Sarah, a sneer on his face. "Beatrice is my wife. I came to check on her."

"You mean, you came to see your handiwork? You nearly killed her!" Her voice rose to an unhealthy volume for a hospital. Sarah didn't care. "How can you call her your wife? You are dead to us."

Josh became alert. "What's going on? Why are you hollering, Sarah?" He rubbed his eyes, focused, then jolted as if he'd been shocked. He sprang to his feet, lunged forward, and with his fist clenched, swung at Father's chest. His knuckles made a thudding sound. "Ouch!"

Sarah realized Joshua's hand must have connected to the time-traveling vest Father always wore. Reaching one arm back, she pushed the red button over Mother's bed.

"Look what you've done to Mother!" Josh yelled. "She may never wake up because of you. You're a monster!" He swung again wildly, but his father ducked, and his efforts were in vain.

"Ha! When will you learn who is in control?" Father thundered as he grabbed Josh by the front of his shirt, his evil face inches from Joshua's. "What did your mother do with—"

The door to the dark room swung open. "You called for assistance?" asked a nurse. She turned on the lights but was still shielded by the privacy curtain.

"Yes!" Sarah and Josh said in unison.

Father released Josh, then reached under his topcoat and turned a dial on his vest.

Josh fell backward but caught his balance. The fire in his eyes suggested he might pounce once more.

"Please call the police. This is the man who injured our mother," said Sarah. She reached out to clutch Father's arm, wishing she were strong enough to keep him there until the authorities arrived, but he jerked it away. Vibrations shook the room.

The nurse lurched forward as she pulled the curtain, but Father had disappeared.

Sarah sagged against the wall. It was true—Father would always be in control, and there was nothing they could do about it.

The nurse stumbled, but Josh rushed to catch her before she fell to the ground. "What in the world was that? It felt like an earthquake," she said, still wobbling. She looked up at Josh, flinched, then backed away. "Is this the man who hurt your mother?" She glared at him, then turned to Sarah.

A split second. That's all it had taken for Father to blast out of the room—a split second. Sarah smothered a moan. How could he escape without being spotted? If only the nurse had pulled the curtain sooner, Father would have been caught with Josh in his grip. Sarah's mind strained to churn out a believable tale. "No, no! I'm so sorry. I must have had a nightmare and hit the call button. Please forgive me for disturbing you."

The nurse looked from Sarah to Josh, then back at Sarah. "Are you sure? I thought I heard loud voices coming from this room. I was almost afraid to enter. Then the building shook…" She exhaled an unsteady breath, and then stole furtive glances at Josh. Sarah realized the young woman must have thought he was guilty and Sarah too afraid to say so.

"Oh yes, I'm certain." Sarah nodded to Josh. "He's my brother and is harmless. Our father is responsible for my mother's injuries."

"And my sister's abrasion, as well," said Josh. "We both have nightmares about him. They can be vivid—as if he were standing in the room with us."

Sarah shot him a warning look.

Worry lines around the nurse's eyes eased. "Your father? He sounds horrible. I hope he's been apprehended." She read Mother's medical chart, then glanced at her watch. "Nearly five. While I'm here, I'll check her vitals. It's almost time, anyway." She put a stethoscope on Mother's chest, then hung a new bag of IV fluids from the pole. "I wonder what caused those vibrations," she mumbled as she worked.

"I—I don't know," stammered Josh at the same time Sarah shrugged and studied the floor.

"Do you think she'll wake up? Or is she in a coma?" Sarah so wanted to hear someone confirm that Mother's state was temporary. Sudden guilt pinched her heart, realizing how petty she'd been about Father's treatment toward her. *Mother has suffered more than any of us.*

"It's still too early to tell," the nurse said.

Her voice bombarded Sarah's musings. "To tell?"

"You asked if your mother would wake up, or if she has slipped into a coma."

"Oh, right."

Mother's countenance was peaceful. *She looks so young and beautiful,* thought Sarah. *No longer haggard and beat down from Father's abuse.* She swiped at a tear. *No longer, that is, until now.*

The nurse lifted Mother's eyelid and aimed a small light at her eye. "Her pupil isn't responding." She frowned.

Josh cleared his throat. "That's a bad sign, then."

The nurse put her light away, then folded her arms, her face expressionless. "I'm really not at liberty to assess her condition. You'll need to talk to Dr. Reed. I'm sure he'll be in this morning."

"Is there nothing at all we can do for her?" Anything. Sarah would do anything to help her mother.

The nurse's face softened. "Being here is good. It's been debated, but I believe our loved ones know we're around—even when they're unconscious." She scribbled something on the clipboard and replaced it at the foot of the bed. "I'll be back every hour. Press the button if you need me sooner."

Sarah closed the door behind the nurse, then turned to see her brother pacing. "Are you all right, Josh?"

"I can't believe Father came here. Is there nothing he won't do? What does he want with Mother? And what was he about to ask us for?"

"I cannot pretend to understand that man." She glanced at her unconscious mother, and ire boiled in her veins. "I loathe him." She didn't believe for a second Father felt any concern for his wife. He was after something.

In an unexpected gesture, Josh strode to Sarah and pulled her in for a hug. "We must band together against him. No matter what, I will stand as a protector for you. I'm sorry about your cheek. He…he just moved too quickly for me to respond."

Tears welled in Sarah's eyes. Not so many years before, Father had caused her to think ill of Josh for his cowardly reactions to Father's abuse. A man now, and having helped with Christopher's nineteenth century rescue effort, Josh had matured and was proving to be anything but spineless. She clung to him a moment longer, stepped back, and tamped down her emotions. "I will stand firm with you as well, Josh."

"We need to let Christopher know about Father's attempt. I'll call him now." Josh located his phone and placed the call.

While her brothers conversed, Sarah found some paper and a pen and began a list—*what is Father after?* She tapped her chin, contemplating.

"I'm coming down there!" Christopher's booming voice rose from Joshua's phone and soothed Sarah's heart.

Of course he would rush to Pueblo to watch over his siblings and mother—Christopher always took the role of protector upon himself. Sarah dropped her pen and rushed to Josh's side. "Put him on speaker."

"Hold on, Chris." Josh covered the phone. "What is it?"

Sarah gritted her teeth, then let out a breath. "I really want him to come, Josh. But he keeps leaving work for us. Maybe we should try to handle this on our own." A shiver of fear had her reconsidering… No. She must brave this storm.

Josh frowned and narrowed his eyes at Sarah. When she didn't say more, he put his brother on speaker. "Christopher, I—I think we're all right. You needn't leave work to take care of us. Sarah and I have got this." He glanced at Sarah with worried eyes.

"Josh is right," she said, though she wished to tell him to rush right over. "I doubt Father is brazen enough to show up during daylight hours." It was about time Christopher stopped feeling responsible for everyone else. Ari should be his main concern now. After all, she was expecting a baby. He should focus on that.

Christopher was silent.

"Please, Chris. Trust us. You've done so much already." Sarah's heart squeezed, longing for his comfort. "Come when you have a day off. In the meantime, think about what Father might want. He is after something."

"I can only think of two things he has ever wanted: wealth and power." Christopher's tone took on a bitter edge. "I'll never forget how desperately he wished for me to lie when I was trapped in Newgate Prison. All so that he could bear the title of Earl of Hemington." A huff of air hit the phone. "Knowing what I know now, I should have gone along with his plan. Then he would have remained in the nineteenth century where he belongs."

"You know you couldn't have done that," said Josh. "Your conscience would have gnawed you to the bone."

"Hindsight—things are always clearer looking backward." Christopher paused. "Well, if you two are certain you are all right, I won't rush down there. But please call if Mother stirs, or if Father reappears." Worry strained his voice.

Sarah knew it was difficult for him to stay put when Father could come and go as he pleased. "Thanks, Christopher. We'll let you know if anything changes."

After ending the call, she glanced at the clock. "Josh, don't you need to go to work soon?"

"I'm not leaving you here alone. I'll use some vacation time. I'm certain they'll understand."

"Especially since the owner of your company is in the room next door and can vouch for your reason for being absent." Sarah smiled, relieved to have the company.

The same nurse who had attended to Mother earlier entered. "Dr. Reed is here and wants to run some tests on your mother. We'll be taking her for an hour or so. It might be a good time for you two to grab some breakfast. The cafeteria here isn't too bad."

Josh shook his head.

"What's wrong, Josh?" Sarah whispered. "Mother won't be here to protect."

"But what if Father comes snooping around?"

"Then he'll be disappointed because there's no one to harass and nothing to find."

Josh's stomach rumbled. "I guess you're right. He just makes me feel uneasy."

Sarah took him by the arm. "Come on. Let's feed you."

They walked out the door, then stopped as a nurse pushed a gurney carrying Mr. Carver near them.

"Good morning, Sarah, Josh." Mr. Carver lifted his good arm, and the nurse halted.

"Mr. Carv—Henry, how are you feeling this morning?" Sarah approached him. Besides the cast on his arm, he didn't look much different from yesterday.

"I feel surprisingly rested. Sleeping in a hospital has its advantages. With all the drugs Nurse Betsy has forced upon me"—he glanced at the nurse standing nearby and smiled—"my spasmatic legs didn't keep me awake. In fact, I was sleeping downright blissfully before that tremor, or whatever it was, shook the building. What do you suppose that was?"

Sarah shrugged. "We felt it, too. How unusual." Heat warmed her cheeks.

"The hospital administration is looking into it," said Nurse Betsy. "But right now, we really must go, Mr. Carver."

"I'll come visit your room—maybe read to you a bit when you are up to it—if you'd like," said Sarah.

"I'd like that very much. Thank you, Sarah."

****

Dear Diary,

Four days have passed, and Mother slumbers on. I fear she may never wake. Father has not returned again to torment us, though we are ever watchful. Watchful I am for news from Hudson, as well. Joshua and I have been given a reprieve from the hospital tonight by dear

Christopher and Arianna, who sent us home to enjoy a night's sleep in our own beds.

I was able to persuade Josh to travel to nineteenth century London to check for a letter from Hudson in the tree hollow. It is now well into the night, and Josh has not returned. It is worrisome, of course. I do hope he has not had a mishap with the device.

A chill snaked through Sarah's veins, and she paused in her writing. Josh had been gone several hours. He'd promised to check the tree, then return immediately. Though she wasn't certain how long time travel took, anxiety pecked at her. She tucked her journal into her bag, then pulled a blanket around her shoulders. Thanks to Christopher and Ari, she'd been given a chance to sleep in her own bed—but sleep was the farthest thing from her mind. Joshua's safety plagued her. *'Tis nearly daylight in London. Surely the ne'er-do-wells have climbed back into their holes.* She stood and began to pace. "What is delaying him?" she whispered. "And what will I do should Father return and find me alone?" Shivering, she pulled the blanket tighter around her. But its warmth couldn't remove the dark fear settling in her soul.

Chapter Fifteen

Clank! Hudson startled awake. His pistol had fallen from his grip and rested on the floor. Had his gun caused the offending noise? After snatching it up, he looked through the window, scouring the surroundings. Outside, the sky had lightened with pink morning rays, yet was still too dim to see anything in detail. His warm breath on the window made a foggy film. How any blackguards thought it worth their while to spend chilly spring nights patrolling his property was beyond his comprehension. The price on his head must be dear.

"If you are wondering what woke you, 'twas I." Mother stood, hands on her hips, tapping her foot. "If you insist on spending your time perched in a windowsill, you must take nourishment." She motioned to a tray of breakfast foods atop a table near his post. The sweet smells of freshly baked breads and sizzling meats wafted through the air, making him salivate.

"Thank you, Mother." He had longed for a decent meal but hadn't dared leave his post for more than a few minutes at a time, lest the thugs outside attack an unsuspecting visitor or sneak toward the house. And Mother, acting more stubborn than usual, would not allow the butler to bring him a plate, claiming he'd created the sour situation and he must fix it. Hudson, however, suspected loneliness, on her part, at the supper table had influenced her actions more than her desire to punish him. Either way, he was hungry. "But what has changed your mind? Until now, you have insisted I eat in the dining room."

"And how many meals have you taken over the course of a week—four, five? Barely enough to keep you alive. I do not enjoy dining alone, but neither do I wish my only son to die of starvation." The hard lines around her eyes softened, and she sank onto the sofa. "I shall tell you what has changed my mind, Hudson—you have." Her voice, gentler now, still held strength. "Your determination to protect"—she waved her hand in the air—"anyone in danger reminds me of your father. When he believed in something, he gave his all to see it through. Just as you are doing." Her lips pulled into a sad smile. "And I loved him for it."

Her heartfelt words touched him more than she could know, yet he didn't feel worthy of such praise. He narrowed his eyes. "But, Mother, I have done nothing but watch. I fear I am wasting my time. And, indeed, all of this trouble is my own fault."

"'Tis your commitment, your fierce determination to thwart an attack I value. But you are correct; days have passed without incident. Perhaps the blackguards have been called off."

He shook his head. "I have seen movement. I believe my foes are still out there waiting for me."

"Then come away from the window. They shan't attack if you remain indoors."

"Perhaps. But what if someone approaches who resembles me?"

Mother cocked her head. "And who would that be, pray tell?"

Hudson shrugged. "Half the peerage share my features—fair complexion, light brown hair, tallish."

"True, you have common British features—except for those brown eyes." She stood and walked close to him, peering into his face. "Which are bloodshot from your uneasy sleep. Break your fast, then nap a while."

"But—"

"I will stand watch for a time."

"Truly?" Had he heard her correctly? She had been especially cool toward him since the ludicrous incident had begun. Her change of heart warmed his. But two questions nagged at him: when would this ordeal end? And how would it end? With bloodshed, no doubt. For now, he would be grateful for Mother's kind offer.

"Yes, truly. Eat, sleep," she said. She gave him a quick hug and patted his cheek.

Appreciative beyond words, Hudson devoured the food on the tray, then went to the kitchen seeking more, while Mother sat in a chair near the window with her needlework. His hunger satisfied, he stretched out on the sofa. "I will be right here, should you need to wake me. Thank you, Mother."

It felt like only moments had passed when he heard his mother's voice.

"Hudson, wake up!" She shook him from his slumber. "There was a gunshot!" Her voice trembled and her face was ashen white. "I saw a man not thirty paces from the door hit by the blast, but he did not die—nor did he so much as bleed."

"What? What has happened?"

"Outside! A man is being attacked!" Mother's wild eyes scoured the room. "Where's your pistol?"

Hudson grabbed the gun, which had been tucked next to him on the sofa, then sprang out the door. "Stop right there!" Still several paces from the men, Hudson aimed the gun at the assailants who had thrown a man to the ground. The ball must have missed the unsuspecting visitor. However, his hair was mussed, and his strange clothing disheveled—the goons had clearly roughed him up. "This man is not who you are seeking. Let him go!"

One of the buffoons narrowed his eyes at Hudson, then peered down at the man on the ground.

"I'm not Hudson," said the stranger. "I only came—"

"Quiet, fool!" One of the brutes kicked the man in the side, then looked at the other. "How d'we know who's who? They both fit the description, they do."

The second thug gave him a bewildered look but remained silent.

Hudson cocked his pistol. "If you do not let him go, it will not matter who's who. You will both be dead." He stole brief glances at the man on the ground, attempting to puzzle out who he was. His face, familiar in some ways…

"Ye forget, there are two of us and one of ye." The blackguard who had been silent raised his own pistol.

"So, it is to be a standoff, is it?" Hudson directed his gun's aim at the man holding the pistol and walked toward the three.

The man on the ground scrambled to his knees.

Hudson willed him away. Whatever he had come for was not worth his life.

Out came the first thug's gun—a second one he'd kept in his boot. Now two pistols were trained on Hudson. This would not end well.

"Who will die first? The odds are against ye," said the first goon. They both advanced toward Hudson.

The man on the ground took advantage of the situation, soundlessly rose to his feet, and took several paces back.

Run, man! Get away from here!

The foolish man didn't run but took a few more silent steps back from the blackguards, whose attention, solely riveted on Hudson, didn't seem to notice. Thank the stars above, the two goons were standing close enough together that neither could escape Hudson's aim. However, it would be impossible to hit them both. His blood ran cold, and his hand shook. He willed it to stop. This would assuredly be the end of him. Visions of Sarah entered his thoughts unbidden. How he longed to see her, touch her, one last time.

Without warning, the unknown visitor spread his arms and lunged forward, knocking both brutes to the ground. But they still had guns in their grips and were quick to struggle back to their feet, yelling and cursing the entire time.

But the man didn't stop there. He kept moving forward until he had hold of Hudson's arm.

"Are you here to kill me, as well?" Hudson stared hard into his face.

"Hold onto my arm and do not let go," said the man. He reached under his coat. "Trust me, Hudson, I am not here to do you harm."

"Thought ye a hero, did you now?" A gun cocked on either side of Hudson and the man holding his arm.

"We've got ye both. Won't matter who's who, weel be collectin' the reward money with the pair of ye dead."

"Don't let go," said the man just as Hudson felt the pistol against his skull.

"Fire on three. One, two—"

A slight tremor shook the ground. Hudson closed his eyes, ready to meet his maker, holding firm to the stranger's arm. But there were no gunshots. There were no goons. There was no…anything—just the man whose arm he clung to. The world spun around him while he remained suspended in air.

Whoosh.

"What—" He attempted to force a question from his mouth but couldn't. What had this stranger done to him? Perhaps they were both dead—floating to their eternal destinies. He loosened his grip. If he was headed to his final reward or punishment, he'd do it alone. But the stranger grabbed his shirt, then secured his hand on Hudson's arm. Wherever they were going—paradise or purgatory—they'd make the trip together.

Chapter Sixteen

Sarah stood aghast, barely breathing.

While waiting for and worrying about Josh, she'd ventured upstairs, through the halls and past Mother's room, then stopped short. Peering into the bedchamber, she gaped at what she saw. Drawers opened wide, clothing strewn on the floor, pictures toppled from their pegs. *Father*, she thought with fresh disgust for the man. *He must have searched here before coming to the hospital for whatever it is he seeks. What is it?*

"You beast!" Knowing he could come and go as he pleased left her uneasy. He could be in the house at that very moment. Her arms prickled with gooseflesh.

Torn with indecision, she scanned the room, then glanced down the hallway leading to the stairs. If she left now, she could reach the hospital in less than thirty minutes—get away from this haunted house and the monster who'd built it. There, Christopher would watch over her, as he always had. She sprinted from the room until reaching the stairs where she halted.

Several long moments passed as she contemplated, her trembling hands twisting and untwisting together. She gulped air as if it contained the nerve she lacked, then let out a steadying breath. "I have run from my ghosts long enough. Father has already been here, and Mother would never abide her bedchamber being askew as it is—conscious or not."

Her courage summoned, she entered the room on wobbly legs and set to work. She held a gown close and inhaled the lavender scent. Mother's favorite. Gathering clothing to replace in the closet and drawers took Sarah on a journey. She blinked back rising emotion. Visions of nineteenth century London swirled through her mind—horse-drawn carriages, candle-lit rooms, lovely floor-length dresses, dashing men...*Hudson.* "If only I could see you again—talk to you..." *But how can we be together when we live in two different worlds?*

She swiped at a tear, hung the dress in the closet, and pushed the memories away. "It does not serve me to live in the past. This is my life now, and I shall make the best of it."

She'd not be part of that world ever again. Neither could she be with Hudson. Seven long years had come and gone without him. Seven years of clinging to hope. Though she'd found a way to communicate with him, it was unsafe for her to return to the nineteenth century, and how could he ever come to the twenty-first? And now Josh's life might be in danger because of her stubborn refusal to move forward. When Josh returned—if he returned—she would never ask him to deliver a letter or check the tree hollow for Hudson's notes again.

Once the room was set to rights, she entered her own bedchamber. While it hadn't been raked through to the extent Mother's had, enough of her belongings were out of place for her to know Father's search had not ended in Mother's room. Her skin crawled at the thought of him touching her personal effects. Thankfully, she'd kept her journal with her, so he couldn't intrude on her private thoughts. When she passed her vanity, she caught sight of her injured cheek. With the help of topical medication, it had nearly healed. She dabbed on some powder to cover it.

It took less time to return her room to order. Still no sign of Josh.

She crept down the grand staircase. Shadows seemed to follow her, frightening her more with every step. Clanks sounded from the kitchen, setting her on edge. She froze, not daring to breathe. Thoughts of Father replaced all reminiscence of the past. Was he here? A few more clinks caused her to exhale, realizing it had only been the refrigerator ice machine. Modern appliances still startled and perplexed her. Perhaps a cup of hot tea would soothe her nerves. She switched on every light she passed, hoping to scare away the darkness which had settled in her heart. *He's been here already. Why, then, am I so afraid?*

While preparing the tea, she chided herself yet again. "I shouldn't have asked Josh to travel back to London tonight." It had been unwise on several counts: first, leaving her alone in the mansion with the threat of Father appearing at any time, then, putting Joshua in jeopardy of being recognized—even though he'd programmed the vest to take him directly to Hudson's property. And last, with Mother in the hospital, she should have never asked Josh to go anywhere he might find trouble. After Christopher's experiences on the time-travel devices, Sarah knew of the possibility of malfunction, or worse, foul play. She squeezed her eyes closed and cursed her selfish actions. What had she done?

She stirred the tea, lost in shadowy thoughts. The essence of herbs from her past filled the kitchen, bringing back the nostalgia she'd just escaped from in Mother's room.

The floor rumbled—not the soft purr of Joshua's improved vest, but the loud vibrations of Father's. She dropped the spoon into the cup, splashing tea onto the counter. Frantic, she scanned the room for an escape or a weapon. A wooden block holding razor-sharp knives caught her eye. She plucked out a butcher knife and stood ready to face her nightmare.

His dark silhouette entered the room before he did. Her hands shook, but she clenched the knife tighter and willed them still. Nervous anxiety sparked in her chest.

"What are you doing here, chit?" Father growled. "Shouldn't you be attending to your mother? Or is she now home and recovering?"

The reminder of Mother and why she was still in the hospital fueled Sarah's anger enough to dissipate all fear. Only hatred for the man remained. Brandishing the knife in front of her, Sarah narrowed her eyes at Father. "On the contrary. Mother is not recovered— Christopher is with her. She may never recover. Is what you are searching for worth the life of your own wife?"

A flicker of astonishment creased Father's face before the mask of superiority returned. "Beatrice provoked me. You witnessed it yourself."

"You struck Mother when she finally dared to speak her mind. And if she dies, I will testify of her innocence." As if he'd ever be caught to stand trial. But perhaps the threat would keep him away. "I also witnessed you pummel your son. Why do you continue to plague this family? Have you not tortured us enough?" She took a brave step toward him, knife aimed at his chest, fearing she'd never use it. How could she be like Benjamin Somerset—a man without conscience or regard for life? But she would threaten him and hope to scare him away.

He snorted. "Sarah, Sarah, Sarah, you do not frighten me. You don't have the nerve to strike me or anyone. And do you think a kitchen knife will penetrate the vest I am wearing beneath my clothes?" He smirked, but she thought she saw fear behind his coal-black gaze. The vest—he might have shed it in the lab.

"Perhaps after years of your abuse, I have changed—become more like you." She *had* changed, but not enough to be a killer. Staring hard into his shifting eyes, she became more convinced he wore no time-traveling vest. "I see no vest. I believe you left it below, wishing to be unencumbered while you toss our belongings to and fro, searching for whatever it is you've come for."

"The vest is beneath my coat, you arrogant brat. Now give me the knife before I put you in the hospital next to your mother. 'Twould be fitting. You are both ungrateful wenches." He moved swiftly toward her, grabbing at the knife. He missed but shoved her against a wall.

He lunged once more, and she thrust her arm forward. The knife sank into his shoulder. He yelped. Blood oozed, and his eyes flashed with rage and disbelief.

Sarah muffled a scream. She yanked out the blade and leapt from his reach but continued to hold the knife in front of her. Heart thudding erratically, she narrowed her eyes in what she hoped looked threatening, then took a deep breath to steady herself.

He clasped the gash on his shoulder to stanch the bleeding. "You wretched girl!"

"Get out! I will kill you...I will—" Her voice, astonishingly firm, caused him to blanch—his eyes filled with malevolence. Shocked at her own words and actions, her heart trembled with fear for the retaliation she knew would come. He would likely end her life now. She had no one to protect her.

"I'm your father. Do you see what you have done to me?" He took a cowardly step back, one hand covering his wound, the other reaching out wildly.

She advanced on him once more. "I said get out!" She waved the blade in his direction, surprised by her steadiness.

He staggered back a few steps, spearing her with a hateful glare. "You will pay for this!" He turned and fled to the bookroom, leaving a bloody path as he went.

Rooted in place until the vibrations had died, she dropped the knife and sank to the floor. She sobbed, her body shaking violently. In her heart, however, pride for standing against the man who had so often tortured her swelled, quelling her emotions.

After pulling herself up and gathering her wits, she took a cleansing breath, located the appropriate cleaning supplies, and wiped up the blood. Tears continued to flow. If only she could wipe Father out of the house and out of her family's life as easily.

Exhausted, she spied her tea. She gulped it down, barely noticing its tepidness. Her stomach lurched, and she fought back the bile rising in her throat.

"Sarah. I'm back—"

She jumped at the sound of Joshua's voice behind her. Relief spread through every limb and vein. He was safe. Josh was home and safe. She must apologize for sending him on the selfish and dangerous errand. Turning, she lifted her arms to wrap him in a grateful embrace. Her heart thudded to a halt. "Hud—Hudson?"

Chapter Seventeen

Hudson blinked, raising a hand to shield his eyes. London hadn't been so bright, especially indoors. He *was* inside, was he not? The faint aroma of tea hung in the air, but nothing else felt familiar in the least. "Where—where am I?" And who had said his name? Still squinting, his eyes darted from one odd contraption to the next. Warm air hit his neck, coming from somewhere above. He glanced up to discover the cause of it, but only saw a metal grate on the ceiling.

"Hudson! It is I, Sarah."

He jolted in response to the woman's voice. It couldn't be Sarah. Not here in London. Eyes fully adjusted now, he stared hard into the girl's face. A frisson of electricity shot through his veins at the sight of her. "Sarah…is it truly you?" He reached out to touch her, then jerked his hand back, fearing something unearthly was happening to him—for without doubt she was not of this world. "Are you a ghost, a specter, sent to reprimand me for my misdeeds?" He stared intensely into her face. "Or perhaps I am dreaming. Surely, you cannot be real. I have searched for seven long years."

Her eyes teared up. "I am real, Hudson. You are no longer in London—or even in the nineteenth century." She stepped toward him, lifting her arms, then halted, dropping them to her sides. Her brow lowered and her lips—her beautiful, rosy lips—turned down.

"What is it? Why did you pause? If I am no longer in London, where am I?" If she were truly real, Hudson longed for Sarah to not only reach for him, but take him in her arms, prove she existed in the flesh, not just his dreams.

She shifted her gaze, then spoke to the man who had forced him to this strange place. "Josh, you shouldn't have brought him here."

Ahh, Joshua Somerset. Sarah's younger brother. Hence the vague familiarity. Hudson eyed him. While he was no longer the childish lad Hudson remembered trailing them around their country estates—now taller, broader in the shoulders, indeed, a man—his coal-black eyes confirmed his Somerset identity. Disappointment at Sarah's words, confusion and joy—so many emotions—dizzied him.

"He was in trouble, Sarah," said Joshua. "We both were." He turned to Hudson. "Forgive me, but—"

"Do not apologize—those men aimed to kill us. You saved my life—unless…is this heaven?" Perhaps this *was* heaven. 'Twas bright like heaven. "Sarah, are you an angel?" She appeared more angelic than a mere mortal. Her raven locks cascaded in gentle waves over her shoulders. Beautiful. So unlike the London fashion—hair pinned up with a few tight curls to frame the face. Though more mature looking, her countenance shone bright and youthful. But what attire did she wear? Trousers. Angels didn't wear trousers; he was certain of it.

"No, Hudson, you aren't dead." Sarah tilted her head and narrowed her eyes. "You are in America—"

"What? I hardly think so. I believe I'd have noticed a two-month journey across the sea."

"Let me finish." Sarah motioned to a chair next to a wooden table—the graven designs of which he'd seen no equal. Wherever Josh had taken him carried an aristocratic air. Perhaps Benjamin Somerset had somehow improved his standing.

He seated himself, Sarah and Joshua settling on either side. Despite the uniqueness of his surroundings and the bright overhead lanterns, which appeared to burn without visible flame, he gave Sarah his full attention.

"What century is it, Hudson?"

"Nineteenth, of course."

"Here, in America"—she glanced at Josh, a question in her eyes, until she received a nod. "Here, in America, it is the twenty-first century. You have traveled not only across the sea, but through time."

"Ha!" Hudson shook his head. "Now I know I have perished, or I am foxed. Hopefully the latter, as I rather enjoy living." He waited to hear the others laugh, but both wore pensive expressions.

"Josh, you must take him back. As much as I wish to be with Hudson"—Sarah's cheeks reddened—"this isn't the right way. His parents will be searching for him—"

"Only Mother. Father passed two years ago." He straightened his shoulders. "You are looking at Hudson Drake, Earl of Alleyne. Though I suppose it is of no import, since none of this"—he waved to his surroundings—"is real." He squeezed his eyes shut and ran a hand through his hair. "Yet I do not feel intoxicated." He opened his eyes and speared Sarah with a pointed look. "Don't sell me a dog. Am I dead, then?"

"No," both Sarah and Josh said in unison.

"Don't sell me a dog?" Josh whispered. "I haven't heard that phrase since Father…"

Sarah shook her head. "Josh, how do we convince him? Better yet, just take him home and let him believe this has been a dream." A tear rolled down her cheek, causing a tremor in Hudson's heart.

He looked from Sarah to Josh and back to Sarah. "Shan't I have a say in what you do with me?" After all, it was his dream, or hallucination. And if he had any answer, he'd opt to stay with the spirit of Sarah until he awoke. Hold her. Kiss her. The thought danced in his mind.

Josh cleared his throat, breaking Hudson's sweet trance. "Sarah, Hudson's property is infested with armed men. They charged me." He pointed to a lump growing on his forehead.

Sarah's eyes widened. "What?"

"They'd have killed me if Hudson hadn't come to my rescue." He paused and rested his dark gaze on Hudson. "Or was it you they were after?"

Heat spread through Hudson's body at the implication—which was entirely accurate. And if Josh remembered the events the same way Hudson did, perhaps he was indeed alive and awake. "Yes, the men were hunting me. Have been for days."

"Hudson"—Sarah placed her soft hand over his, and his heart soared—"why would anyone wish to harm you?"

Perhaps he'd alter the details—pick and choose a few. She needn't know everything. "Seems I am a keen card player. Those thugs were hired to take back what

I'd rightfully won from…whoever hired them in the gaming halls."

Her nose wrinkled. "Gaming halls? You were never a gambler."

If only that was the worst of it. Hudson shrugged. "Just a bit, now and then."

Josh quirked a brow. "Men don't kill men over their losses, unless…did you cheat?"

"Josh!" Sarah's brows drew together. "Hudson is no swindler!"

"I needn't cheat when I am playing cards with the likes of Lords Finley or Burke. They are sour losers is all." He must change the topic before he said too much. "Nevertheless, Joshua is correct—I cannot return home until the men are convinced I have utterly vanished."

"Well, that you have certainly done." Josh shook his head. "With so much room, we can keep you here until the trouble blows over."

"How far are we from London? Will it be difficult to—"

"We're in America, man." Josh huffed. "As much as you kick against the truth, facts cannot budge. I brought you to the twenty-first century. In America!" He stood and began to pace, tapping his chin in time with each step. "The only way to find out what's happening in London—two hundred years in the past— is to give it a few days, then return."

Hudson rubbed the back of his neck. "I do not understand. How is what you are saying possible?"

Josh reclaimed his chair. "Through time travel." He let the words hover in the air before going on. "Our father invented a device that travels through time. He did it for nefarious reasons, and his first machine, crude as it was, worked, but dumped us here. He had little control over time or location."

Hudson smothered a scoffing grunt. They must think him daft to believe such a fable. But if he played along, perhaps he would wake up, sober up, or work out the truth in time. At least he'd enjoy Sarah's nearness in this strange state in which he now existed. "I do not recall mounting a device to travel here."

"That's because I was wearing the vest—a modern version of Father's original machine."

"What nonsense! Utter nonsense!" He looked at Sarah for confirmation of his doubt.

"Show him, Josh." Sarah tilted her head toward the hallway. "He'll never believe you until you show him. If he still doesn't believe you, take him somewhere."

"Why must he take me anywhere other than here?" Anguish rent Hudson's soul at the thought of being separated from Sarah now that he'd finally found her. "Can I not simply walk outside to see the difference between two dissimilar continents and centuries?"

Sarah sighed. "Not here. Father had this house built too far from civilization. But maybe you could—"

"No need to take him back down the ladder. I'm still wearing it." Josh opened his coat, exposing a silver vest, the likes of which Hudson had never seen.

"Josh," Sarah narrowed her eyes and peered closer at the strange apparatus, "did you create another vest? As I recall, Mother sewed a cover for the one you and Christopher constructed. This one is so sleek."

Josh closed his coat, cutting off Sarah's and Hudson's view. He looked away.

"This is what you've been doing in the dungeon all this time, constructing more of these evil devices?" Sarah took a step back and scowled at Josh.

"This *evil* device brought Hudson here, Sarah! And it purrs rather than vibrates. I've improved upon Father's invention. And, no, I'm not robbing and pillaging, if that's what you think I am using it for."

"Please, may I view it again?" Hudson needed to get a closer look at something so unique.

Josh and Sarah stared at each other, but Josh finally broke the glare and complied, shedding his coat and allowing Hudson a closer look.

"I've seen nothing like it." He ran his fingers over the fine material. "From what cloth or…substance is it constructed?"

"A metal alloy." Josh unfastened the front by pulling it apart, creating snapping sounds. Inside he viewed a large pocket containing curious vials and some sort of control mechanism.

"Alloy. A blend of metals," Hudson mumbled as he moved his fingers toward the buttons.

Josh clasped a hand over his. "If you push one of those, you'll send me somewhere I won't want to go. Especially at this hour." He chuckled, then yawned. "Which reminds me, Christopher has given us a reprieve from sleeping in hospital chairs, and I intend to find my bed at once."

"You're right, it's the middle of the night." Sarah squeezed Josh's hand. "I apologize. It is late, and you have lost sleep tending to my errand."

"Perhaps, then, Sarah," said Hudson, "you and I can talk…you can explain more…" He wished to reach for Sarah's hand, but instead just stared at it.

Sarah hesitated long enough for Hudson to worry he'd made a misstep. Being unchaperoned together, even if they only planned to talk, was inappropriate. He glanced up to see that Sarah's cheeks had turned a charming shade of pink.

"All right. I'd like that." She turned back to her brother. "Then I will show Hudson to a guestroom. Go on to bed, Josh."

Josh nodded, then hustled from the room.

Hudson exhaled a breath of relief. He kept his attention on Sarah, who had a gleam in her eyes. "What is it?"

"Nothing at all." She clamped her mouth shut, as if squelching a smile. "Come this way, and I'll show you to the parlor, where I think we will be much more comfortable."

Hudson followed until they reached a curious panel on the wall. Sarah pushed against a small lever, and the room plunged into darkness. The invisible flames of the bright overhead lanterns had been doused with only the flick of a switch. Curious. Before he could adjust to that, another lantern lit up above him in the hallway. "What—what is happening? Are you a witch?"

Sarah laughed. "Wait until you see your washroom."

Perhaps he'd hit upon the truth. Sarah was a witch. Her beguiling blue eyes had cast a spell on him—he was certain of it. But the strangeness of his surroundings amounted to nothing compared to her beauty and charm. He wished above all to take Sarah into his arms and show her how much he'd missed her. Would she look kindly on that, or think him too forward? The desire grew in his chest until he could take it no longer.

"Sarah." He reached for her hand, halting her in her movement toward the parlor. Her velvet-soft skin sent chills up his arm.

She turned around, her brows lifted.

"I cannot claim to understand anything I have seen or heard tonight, but"—he pulled her close to him and peered into her azure depths—"if there is one thing I long to be real, 'tis you. Your letters have given me hope and now—" Unable to hold back, he closed the space between them and slid his lips over hers, hesitantly at first—waiting, wanting a response. His nerves zinged, hungry with anticipation, hungry for her.

She stiffened at first, then her muscles relaxed in his embrace, and her mouth melded with his in answer.

"I have sorely missed you, my love." He captured her lips again, pouring seven years of pent-up emotion into more kisses. Each time their lips met was sweeter than the last. A feeling of completeness settled in his heart as sparks sizzled from head to foot. Never had he experienced such sensations.

Chapter Eighteen

Sarah lay in bed, her fingers resting on her lips—the lips that had been so thoroughly kissed by Hudson just minutes earlier. *My first kiss.* She sighed. Her heart still raced from the exhilaration of his touch. Sleep wouldn't come no matter how exhausted she should be. She had only one thing on her mind—Hudson.

Even more handsome than he'd been seven years ago, though she hadn't thought it possible, his features had filled out to perfection. His rich brown eyes, a few shades darker than his hair—which she'd been tempted to run her fingers through—shone like spoonfuls of treacle. And his kisses tasted better than the cobblers Mother made with the sweet, brown syrup.

Speechless. Her reaction to his affection had not only taken her breath away, but also stolen her ability to form proper sentences. He must have thought she sounded ridiculous in her attempt to make conversation after he'd kissed her. Once she'd realized she could think of nothing beyond her desire for more kisses, she'd feigned exhaustion and showed him to his room.

She did recall his reaction when she'd told him there were no chamber pots or servants in the house. His eyes had bulged. "Then how does one"—he turned, scanning the room—"relieve themselves? Is America so old-fashioned that they must do their business outside in the trees?" She giggled, thinking about his embarrassment, then the amazement on his face when she introduced him to running water and a toilet.

The magical musings continued to twirl in her heart until she remembered what had occurred before Hudson arrived. "Oh, no!" She sat up bolt straight. "Father!" She'd forgotten to tell Josh about the uninvited, unwanted, and unwelcomed visitor. *Should I wake him now with the news?* Earlier, she had crept into his room to borrow a nightshirt for Hudson and had found him peacefully slumbering. Waking him seemed cruel. She cursed Father for ruining both her reflections and the rest of Josh's sleep.

Quiet to avoid disturbing Hudson, she padded down the hall toward Joshua's room. She kept the lights off and felt her way along the wall.

"Oomph! What? Who? Sarah, is that you?" asked a man—undeniably, the voice of her dreams.

She clung to his arms to steady herself. "Hudson, what are you doing up? You should be sleeping." *And not standing with me in a dark hallway in my nightclothes.* At least her silk pajamas modestly covered her.

In the dim moonlight that filtered through his room and into the hallway, she could see him shrug; then he put both hands on her shoulders, sending shivers of desire down her spine. "I have been exploring. If I am truly in a different era, I wish to see everything. Do you know there is a cooling box in the kitchen that lights up when you open the door? And it is filled with food!"

She smiled. "Hudson, there will be plenty of time to discover the inventions that have happened since *our* time. There's no need to lose sleep over it tonight."

Hudson didn't say anything, just squeezed her shoulders. His intense gaze sparked an electrical current through her body.

"Are you all right?" she asked.

He shook his head. "I apologize. You are just so beautiful. I—I still cannot believe you are real. And I daren't go to sleep lest I wake to find this—you—have been a dream. I fear it shall break my heart all over again."

It is real, and yet it is not. She swallowed against a knot forming in her throat, knowing she couldn't keep him in her arms forever. Having Hudson with her only heightened her desire to share a future with him. But she couldn't risk living in his world, where she might be discovered as Benjamin Somerset's daughter—thief and murderer. Christopher's experience had taught her that. And Hudson's visit to her world must be temporary. His mother, alone now and unaware of his whereabouts, surely missed him.

"What is it, love? Your eyes are sorrowful, bewildered. Did I overstep by my actions earlier? If so, I apologize—"

"No, Hudson. No. I have waited so long for you— for your touch, your kisses. Everything about *this* is real… Perhaps too real." She tried but failed to keep a tear from falling. "Yet a few days together will only bruise my heart further. That is why I am disheartened."

He wiped the tear from her cheek, then pulled her into an embrace. "Sarah, my darling Sarah, there is a way for us to stay together—there must be. If your father could invent a machine that travels through time—"

"Father! I'm sorry, Hudson, I was headed to Josh's room just now. I must speak with him."

"But—"

"I will explain everything in the morning. You should try to sleep." More than anything, she wished to remain in Hudson's arms.

He searched her eyes. "You really mean to leave me and wake your brother, then?" His forehead creased.

She should warn Hudson about Father, too. Yet the amount of explaining involved… It could wait until morning. "I vow I will be here when you wake." She stood on tiptoes and pulled his face down to meet hers, then pressed her lips to his. "I promise."

He kissed her again. "If this is a dream, may it last forever." After one more passionate kiss, he let her go and moved aside.

Sarah slipped into Josh's room but didn't immediately wake him. The tears she'd mostly held at bay now flowed down her cheeks. How could she ever let Hudson leave?

"Sarah? What is it? Has Hudson done something to upset you?" Josh's voice was groggy.

"Sorry to wake you, Josh. I didn't…I mean, no. Hudson didn't upset me." She dried her face. "With all the excitement tonight, I forgot to tell you that Father was here earlier."

"What?" Josh threw off his blankets and sat up, then turned on his nightstand lamp. "When?"

"By the condition of Mother's bedroom, he must have come days ago, then again just before you arrived home with Hudson."

Josh scowled. "Did he hurt you?"

The door burst open wide. "Did who hurt Sarah?" Hudson entered the room, brows pulled down.

Sarah glanced at Josh, who shrugged. "I suppose you will find out soon enough," she said. "Our father has become a brute—"

"And a thief and even a murderer," Josh cut in. "And though we thought Christopher had freed us from him, he has found his way back."

"He's searching for something," said Sarah. And to answer your question, no, he didn't hurt me. But…"

"But what?" both men fairly shouted.

"It's just…well, he pushed me too far…"

"Say it, Sarah!" Josh was out of bed and walking toward her now. "What did he do?"

"Not him. It was me…I stabbed him."

The silence in the room was palpable for a long moment. Sarah's heart quickened at the memory. But she felt no shame, no remorse.

Josh broke the stillness. "You stabbed him?"

"He lunged at me. I only wounded his shoulder. I fear he will be back to make me pay. He promised as much."

Hudson wrapped a protective arm around Sarah. "He will have to slice through me before I let him near you." His words were laced with anger and anguish. "How could a father harm his child? When we all resided in the country, he bragged about your sweet disposition and beauty incessantly. He once told me not to get too fastened to the idea of marrying you because after you were presented to Society, you'd have your pick of the gentlemen of the *ton*."

"He has changed," said Josh. "Nothing remains of the father of our youth. That is why we're here."

"Please, enlighten me," said Hudson.

Rather than getting their much-needed sleep, Sarah and Josh spent the next hour describing the events of the last seven years to Hudson—from the jewelry heist, which landed them in the twenty-first century, to the most recent events.

"Your mother is unconscious by the hand of your father? Is she here? Where is the physician?" Hudson looked out the door and craned his neck.

Sarah tugged on his hand. "Mother's not here. She's being taken care of by a doctor in a hospital."

Hudson's brows furrowed.

She knew that look—information overload. Sarah recalled the shock of arriving in the twenty-first century—so many new things to learn. "Christopher and his wife are with her now."

"We should go there in the morning to tell Chris what Father's been up to," said Josh.

"Christopher has wed? Mother will be so happy to hear the news. She has always liked him."

"Yes, Hudson, he has," said Sarah. "Arianna, his wife, saved Christopher from being hanged for Father's crimes. But that's another story."

Hudson's brows arched. "It appears I may have to stay in your strange world for longer than a few days to hear everything." He chuckled. "For now, though, I believe the two of you should sleep."

Josh yawned and eyed his pillow. "You'll get no argument from me."

"Come, Sarah. Let me walk you to your bedchamber." Hudson placed his hand under her arm and led her out of the room.

"I can—" Sarah began to protest. She certainly didn't need help finding her own bedroom. But the sensation of his touch caused her to swallow the words and enjoy a few more moments with him.

"You may be able, but you shan't as long as I am here." When they reached her room, he closed his arms around her. "If you need me, just shout. I am at your beck and call." He kissed her, then held her head next to his heart, stroking her hair. "These raven locks have haunted my dreams for so long now. I love the way you let them fall around your face and down upon your shoulders. He rubbed her back. I cannot believe you are in my arms. I feared I'd never see you again." Releasing his grip, he tilted her chin up and kissed her once more. "Until morning, my love."

Sarah floated into her room and closed the door. Speechless. Again. How had he learned to kiss so well? She took a few steps toward her bed before the thought struck her: *Unless, while I have been pining for him, he has been...no, no.* She pushed the thought away. He'd left notes in the tree hollow, told her of his determination to find her, proclaimed his love.

But Hudson came from a different century. And times had changed...

Chapter Nineteen

A beautiful woman slipped in and out of Hudson's dreams. He longed to caress her porcelain skin, rose-petal-tinged cheeks, and locks of shiny, deep-brown hair. Even more he longed to gaze into her hypnotic sapphire eyes, which cast him into a trance each time they fell upon him.

Sarah. She had found him in his sleep. Not the Sarah he'd dreamt about most nights—the pretty, young girl he'd fallen in love with in his youth. No, this Sarah was a woman in every sense of the word. Her disposition was still sweet, while age and maturity had combined to create a stunning creature. Such a being could not be mortal.

Each time she appeared, he tried with desperation to capture her in his arms, but without fail she'd vanish, leaving an ache in his soul.

Oomph. The surface he'd fallen asleep against gave way, and his dreams—bittersweet—came to an abrupt halt.

"Hudson, what are you doing?"

He scrubbed at his eyes. It couldn't be her.

"Hudson?"

He rose from his tumbled-over position, rubbing his wrenched back as he sought a better look. Even more beautiful than before—dressed in a flowing pink frock, hair cascading over her shoulders—she took his breath away. "You smell of roses and lavender." His only thought was to move closer to her. Hold her. And not allow her to vanish this time. "You look lovely this morning." His eyes remained riveted on her. The woman in his dreams had come to life. His arms ached to pull her into an embrace.

Her brows lowered. "Did you sleep in the hallway?"

"Uh…" The reason he'd slumbered against the door of the woman he loved crawled through the cobwebs of his dreams, inching to the forefront of his mind. "I—I had to. Your father has threatened you. At last I have found you, Sarah. I shan't lose you again to that monster."

"You were guarding me?" Sarah's lips curved into a soft smile as her eyes filled with moisture. "That"— she swallowed—"that means so much. No one has ever—" Her voice hitched, she shook her head and wiped a few tears away. Once she gained control, she cleared her throat. "Thank you, Hudson. Hopefully, Father won't come back, but if he does, we'll know by the heavy vibrations. They shake the entire house."

"The vibrations? I do not recall vibrations such as you are describing."

"That's because Josh has created a new vest that improved upon the original invention. Father only possesses the old version, thank goodness. At least we get some warning before he arrives."

"But can he not show up anywhere he chooses— such as in your bedchamber?" That had been Hudson's fear during the night. Yet he hadn't dared enter. As a maiden, which he hoped she still was, Sarah most likely thought him brazen to sleep outside her room. Forward or not, he had to protect her.

"He always enters the house in the dungeon—uh…I mean his lab in the basement…below stairs. I believe he only has certain settings on the old machine. Josh has figured out how to program the new device to land just about anywhere. He's even smarter than Father." Her face grimaced, then just as fast, smoothed back into a smile.

Curious. This new world continued to amaze and confuse him. "Still—"

"It was gallant of you to guard my room." She kissed his cheek. "Are you hungry? I am headed to the kitchen to fix breakfast."

He closed his eyes for a moment to savor her nearness, then angled his head. "Will your cook not do—" He exhaled. "I nearly forgot; you have no servants." Lifting both hands, he motioned to the expanse of the mansion. "Surely in a manor such as this, you require servants."

"We do fine without them." Sarah looked him over, her eyes pausing on bare manly legs and feet. "If you locate Josh, I'm certain he will provide you with some clothing." She raised a hand to her face but was unsuccessful at hiding the blush spreading across her cheeks.

He'd slept in one of Joshua's soft cotton shirts and something Sarah had called sweatpants. She had been correct about the sweat portion of the breeches. He'd been uncomfortably warm and had tugged them up over his knees during the night. Ahh, now he had embarrassed her. No wonder she blushed. He backed away. "I apologize. I shall find Josh straightaway, then."

Sarah giggled and brushed past him, aiming for the grand staircase. Her scent lingered. He breathed it in, wishing for more.

After savoring her a few seconds longer, he knocked on Joshua's door.

"I'm up. Come in." Josh appraised Hudson. I suppose you'll be needing some modern clothes. It's good we are near the same size. There's a washroom through that door, where I am sure you can determine how to bring fresh water through the pipes, perhaps take a shower."

"Yes... Sarah acquainted me with that marvelous room last night. And I am indeed in need of a wash—but shower?"

He followed Josh into the strange water closet.

"This turns the water on." Josh tugged a silver lever. "Move it around until it reaches the temperature you like."

Hudson held his hand under the spraying water. "Extraordinary."

"And here's a toothbrush...to clean your teeth." Josh opened his mouth and made a brushing motion with the odd apparatus. Then he glanced at Hudson's exposed knees. "Did Sarah see you like that?" He raised his brows and widened his eyes. Hudson couldn't tell if Josh was appalled or if he was mocking him.

Hot with embarrassment, he wasn't certain how to answer. "Sarah...sweat trousers..." He tugged the stretchy cloth down to his feet. "I became fiendishly hot during the night, is all." At last he formed a coherent sentence.

"She *did* see you. Otherwise, why would you be so tongue-tied?" Josh's lips pinched together as he handed Hudson some clothing he referred to as jeans and a pullover. The corner of his mouth twitched.

"It was not my intention. I vow I did not ruin your sister."

Josh chuckled. "I'm jesting with you. Times have changed, my friend."

Hudson blew out a breath of relief. "What do you mean by that?"

"I mean that I haven't heard that phrase since I was twelve. And I believe Sarah can take care of herself." Josh turned to leave but stopped and threw him a soft towel. "Take a shower."

As a child, Hudson hadn't known Joshua Somerset well—he'd found him studious and awkward. But now Hudson was getting acquainted with the mature Joshua—a man of intelligence, wit, and sarcasm. He liked him.

Heavenly—the instantly warm shower not only washed his filth, it soothed his kinks. Once Hudson was properly attired, he glanced in Joshua's mirror and wrinkled his nose. "You say men wear this clothing out of doors?"

"Yes. In fact, you will get laughed at in your own clothes."

The delicious aroma of bacon floated up the stairs, making Hudson's stomach growl. "Does Sarah cook often? It smells divine."

"She does cook. Even more than Mother. Mum spends a lot of time in the gardens. That might change, though, now that Sarah has a job... Of course,

everything has changed since Mum is in the hospital."
Josh's shoulders slumped.

Hudson narrowed his eyes as he tried to
comprehend this world of strange clothing and no
servants. But wait— "Did you say Sarah has a job? As
in Sarah is employed?"

"I did. She's quite good at it, too."

Hudson puckered his face. "She can leave that
behind now. We will wed, and she shan't need the
employment any longer." He followed Josh down the
stairs.

"I'll let you tell Sarah that yourself." He smirked.

They entered the kitchen where Sarah stood,
dishing up riced potatoes, bacon, and fried eggs.

"Hudson, would you like tea, coffee, or something
else to drink? My favorite is hot chocolate." Her eyes
sparkled.

"Tea, please." He couldn't move his gaze from her.
Even doing something as menial as serving food—
enchanting. He watched as she filled a teacup, then
motioned for him to sit at the table. "What is that
sound?" Accustomed to his own townhouse being
silent, except for occasional servant chatter, this manor
had subtle background noises.

Sarah shook her head. "You'll need to be more
specific. I remember first arriving in this century and
noticing so many unfamiliar sounds. It could be the
hum of the kitchen appliances, the heater, anything
electric, really."

Hudson gaped at her. The only things remotely
familiar to him were the people and food. And heaters?
Where were the fireplaces? He sniffed. No fire. Nothing
but the aroma of food and a hint of Sarah's sweet scent.

Both Josh and Sarah laughed. "You'll get used to it," said Josh.

Sarah's smile flattened. "No, he won't, Josh. He must return to his time. The sooner, the better." She turned her attention to the food on her plate, spearing a bite of eggs so hard Hudson feared she might break the dish. She swiped at a tear. "I know his mother. Gwen— Lady Alleyne has always been kind to me. I cannot in good faith leave her wondering the whereabouts of her son—whether he lives or has perished at the hands of the thugs from whom you rescued him."

His heart ached at her words. He longed to spend the rest of his life with Sarah. There had to be a way, and he'd think of it.

Once breakfast had been cleared, Josh and Sarah led him to a cold, cavernous room housing large machinery with strange, thick wheels. Never had he seen the likes of such contraptions. *Modern carriages, perhaps.* Josh pushed a button on the wall, lifting a monstrous gate. Hudson wished to explore each vehicle but only managed to run a hand over the sleek metal before Josh told them to hurry.

Sarah opened a door on the smaller of the machines and motioned him to enter it. He complied, and she slid in next to him. "Christopher will be surprised to see you. And I can't wait for you to meet Arianna."

We are meant to travel in this strange contraption? "But where are the horses?"

"It appears I am to act as the chauffeur, then." Josh, who sat on a seat in front of them, did something with his hand, causing the machine to roar to life, and Hudson's heart to leap to his throat. "And about the horses, Chris keeps one here, but only for pleasure riding. Horse-drawn carriages are not part of this century. Now we have cars, or automobiles." Josh glanced at a looking glass above him, then craned his head back.

Before Hudson had time to respond to the horses—or lack thereof—the car jerked, rolling backward and onto a road. He clutched the handle to his left and Sarah's hand on his right. The car moved fast. He sucked in a breath and gritted his teeth. He wished to keep her fingers captive but cleared his throat and let them go.

Trees and fields blurred together at the speed they traveled. He feigned nonchalance. "At least foliage still exists in this century. And though the variety appears to be different from that of England, the countryside is similar."

Josh glanced back at Sarah.

She smiled, then looked out the window. "Just wait," she said.

Hudson followed her gaze. Only moments later, where the landscape had consisted of trees and lawns, buildings now crowded the area, along with more cars. His eyes bulged, and he grasped Sarah's hand once more. The car moved forward and stopped again and again, according to colored streetlamps. A million questions flooded his brain. "How do those—"

"Here we are." Josh cut his first of many questions off.

He parked the fast-moving vehicle next to a row of others much like it. Not a horse in sight. And the ground was black with white lines—no granite setts.

"Follow me. This is the hospital."

Hudson tripped over his too-large shoes Josh had called loafers, trying to keep up as they pushed through the doors of the gigantic building. It was difficult to see all the new sights while being led through a remarkably brightly lit maze. But he had retained his grip on Sarah's hand and knew he wouldn't get lost. The smell in the air reminded him of oils and ointments his own physician used, only much stronger. He stumbled more than once, attempting to take everything in.

"Whoa, Hudson." Sarah let go of his hand and pushed on his chest to stop him from barreling into her. "We need to go up here."

Josh pushed a button on the wall. A set of strange, silver doors opened without anyone's help. Josh stepped in. Sarah stepped in. Both looked at Hudson, eyebrows raised. He hesitated.

The doors began to close, and Hudson jumped back. "Oh, no! Now I've lost them." Panic jittered through his body. Any other day, he would have had his surroundings memorized, but today, too many unfamiliar items had caught his attention. Who knew where the small room behind the silver doors led? As he reached up to bang on the door, it re-opened. There Josh and Sarah stood, both smiling broadly. Josh flat-out chortled, not holding his amusement back.

Hudson blew out a breath. He could not deny he found this world disconcerting, even though he had been confident—cocky, even—in London's most prestigious edifices.

Sarah held out a hand. "You've got to step in, or you'll be left behind. Sorry about that." Her beautiful smile washed the whole unnerving mishap from his mind.

The little room rose up; Hudson's stomach went down. How he'd survive this new life of fast-moving objects, he didn't know.

He caught his breath when they exited the tiny space, ready to be on solid ground. "Where are they keeping your mother, in an amusement asylum?"

Josh snickered again. "Her room is right around the corner." He continued to lead the way.

Sarah tapped on a door, then entered. "It's us."

Hudson followed her around a curtain. "Christopher!" He wasn't certain why he was so surprised to see Sarah's brother. She had mentioned him several times. Perhaps the physical changes and mature countenance had initially thrown him.

Christopher narrowed his eyes at Hudson, then shifted his gaze to Sarah. "Hudson Drake, is it you?" He stood and extended his hand. "Sarah, how did you manage that?"

"I didn't. Josh did. But you won't hear me complain." She turned to Hudson. "Meet Christopher's wife, Arianna."

A pretty woman stood next to Christopher, a smile spread across her face. "Nice to meet you, Hudson." Her eyes twinkled when she glanced at Sarah.

"Hudson Drake!"

Everyone turned at the sound of Mrs. Somerset's voice.

"She's awake!" said Arianna.

Sarah sat next to the bed. "Mother, we are all here. I'm so happy you've come back to us."

"Hudson Drake!" she repeated, her voice firm and insistent.

"Yes." He moved closer. "What is it?"

"You must warn Gwenillen. She is in danger."
"Mum's in danger? But—"
Mrs. Somerset's eyes fluttered, then closed.

Chapter Twenty

"Wake up, Mother. Wake up!" Sarah curled her hand into a fist, then squeezed her eyes shut and pushed out a breath. Mother had spoken. She'd not even sounded groggy. Why then had she fallen back into that void?

Christopher gave Mother's shoulder a gentle shake. "Come back to us. Tell us what dangers Hudson must warn Lady Alleyne of."

No response. Only the constant beep of her monitor echoed through the room.

Like a stormy sea turned abruptly calm, the sharp lines of Mother's face smoothed as her pallor, pink just seconds ago, returned to white.

Deep despair crept into Sarah's soul. Mother—awakened from her coma for a brief moment—gone again. She ran her fingers through the locks framing Mother's face. So peaceful. Too peaceful.

Hudson peered down at Mother. "I shall do as you ask, Mrs. Somerset. I shall warn Mum, but I must know why she is in danger."

Mother stirred at Hudson's voice, but did not wake.

A spark of hope. Sarah clutched Hudson's hand. "Keep speaking to her, Hudson. Yours is the only voice to which she responds." Sarah squeezed his fingers.

"Ahem."

Everyone's heads turned toward the voice. A nurse stood at the foot of Mother's bed.

"Dr. Reed needs to run more tests. Did the patient wake up? Is that why you are crowded around your her?"

"Yes. She did, but only for a moment. Does it mean she'll be all right?" More than anything, Sarah hoped it did. "She even spoke."

The nurse's brows arched. "What did she say—anything coherent?"

Uncertain how to answer, Sarah looked to Christopher for help.

"Nothing that made much sense." Chris glossed over the question and kept talking. "But can you answer my sister's question? Does her waking—even for just a moment—indicate she'll be all right?"

"I hope so. We'll likely know more after we get the results from the scans Dr. Reed ordered." The nurse glanced at each person. "Is this your whole family?" she directed her question to Sarah.

"Yes, we're all here. I believe you have met everyone but Hudson." She nodded in his direction. "He is…"

"Her fiancé." Hudson gave the nurse a slight bow.

Sarah tingled all over, hearing those words spoken aloud, and to a stranger. Oh, how she wished she could truly be Hudson's fiancée. There was nothing she longed for more. But circumstances as they were made the prospect doubtful. Her heart bruised at the reality.

"Nice to meet you, Hudson." The nurse turned back to Sarah. "I need to prep your mother for the tests, so if you'd all like to grab a bite, it's going to take a while."

Sarah coiled her fingers together. They couldn't leave now—right after Mother had spoken. "But what happens if she wakes and no one is with her?"

"Someone will *always* be with her." The nurse tilted her head, her expression softening, then handed Sarah a clipboard. "Write down your phone number. If she wakes up, I will call you immediately."

Worry still gnawed at Sarah. She looked at Christopher and Josh to gauge their reactions.

"She is not stirring, Sarah. And I believe we have much to discuss." Christopher glanced at Hudson. "Perhaps now is the best time to do it... Oh, I nearly forgot, Sarah, you have a new phone number."

"What? Why? My phone—"

"Your boss in the next room had his secretary bring those for you and Josh." Christopher pointed to a table in the corner. "Mr. Carver came in earlier with them. They're satellite phones—the newest, most advanced phones on the market. Sleeker than the old models and very sophisticated, he said. I guess he would know since his company makes them. Mr. Carver said in this day and age, there is no reason you should be without cellular service—even if you live in the boondocks." He chuckled. "Nice man. We should have invested in satellite phones before now, but..." He shrugged.

Sarah knew what Christopher was thinking but couldn't say in front of the nurse. Without Father's dirty money, none of them had the means for fancy phones. Living expenses, including upkeep on the mansion, took donations from each family member. She crossed the room and analyzed the new phones. "I must thank Henry."

The nurse shook her head. "Mr. Carver isn't in his room right now. He's in surgery."

"Oh. Later then." Sarah wished she'd been able to see Henry before he'd gone under the knife. She hoped it wasn't a complicated procedure. The dear man had already been through so much.

****

Five chairs scraped against laminate flooring as trays clanked one by one onto the round cafeteria table. Aromas of soups and burgers rose from the plates. Sarah scrutinized Hudson's every reaction to his new environment, hoping he wasn't being overwhelmed. She'd lost count of the number of times his eyes had bulged—in Mother's room, where the TV was playing in the background; when he'd asked to see her new phone and it lit up, causing him to jerk and nearly drop it; at the vending machine, where Josh had stopped for a candy bar; every single time they'd used the elevator; and as they'd entered the cafeteria, when he'd seen the variety of food available. She smiled but never laughed at his amazement. She'd been there. A brief vision of him remaining in the twenty-first century and becoming her husband warmed her soul.

"Why would Mother feel the need to warn your mother about impending danger?" Christopher began grilling Hudson, cutting short Sarah's sweet ruminations.

Hudson lifted his hands. "I am as unclear about that as are you."

"Our mothers were dear friends in the country," Sarah said. "Mother confided in Gwenillen—Lady Alleyne—often."

"'Tis true enough. Before your family was evicted from your estate, Beatrice and Mother shared daily visits. I wonder what else they shared." Hudson bit into his burger, and his eyes bulged again. After swallowing, he wiped his mouth. "I must get the recipe for this sandwich for Cook."

Everyone laughed but Christopher, whose forehead wrinkled and eyes narrowed. He directed his focus on Hudson again. "Do you know if our mother gave anything to yours for safe keeping during that time—anything she may have held dear, and wished to keep from the creditors?"

Hudson stared at his plate, closed his eyes for a moment, then shook his head. "I would remember if she had told me of such a thing, but I was only a lad at the time. She wouldn't have confided your mother's secrets with me. What sort of treasures are you referring to? Anything specific?" He met Christopher's gaze.

"Although untitled, Mother came from a wealthy family. From her parents she inherited valuable artifacts such as rare, oriental vases—Qing, I believe. Priceless in today's market. She also had unique jewels squirreled away from Father. His drinking drained his inheritance. Mother didn't wish for hers to vanish, as well." Christopher glanced at each sibling's face. "Do either of you know what became of those vases or jewels?"

Sarah tapped her chin, concentrating on the beautiful country estate in which they'd once resided. Her life then resembled a fairy tale—beautiful and surreal.

Chris didn't give her a chance to answer before continuing. "A couple of years ago, I recall reading about someone finding a Qing vase in their attic. It sold in Paris for millions of dollars. Imagine what Mother's entire collection is worth."

Josh blew out a whistle and shrugged. "I think I remember them. Mum kept them on a shelf, out of my reach."

Sarah gasped. "That's right! I recall those vases. So colorful, they mesmerized me. I don't know what became of them, nor do I recall the jewels. But I stood watch as our belongings were crated and carried away, and those vases"—she shook her head—"were not among them, unless I missed something. I doubt Father knew what became of them, as he was foxed through those dark days. Surely he believes the creditors had seized them…"

Josh swallowed a fry, then gulped down some soda. "What if Mother did give them to Lady Alleyne to hide?"

Hudson also gulped his soda, then sputtered. "What sort of ale is this?" With watery eyes, he put the drink down and coughed into his napkin.

Christopher chuckled. "One of many surprises the twenty-first century has to offer."

Sarah patted Hudson's hand. "I'm sorry. I should have warned you about the carbina—the bubbles." She smiled up at him. "Sip, do not gulp."

Hudson belched, then covered his mouth. "Please pardon me. Good advice, Sarah—though a bit late." His lips tugged into a grin.

"Back to the predicament—the vases and jewels," Sarah said. "After all this time, why would Father think to seek after Mother's belongings?" She stirred her soup to cool it. "Surely he has stolen jewels more precious than hers. But the vases—if what you're saying is accurate, Chris—he might be searching for those. Still, couldn't he go back to before Mother hid the vases to retrieve them?"

Christopher shook his head. "He could, but if it was before he had constructed the machine, he might not have had the components or chemicals available yet, should something go wrong. Going back would be a huge risk. And as far as the article about the vases goes, I believe it was credible." He bit into his burger, then speared a lettuce leaf and twirled it on his fork. "And if he did get wind of Mother hiding them without his knowledge, he'd be furious. Father's ego is bigger than his bank account."

Sarah shrugged. "I've not seen any vases or jewels in the mansion. But Father tore the place apart—"

"He what?" Christopher dropped his fork. "Father has been in your home, rummaging around?" Anger sparked in his eyes.

"Yes. But his pursuit thus far has been futile."

"How do you know that?" Christopher huffed.

"Because he came back only last night to continue his search."

The storm in Christopher's countenance escalated to a hurricane. He looked from Sarah to Josh. "What happened when he saw the two of you?"

"I—I was alone. Josh was on an errand for me—which is why Hudson is here." Sarah glanced at Hudson, who was giving her his full attention. In fact, everyone was. "We had a confrontation, of sorts." She exhaled a deep breath. "I should have told you sooner, Chris, but with Mother waking up…" She shrugged. "I would have called you directly after the episode, but with no cell phone service at the mansion…" Her voice trailed off, but her thoughts remained on the bloody scene caused by her monster of a father.

Josh smirked. "Sarah stabbed him in the shoulder." He grunted. "I wish she'd aimed for his heart."

Christopher gasped, his eyes wide. "Sarah, what happened? Are you all right? Did he hurt you?"

"No, he didn't hurt me. I will admit to being shaken from it all. Father cornered me in the kitchen. Thankfully, I had the presence of mind to grab a butcher knife."

Arianna's mouth dropped open. "Are you kidding me, Sarah?"

Sarah proceeded to relate the whole incident.

Fear, worry, and pride crossed each person's gaze through the telling. Her core strength and confidence grew from an anthill to a mountain from everyone's awe and kind comments in reaction to the events.

However, the indiscernible pallor of Christopher's face did not sync with the pride in his eyes. He had guarded and protected his family for as long as she remembered. *We are all adults now. Perhaps it is time we stepped up and stopped relying on him for everything. The burden we lay on his shoulders must weigh him down.*

He'd been her knight, her protector, her savior. Could she allow him to relinquish the role and concentrate on his own little family? She glanced at Arianna's growing stomach—a new babe to add to the family. No, Christopher wouldn't want to give up the lead to bring Father to justice, nor would he leave his siblings and mother to fend for themselves. He had worked too hard to reclaim his family after Father had thrown him out of the house and out of their lives. And Arianna—she was as much family as if she'd been born a Somerset. Sarah exhaled a quiet breath. They must continue to work together, but her bolstered confidence would now aid in the cause instead of adding to the worry.

After a pause, Sarah continued. "We all know Father will stop at nothing to get what he wants. He knew how close Mother and Lady Alleyne were. If he believes Mother asked her to hide her valuables, dear Gwenillen"—she looked at Hudson—"your mother, will be his next target." A cold chill settled over her as she watched Hudson's face pale. "I do not know what we can do, however, with a price on your head. For you to go back to the nineteenth century would be perilous.

All eyes turned to Hudson. He pushed his half-eaten burger away. "Perilous or not, I must return home. Now."

Chapter Twenty-One

Hudson's nerves soared to high alert as he listened to the Somerset siblings speak of possible danger encroaching on Mother. He must return home to protect her—the sooner the better. Scrutinizing the cafeteria, he searched for an exit. He must find one at once.

"It's too dangerous, Hudson." Sarah's eyes grew wide as she clutched his hand. "Please, give it a few days. Wait for the ruffians surrounding your house to retreat—believing you have vanished forever. I beg you." Her grip tightened as a dark cloud settled over her countenance.

"But Mother—"

Josh cleared his throat. "I don't know if it's possible to accomplish remotely, but I can attempt to program the machine to land inside your manor, Hudson." He looked toward Christopher, then glanced at Sarah.

Christopher flinched and lowered his brows. "Josh, have you been experimenting with the device? Is that why Hudson is here now?"

Awkward silence fell over the group. Arianna reached for Christopher's hand.

Josh exhaled a deep breath. "Yes. I've experimented. But had I not, Hudson might be dead. Someone has put a bounty on his head, and I snatched him from their grasp with no time to spare. Their pistols were cocked." He huffed. "I was only helping Sarah. Is that so bad? She had it in her head to find Hudson on her own and would have blown herself up trying if I hadn't discovered her in time."

Christopher sputtered. "What?" He turned to Sarah. "You must promise to never toy with those chemicals or the device. They are dangerous."

Hudson's mouth fell open. Sarah had risked her life to find him. Ice slithered through his veins at the notion, and the delicious burger now soured in his belly. The thought of the woman he loved dying in her attempt to soar through time to locate him—a man so unworthy of her—caused bile to rise in his throat. Clamping his lips shut, he swallowed it down, then inhaled a deep breath. "Is it true, Sarah?" His voice hitched. "Did you set out to find me on that traveling device?"

She nodded, then closed her eyes. A single tear dripped to her chin. "I was desperate." She blinked several times and swiped at the tear, then straightened. "We can waste time discussing what might have but didn't happen in the past, or we can come up with a way to help Lady Alleyne."

Hudson squeezed her hand. He lowered his voice to a whisper. "I was desperate, as well."

Christopher's lunch had gone mostly ignored. Ari nudged him. "You should eat. It might be a while until our next meal." She patted his hand, then turned to the group. "Before you run back to the nineteenth century, shouldn't we return to Beatrice and see if Hudson can coax more information from her? Not to mention, hear what the doctor has to say about her test results?"

Anxiety zinged through Hudson. "But—"

"Ari's right," Christopher said. "We can't act rashly—especially when it might get you killed, Hudson. Father's machine is not programmed to land anywhere near your home. If he approaches, let us hope the thugs scare him away. In the meantime, we should listen to Ari. We can't leave Mother now."

"Sorry, Hudson," Sarah whispered. "But I believe they are correct. Although I do hate the idea of your mother fearing something untoward has befallen you."

Hudson dipped his head. If not for the goons skulking his property, Mother would scarce bat an eye at his absence... But he would not share such information. "I worry more for Mum's safety than my disappearance."

A chime sounded, startling Hudson. Sarah tugged her new phone from her pocket.

"What is it, Sarah?" Christopher cocked a brow. "Is Mother awake?"

Sarah shook her head. "The nurse. Testing is complete, and Mother is back in her room. No signs of change." She sighed. "I wish she were awake; then perhaps she could enlighten us about the vases, or whatever spooked her when she heard Hudson's voice."

"Let's get back up there. Everyone ready?" Christopher glanced at the half-empty plates cluttering the table.

Arianna began stacking dishes on trays. "I'll take care of this mess. You all go. I'll catch up in a few."

Christopher gave his wife a quick kiss. "Thank you." He led the group to the sliding silver doors.

As they passed the nurses' station and approached Mrs. Somerset's room, a man's voice floated through the open door. Christopher held a hand up, halting the group.

Is it Benjamin? Hudson's heart thudded. But as they rushed toward the open door, he heard the most soothing voice—gentle, not threatening.

"Then, in my teen years, I found myself in one scrape after another. My mother once predicted I would either end up in jail, or as the CEO of a large corporation. I believe those words prompted me to prove her right." He chuckled. "That is to say, I determined to one day start my own company and become a success. And I have. I give all credit to a mother who loved me no matter my sometimes-grievous actions." He laughed again.

"It's Henry." Sarah pushed past Christopher and into the room. The small group followed her.

The man startled and, with his good hand, turned his wheeled chair to face them. "I'm sorry to intrude. She rests so peacefully. Something I envy." He turned and graced Beatrice with a longing gaze. "I only wished to keep her company while you were away. I said I was a relative, and the nurse let me in."

Sarah approached the man and placed a hand on his shoulder. "Henry, there's no need to apologize. Thank you for watching over her."

Henry nodded. "She looks angelic."

Christopher cleared his throat. "Has the doctor checked in with the test results?"

Although Benjamin Somerset had been out of their lives, Hudson assumed there had been no bill of divorcement between Mr. and Mrs. Somerset. A man such as Benjamin would never agree to such a thing. Therefore, the open adoration expressed from this patient—innocently spoken or not—would rankle the Somerset children—especially the eldest.

"No, not yet. The nurse said she'd be back shortly with results," said Henry. He didn't act affronted by Christopher's pointed looks. Instead, he continued to gaze upon Beatrice. Her hair flowed in waves over the sheets, framing her heart-shaped face—smooth and free from the cares of the world. "If someone will push me"—he lifted his casted arm—"I will retire to my room and leave you with your mother. Again, I apologize for the intrusion."

Christopher stepped forward, but Sarah raised her hand, stopping him. "Allow me, Christopher. I must thank Henry for his generous gift. The satellite phones will be a godsend for us—especially with Mother here in the hospital." She grasped the handles of the wheeled chair, and the group cleared a path to the door.

Henry smiled, though Hudson saw pain in his eyes, perhaps due to the injuries which had brought him to this place. "My dear Sarah, providing you and Josh with phones was the least I could do. You're most welcome."

Sarah rolled him away, and the Somerset siblings gathered around Beatrice once more.

Christopher clasped her hand. "Mother, we are here. Will you not wake—come back to us?" He turned to Hudson. "Please, Hudson, will you speak to her again?"

Sarah returned to the room and placed a gentle hand on Hudson's arm. "Just say anything to her. Yours is the only voice to which she has responded."

Hudson patted Sarah's hand, then stepped closer to the bed. Christopher moved, motioning him to take his spot, and to hold Beatrice's hand.

Though awkward to do so, he submitted. "Beatrice…er…Mrs. Somerset, it is I, Hudson Drake. If you can, will you tell me why my mother is in danger?"

A silent moment passed. Hudson held his breath. Beatrice's body gave a slight twitch, causing his heart to skip a beat. What contemplations troubled her? He must know.

Squeezing her hand, Hudson tried again. "Please, Mrs. Somerset, I must know how to protect Mum—" His emotions rising, he stopped.

Beatrice's eyes flew open at the same time as her mouth. "She is in danger!" The slopes of her face creased into sharp lines on her forehead. "Benjamin will stop at nothing. You must hide her away, Hudson. If you do not, he will find her and terrorize her as he has done me!" Her icy-blue gaze never left Hudson's.

His pulse quickened as fear spasmed through him. He must help Mother. "Are you certain? How do you know?"

"Hudson, attend to her at once!" Beatrice's grasp on Hudson's hand tightened.

"Does she have your vases? Where are they? I shall conceal them from your husband. Is that what he is after?" The words spewed out in an urgent fervor.

Beatrice's hand went limp and her eyes closed. Her face placid once again. Silent.

Hudson dropped his head. Defeated. His body shuddered. No answers. More questions.

Sarah rushed to Mother's bedside. "Wake up! You must stay with us!" Tears ran down her cheeks. "Please, Mother, we need you."

Hudson pulled her into his arms as she wept desperate tears. He held her back. "What is it, love?"

She shivered. "I am not entirely certain, but I think Father is infiltrating Mother's thoughts while she sleeps. I know it sounds preposterous—crazy, even—but Mother clearly has a message, as if from beyond."

"Mother isn't dead!" Josh shouldered his way to Sarah. "You speak as if she is rising from her grave to save Lady Alleyne. Have you given up on her, Sarah?" His voice, firm and edged with anger, demanded an answer.

"Of course not!" Sarah jerked toward Josh. "I shall never give up on her. I am only wondering what causes her to wake for Hudson and no one else."

Hudson moved his hands up and down her arms, hoping to soothe her anxiety.

Sarah relaxed under his touch. "What is our next move?" She held Joshua's gaze. "You said you can possibly program a device to land inside the Drakes' townhouse. Are you referring to the new vest you constructed, or can you do the same with the disc?"

Josh narrowed his eyes. "Not the disc. I was able to get Hudson here well enough with only the vest."

"But will it transport me, too? For I have no intention of being separated from Hudson…ever!"

Josh grunted. "Three of us is too much weight—I struggled keeping Hudson with me. And I can't construct a new disc so quickly. I'll just go with him."

Sarah didn't waver. "I waited with Mother for days while you and Arianna made the perilous journey to the nineteenth century in search of Christopher." Her voice rose, and the volume increased with each word. "And I have waited to be reunited with Hudson for seven tortuous years. The only thing worse than experiencing whatever unknown danger is lurking in the shadows is *waiting*!"

Hudson's heart quaked. If she came to the nineteenth century, she risked discovering Hudson's past behavior. "But—"

"Hudson has an eidetic—photographic—memory. I studied it in a college class last year. Josh, if he even glances at yours and father's notes, he'll never forget them. We can go without you. I know I messed up mixing that vial of dangerous chemicals together—you can't even dispose of because of their volatility—"

Christopher and Arianna gasped.

"But Hudson is the most brilliant man I know. He shan't put my life in danger." She glanced at Hudson, a plea in her eyes.

He nodded. He couldn't deny her—risk or no risk.

Joshua's shoulders slumped. "Very well."

Chapter Twenty-Two

Darkness had fallen when Hudson's boots thudded against the marble floor in his nineteenth century townhouse. Joshua had been correct in his estimation—they landed just inside the foyer. Hudson had tried but failed to communicate with Sarah in transit. The traveling vest had caused a paralyzing effect on him.

Sarah gasped.

"Are you well, Sarah?"

She blinked against the darkness. "I shall be. It's—it's nothing, really," she said, keeping her voice low.

"I do not recall you ever coming inside our London home." His eyes adjusted, and he saw an array of emotions in Sarah's wide eyes. She must be experiencing a sense of recollection after so many years away from her original time.

"I've not been inside, yet everything is familiar." She sniffed. "The scents of this century bring back a flood of memories."

"I hope good ones."

"…Yes, some. But Hudson, though we communicated through letters during those years I lived in London, I never confided in you the abuse Father inflicted on our family."

Hudson flinched, and his muscles stiffened. Sarah's letters had been filled with poetry and magic. She'd said nothing of abuse. "Why did you keep such a thing from me?" He gripped her arms firmly and sought her eyes.

"I feared you would do something rash. And by your reaction, I believe I was correct. 'Tis all in the past now—mostly."

A growl rumbled in Hudson's chest. He must protect her from that monster. And that she lived with his abuse without an outlet or anyone to protect her... He emitted a low groan. "I am profoundly sorry, Sarah. Sorry for the abuse you endured, and sorry you felt you must withhold it from me." He kissed her forehead. "I'm an impulsive dolt." In the country Hudson remembered Mr. Somerset being distracted with his work, but not cruel. "What happened to your father to produce such a change of character?"

She lifted her shoulders and let them drop. "Disappointment and discouragement, I suppose. His inventions failed one after another; he could not retain employment; and, instead of turning to Mother for comfort, he turned to the bottle. Sober, he was unkind. Foxed"—her voice cracked—"his actions were unforgivable. When we lost our country estate, Father became a stranger to us—worse, he became a drunk and a tyrant. Christopher, forced home prematurely from Cambridge, did his best to protect and provide for us...until that dreadful night."

"The night of the London Diamond Emporium heist?"

"Yes—"

"Do not move a muscle or I'll shoot."

Hudson startled at the woman's voice. "Mother? Is that you?"

He heard a loud breath being expelled. "Hudson. Where have you been? I thought the blackguards had carried you away."

He lit a lamp and removed the pistol from Mother's quivering fingers, then clasped her in a hug. "I am fine, Mother, and look who is here."

"Sarah? Sarah Somerset—is it you?"

Sarah dipped a curtsy. "'Tis I, Lady Alleyne. I am sorry we frightened you."

"Except for your hair color, you've grown to be a mirror image of your beautiful mother. How I miss Beatrice. I hope she is well."

"Uh…" Sarah's lips flattened to a tense line.

"Beatrice is presently unwell, Mother. But her family is with her, and I am certain she will return to full health soon." He reached for Sarah's hand and squeezed her fingers.

"Oh, how dreadful. I shall write a missive to her, expressing my concern. I do hope she recovers from her ailment rapidly." Mother looked from Sarah back to Hudson. Her graying hair, woven into a long plait, hung over her shoulder. "I've slept not a wink since you disappeared, son."

"I've returned, Mother. You can sleep now."

"Not without an explanation." She located the nearest bell and gave it a good clang. "I sense this story will require tea. Shall we retire to the parlor, then?"

Hudson had stewed over what to tell Mother, should she demand an explanation. In truth, he'd hoped to arrive as she slumbered, then have a viable story when she awoke. A worried glance from Sarah confirmed she shared his concerns.

Jeanie R. Davis

Seated with steaming cups of tea in their hands, Mother turned to Hudson, her forehead wrinkled. "Son, what happened after you shot those men?"

Sarah flinched, spilling a few drops of tea. "I—I'm sorry." Placing the cup down, she lowered her brows. "You killed someone?"

Hudson handed her his handkerchief to dab up the tea from her frock. "I didn't kill anyone. Two goons were after me—and Josh." He turned to Mother, "You remember Sarah's younger brother, Joshua. He was the man who delivered Sarah's notes." He didn't wait for her response. "Those thugs outside meant to kill us, but we—" He stopped short, realizing what must have happened. "They shot each other when we disappeared," he said more to himself than to the others. What a terrible mess he'd left on his front walkway. He bunched the cloth in his hand. "Oh, Mother. I didn't know…that is to say, the men had pistols trained on either side of us, but Josh hit the button, transporting us. When they pulled their triggers, they must have…killed each other."

Mother's wrinkles deepened. "Transporting you? Transporting you where?"

"To another time. Mother, you shan't find my explanation believable. I scarcely do. But the important thing is I have returned to save you."

"Son, you had better come up with a better story than that. And from whom, pray tell, are you back to save me? Only a day ago, *you* were the target."

Has it only been a day? It feels more like a fortnight. Hudson rubbed his temples.

"He's here to protect you from my father." Sarah twisted her fingers together.

164

"Your father! I haven't seen Benjamin in years. Even if I had, I've done nothing to provoke the man."

"Let me start from the beginning." Hudson huffed out a breath and began the retelling he'd recently learned himself. With his keen memory, he didn't believe he'd left anything out of the narrative, but he looked to Sarah for approval.

She nodded. "When creditors boxed up our belongings and hauled them away from our county estate, do you recall Mother asking you to hide jewels or a set of valuable vases, Lady Alleyne?"

"Or anything else of worth?" Hudson added.

Mother pursed her lips. "What has come over you, my boy? Time travel? You expect me to believe this fable? Well, I do not. Moreover, I demand the truth."

Frustration gnawed at Hudson. Beatrice's life hung in the balance; Mother's life hung in the balance. He'd gone about this all wrong. "Suppose you are correct, Mother, and we have just been hiding out...with my chums. Will you listen to me?"

Mother narrowed her eyes. "Then why tell me you traveled through time with some vest? And is Beatrice at your chum's house, too?" She waved a hand in the air. "None of this makes sense."

Sarah stood and began pacing. "Time is running out. I feel it in my bones—Father is coming." She stopped and faced Mum. "Please, Lady Alleyne, did my mother ask you to keep anything for her? I fear my father has discovered that some of her valuables were not confiscated from the country estate, as he'd presumed. He has torn our home apart searching for them; he has threatened his family, and I now worry for you." Sarah's voice broke into a sob.

Hudson wished to take her in his arms, comfort her.

The harsh lines of Mother's forehead flattened at hearing Sarah's earnest plea. "You dear girl. Has Benjamin become so bad as all that?"

Dabbing at her eyes, Sarah nodded, then seated herself next to Hudson again.

Mother placed her teacup on its saucer. "Suppose Beatrice did ask me to care for her valuables but made me vow to tell no one of their whereabouts?"

Sarah clasped her hand. "I do not care about their hiding place. I'm not trying to gain access to them. I only hope they are hidden from my father, and that you are safe. If he has discovered you have them, he will stop at nothing to find them. Father has changed. He has done unspeakable things, including rendering Mother unconscious. She wakes for no one but Hudson. And only to warn him to safeguard you. That is why we are here."

Mother's mouth dropped open and her brows arched. "Benjamin beat Beatrice?" She stood and let out an ungraceful snort. "The man should be drawn and quartered. Where is he?"

"We do not know, Mother." Hudson also stood. "But we believe he will find you—"

Sarah cut in. "And terrorize you until you give him what he wants."

"That man will get nothing from me! Nor will he from you. 'Tis why I shan't divulge the valuables' hiding place." Anger Hudson had never witnessed sparked from Mother. "What shall we do? Where shall we secrete ourselves?"

Hudson tapped his chin. "Not here. Not in one of our country estates—" He stopped, a grin spreading on his face as an idea formed. "Mr. Somerset knows of all our residences, but he does not know of my newly acquired estates—the estates I won at the gaming halls. Tell me, Mother, are the goons still patrolling our property, or did they scurry off after I disappeared?"

"I've seen no one since the gunshots sounded and the bodies were hauled away."

"Then those men who put a price on my head either think I killed their thugs, causing them to fear me, or they believe I have escaped to a different location." The wheels in his head whirled like bobbins of spinning wheel thread. "I lay bets on Finley's country estate sitting desolate, without so much as a footman. His gambling has cost him dearly, yet he refuses to stop. We shall go there. Just allow me to locate the key."

Before anyone could protest, Hudson sprinted from the room, but froze when he heard a knock at the door. Changing direction, he returned to the ladies. "Who has come to the manor at this time of night?" His blood ran cold. Perhaps Benjamin Somerset?

Chapter Twenty-Three

Sarah's heart thudded so hard in her chest, she feared whoever stood outside the door might hear it.

"Hide. It might be your father, Sarah." Hudson kept his voice low, but she felt the urgency in his words.

She clutched his hand, stopping him. "Shan't we all hide together?" She worried for Hudson as much as for his mother.

Another loud knock made her jump.

"Lanterns are burning. Whoever it is knows someone is here. I will slip to the window to discern his identity. If it is your father, I shall claim to be here alone."

Sarah reluctantly released her grip on his hand. An aura of foreboding whispered through the candlelit room. She and Lady Alleyne moved into the shadows of the parlor, while Hudson peered out the window.

"Is that...I believe it's... Stay where you are." Hudson sprang from his perch, and the front door creaked open.

"You are here. And you're alive!" boomed a loud voice.

Relief blanketed Sarah's soul. Not Father.

Hudson greeted the man in a like manner, soothing her fears. Yet, he didn't invite him into the parlor.

She continued standing next to Gwenillen—separated from Hudson by a thin wall—listening. Was this man friend or foe?

"Eddie, why are you here at such a late hour?" asked Hudson.

The man scoffed loudly. "Everyone has taken an interest in your whereabouts. Wagers are being placed throughout London on whether you have perished or not. I came to see for myself. As I approached, I noticed—unlike last night—lanterns burning. I do not believe your mother keeps late hours, so I knew it must be you."

"Yes, well—"

"So, tell me, Hudson, where have you been?" the man he'd called Eddie asked. "I mean if rumors are correct, you killed a couple of goons, then disappeared. But here you are."

Sarah turned to meet Lady Alleyne's gaze. "Who is Eddie?" she whispered.

"He's Hudson's chum. They have been best mates for years."

"Why doesn't Hudson invite him in?"

"If I must speculate, I'd say 'tis because of you."

Sarah blanched. Hudson didn't want his closest friend to meet her?

Lady Alleyne narrowed her eyes at Sarah. "Do you not think your presence would raise questions?"

"Oh. Of course." She smoothed down her clothing—a long, pink tunic-style blouse with leggings, worn intentionally for Hudson's sake—the closest thing she had to a dress. Lady Alleyne must think her scandalous to wear such a thing. If so, she had made no mention of it.

She stopped dwelling on her apparel and glanced back up at Hudson's mother. "But why are *you* hiding with me? Surely you wish to greet him."

Lady Alleyne's lips curved into a sly smile. "I learn more about my son from his friends than I do from him. Do not misunderstand; Hudson and I get on delightfully well. However, there are always secrets between chums." She winked.

Sarah smothered a giggle. She'd always loved Gwenillen Drake. The man's loud voice drew Sarah's attention back the foyer.

"Why are you not inviting me in?" asked Eddie.

"'Tis late. I was preparing to retire."

"Ha! Late? Have you forgotten who you are speaking to, Drake the Rake?" He roared with laughter. "The word 'late' is not in your vocabulary."

Lady Alleyne began to fidget. Sarah turned to see that her demeanor had changed. She'd paled and now had a predatory glint in her eyes.

Hudson chuckled. "I told you, Eddie, I am changing my ways." His voice sounded playful, yet unnatural.

Between Lady Alleyne's unease beside her and the strain she heard in Hudson's voice, Sarah knew not what to think. Hudson had never been referred to as Drake the Rake. Why did his friend…unless…no, it could not be true. She strained to listen as the conversation continued.

Eddie grunted. "So you said. But as I recall, you were referring to the gaming halls. Shall your new life keep you out of public houses and exclude wo—"

Lady Alleyne sprang from their dark corner and entered the foyer, effectively cutting him off. "Eddie, how nice to see you."

Sarah froze, absorbing the ugly phrases boring into her brain. Then her body shook from limb to limb as her mind finished the word Eddie had begun— "women." Hudson had frequented public houses, gaming halls and, worst of all, brothels. Squeezing her eyes tight, she swallowed down bile roiling in her belly and oozing up her throat. Her perfect memories of the man she loved shriveled like a piece of rotted fruit.

Rooted in place, she remained in the shadows with the harsh reality she'd just learned. Information of Hudson's years without her hit like a modern-day Mack truck, running her over and dragging her heart down a gravel-riddled road. But she had nowhere to run— nowhere to hide.

"Lady Alleyne. Forgive me. Did I wake you?" Eddie's voice lowered to a polite, gentleman-like tone.

"No, no," she said. "Hudson and I were just discussing our next move, for surely those blackguards won't keep their distance long. Tell me, Eddie, have you seen Charles Finley recently?"

"Yes, just this evening. He has been quizzing everyone in London of Hudson's whereabouts. He's desperate to retrieve the deed and keys to the country estate he lost to you, Hud. Not that he intends to occupy it. I suspect he is in want for something else to gamble away."

"Has he continued to gamble, then, or just make enquiries?" Hudson asked.

Eddie snorted. "The man will continue to frequent the tables until he's lost his last boot."

"You are brilliant, Mother. I should have thought to ask Eddie about Finley myself." He paused for a moment. "Eddie, I killed no one. Those goons shot each other, but I have no proof. For now, Mother and I shall lay low and soon leave the city. If for any reason you need to find me, only you will know we are at Charlie Finley's country estate—er…my newest estate."

"That's it, then? That is all the explanation I am to receive? Hud, we have no secrets. Where have you been?"

"That tale will keep for another day. As Mother said, we must make our escape a hasty one." The door scraped open. "Keep me apprised, Eddie. But address your missives to Lord Finley…Rovenal. Best not raise suspicion."

The longer Hudson talked to Eddie—as if Sarah's world hadn't just shattered—the angrier she became. Too livid to cry, she exhaled long breaths, her hands balling into fists, then releasing repeatedly.

The door shut. Hudson said something to his mother in a hushed tone. Secrets—from Sarah. The woman he'd just declared his fiancée.

Chapter Twenty-Four

Hudson had inwardly cringed when his friend recited his vices—abysmal behavior—of the past seven years. Mother had attempted to cut Eddie off, for which Hudson was grateful, but he feared Sarah had overheard enough to get a sufficient delineation of his debased existence. The possibility did exist, however unlikely, that Sarah had not listened, or hadn't discerned what Eddie meant… Again, unlikely.

"Mother—" He gulped, though his mouth was as dry as the Gobi Desert. "Did Sarah hear…" Though his voice was hushed, he could not complete his distraught query. Mother understood his lifestyle. He'd not shared intimate details with her, but she knew the ways of men with power and money—especially men who ached for their lost love. She knew *him*.

And he knew the answer to his unfinished question when he peered into her pained eyes. His heart cracked open as his hopes of sharing a future with the woman he loved fizzled into despair.

"Go to her, son. You cannot blame her if she turns her back on you, nor can you give up without a fight."

Hudson stared down at the meandering grain of the wood floor. "Suppose she did not understand Eddie's meaning—"

Mother's hand shot up. "Sarah is an intelligent girl—very perceptive since she was a child. I am certain nothing has changed. But you shan't know or fix the situation by standing in this foyer whispering about it." She gave him a gentle shove toward the parlor. "Go to her."

Visions of blades brandished, guns cocked and ready to snuff out his life, blackguards hauling him to destinations unknown—none of those incidents had incited as much fear and trepidation that now pounded in his chest. To have found Sarah only to lose her because of Eddie was unacceptable.

He walked in a slow circle before braving the entrance to where he'd left her. He stopped short. *I am an idiot.* Eddie was not at fault. No, he amended: to have found Sarah only to lose her because of his *own* foolish actions was unacceptable. The truth was destined to come out, whether through Eddie or someone else. He only had himself to blame. Mother had cautioned him about his behavior, but using Sarah's absence as an excuse, he had chosen to live a life of self-indulgence. *Is redemption possible for me? Can Sarah forgive me?* There was only one way to find out.

He crept around the corner, entering the parlor. "Sarah…I…" The lantern still burned, but Sarah no longer occupied the room. "Sarah!" he shouted, while darting from room to room, frantic to find her. She'd surely fled back to the future—away from him. He patted his chest and exhaled relief. He still wore the vest, though hidden by his clothing.

Mother stopped him. "What is it, Hudson?"

"I cannot find her."

"Perhaps she had to make preparations for our trip to the country. We are still traveling to the country, are we not?"

Dire fear of losing Sarah caused Hudson to almost forget the reason they had come in the first place. "Yes, of course. But Sarah had nothing to prepare. She'd packed a few articles of clothing and brought them here in the bag she carried."

Mother pointed to a satchel just inside the parlor. "You mean that? 'Tis a curious sort of traveling bag, is it not? I've never seen such cloth, and all those straps…"

"Sarah called it a backpack." A portion of relief washed over Hudson at seeing Sarah's bag. She hadn't left him for good. But where would she go? Wild thoughts whirled through his brain, making little sense.

"I shall help you look for her. You search the grounds, I'll scour the house." Mother gathered her skirts and swished from the room.

The grounds, yes. Hudson took the lantern from the parlor and headed out the back door. Perhaps Sarah had needed to take some air. He stopped. Trepidation made his heart race. Was it fear of the thugs? …No. It was the fear of facing Sarah. Breathing in a deep breath, he prayed for courage to own up to his guilt. He took a cautious step out, hoping Eddie was correct about the goons having left his property. Sarah should never encounter the likes of those foul men. He shivered at the thought and sped his pace.

The night air was cold and damp. Wearing nothing but a thin frock, Sarah would catch her death if she were outside. "Sarah? Are you there?" Holding the light aloft, he scanned the great expanse. Large trees surrounded spring blooms weaving alongside walking paths, made it difficult to discern anything, or anyone.

Then his eyes landed on her, huddled on a bench near the fountain.

"Sarah!" He ran toward her, but with each step, the hopelessness on her face became more apparent. Tears wetting her cheeks glistened in the moonlight. He must kiss those tears away.

He opened his mouth to speak, but she stopped him. "You have betrayed me in every way possible, Hudson." She rubbed her hands up and down her arms.

"I—"

"In your notes you declared that I was your one true love." She sniffed. "And you never stopped writing the letters—even when they went unanswered. Your words sustained me." Her voice cracked on the last word.

"Yes, but—"

She composed herself once more. "I—I cannot be here."

Frantic, Hudson moved toward her, but she raised her hand, halting him. His insides screwed into knots.

"We came here to protect your mother, but you can do that without me. Just get her to the country estate you spoke of."

Hudson closed his eyes. He wanted to close his ears, fearing what she might say next. Wishing to talk—to apologize for his misdeeds—he focused on organizing his thoughts. But she continued.

"I only ask one thing—will you spare me the humiliation of seeing the pity in Lady Alleyne's eyes, and give me the vest so I may return home?"

"No… Sarah, you cannot mean to leave me."

She averted her eyes.

Finally allowed to speak, the words jumbled up in his brain. "You must know, *every* gentleman frequents public houses and gaming halls."

She jerked her head toward him again and narrowed her swollen eyes. "You are right. I must know. My father was among them. But I shan't live my life in fear, as my mother does. And though I've been away these many years, I have not forgotten what a rake is." The disgust in her voice struck his very core.

Her eyes filled with more tears, but she held his gaze, piercing him with guilt and racking his soul with sorrow. Only Sarah could summon such emotion from him.

"They were only words, Sarah…Eddie…" He choked on the phrase. "Eddie made more of it than there is."

"Then, Hudson, tell me, what is it?"

He motioned to the bench she sat upon. "May I?"

She hesitated long enough for him to know where he stood, then scooted to the far side and nodded. He noticed her shivering. She needed his warmth—physically and emotionally. Having been transported without a cloak, he had little to offer besides his arms. He reached toward her, but she recoiled.

He sat, keeping distance between them, but longing to close it. "You are chilled. Can we not speak inside? I can call for more tea and bank up the fire."

She shook her head. "Just, please give me the vest, and I will be on my way."

Not without a fight. He folded his arms across his chest. "You said to tell you how it is. Before I give you the vest, I beg you to listen—give me an opportunity to explain."

Sarah buried her face in her hands, shoulders shuddering—from the cold or from emotion, or more likely both. Either way, he ached to pull her into his embrace. Again, he reached out an arm, but she didn't respond.

"Sarah, my love—my one and only love"—he swallowed—"I've not lied to you about my determination to find you. Ever since you vanished, I held nothing back in my efforts—spared no expense, spent numberless hours—searching. Then Father died, adding to my bereavement, and leaving me his earldom—an enormous responsibility, which I admit I have not handled well. I needed you by my side."

"I believe you, Hudson. But regardless of your efforts on my behalf, it seems you had time for other distractions."

"That is precisely what they were—distractions. I was distraught beyond consolation." His voice rose. He paused and lowered it, realizing his defensive tone didn't aid in placating her. "I admit I have gambled, indulged in imbibing spirits too often, and…" The rest of the sentence caught in his throat.

"Spent time *consoling* yourself with other women." Her shoulders shook with increased force.

"I swear to you, I have quit those things—I…I *will* quit those things. All of them. Please, Sarah, give me a chance to prove it."

Silence, except for Sarah's sobs.

His heart tore a little more with each whimper. "Come to the country with us. Allow me to atone for my—my many mistakes. Please, Sarah. I beg you."

She turned toward him. "Anyone"—she hiccupped a sob—"anyone can be on their best behavior for a few days." She hiccupped again. "But, Hudson, we are—*were*—talking about spending a lifetime together." She lowered her voice to a whisper. "How long will it take you to tire of me? To seek distractions, or thrills?"

"I could never! You must believe me! Other women—they meant nothing to me. My past actions were deplorable. But until I received your letter in the tree hollow, I thought you were dead."

"The boy I grew up with—the man I loved—had character. He had integrity. He would not need to drink away his problems." Her voice grew louder with each word. "He would not use his keen mind to profit at the gaming tables—especially at the detriment of others. And he most certainly would not turn to another woman—nay, women—for comfort."

She fully faced him now. Angry darts pierced his soul. "I was thrust into an unknown time and place," she continued. "I sulked and cried over my loss—my loss of you, Hudson. I even attempted to end my life. Father seized every opportunity to remind me of my weakness. He told me I wasn't good enough for you—that I should be grateful you couldn't see the shell of a person I had become. And besides his verbal insults, he slapped my face when I tried to speak my mind. Perhaps I am everything Father accused me of. But I *never* betrayed you." She stood. "I do not believe I know the man sitting before me." She turned and strode toward the house.

A knife thrust into his heart would not have cut as deep. But how could she say such things? Of course she had not behaved as he had—men and women were different breeds. For her to have given herself to another man—unthinkable. Sarah was no light-skirt.

Grief and an edge of irritation settled over him like an angry cloud threatening to burst. "I shan't give you the vest until we have secured Mother in the country." He hated himself for saying it, but if she left him now, he'd never see her again. Having her near quelled any desire he had to do the things which had earned him the reputation of a rake, a swindler, or a man too much in his cups. Sarah made him Hudson once again. The Hudson he knew he was meant to be. *I will prove my worth to her.*

She stopped walking at his denial of her request but didn't turn back. Dropping her head, she stood silent for a moment, then continued down the path.

Chapter Twenty-Five

After six uncomfortable hours of being jostled over bumpy roads in a carriage—silent, except for occasional chatter between Hudson and his mother—Sarah longed for modern-day automobiles. Other than a few stops for fresh horses, she'd had little interaction with anyone—especially Hudson. She'd feigned exhaustion and had curled against the side of the coach, pulling a lap robe high enough to hide from the Drakes. Although in Colorado the sun still shone...she thought—time travel did strange things to one's mind—her emotions had left her drained.

A second carriage trailed them, transporting a sleepy staff. The poor servants, having been rousted from their slumber, had given no complaints about the abrupt disruption to their routine. Sarah had noticed the respect and courtesy they'd shown to Lady Alleyne and Hudson. Cook even wrapped her arms around Hudson and kissed his cheek, proclaiming her joy at beholding him alive.

"Miss." Someone nudged Sarah awake. She must have slept after all. "May I help you down?" A footman extended his gloved hand.

Sarah wiped the sleep from her eyes, then clutched the man's hand and descended the coach's steps. Pink-tinged clouds in the eastward sky promised daylight soon. Fresh country air confirmed their distance from

London. She let her eyes take in her surroundings—beautiful, even in the pre-dawn hours. Rolling hills, lush with spring foliage, bordered the large country manor. So much like the home in which she'd been reared—the estate next to Hudson's. She glanced back to see Hudson helping his mother from the coach. So handsome and chivalrous—and such a cad. Her mood made a hairpin turn from nostalgia to nausea.

Hudson led the troop to the front door, opened it, and with a grand sweeping gesture, motioned them to enter. As she passed him, Sarah avoided his gaze, but thought she glimpsed bloodshot eyes. He must be exhausted.

He'd been right about the previous owner—Finley, he'd called him. No servants rushed to greet them, the furniture hid beneath large cloth coverings, and the cavernous manor smelled fusty and stale.

"I shall set to work laying the fires," said one of the Drakes' maids, who rushed from the foyer.

"And I shall begin preparations for you to break your fast." The cook looked to Hudson, perhaps seeking his approval.

Hudson shook his head. "Get some sleep first, Cook. We'll not perish without food for a few hours. I forced everyone from their beds—I shan't ask you to work without needed rest."

The cook curtsied. "Thank you, m'lord. At the very least, allow me to prepare chamomile tea to aid in your sleep." She didn't give Hudson a chance to respond—just vanished. How strange to hear Hudson referred to as a lord. He was an earl. The title was his. Still odd for her. Sarah had only ever thought of him as a boy she loved and never wished to live without. But he was indeed a man. A man with power, privilege, and money. So small she felt, standing in the cavernous manor, which now belonged—as so many other estates did—to the Alleyne empire.

During the exchange between Hudson and his cook, the other servants scurried off. Sarah assumed they'd either gone in search of the staff's sleeping quarters or had rushed to prepare rooms for the Drakes—and hopefully her.

Sarah dropped her head and studied the marble floor. Why was she here? She should be in the twenty-first century keeping watch over Mother. It had been selfish to leave the burden on Josh and Christopher, all to be with Hudson. He didn't need her. He had a life filled with friends, family, and purpose. Not to mention diversions. She—just another woman in his collection—was of no significance. Why, then, would he not give her the vest and permit her to return home?

"Sarah." Hudson's voice jolted her from her thoughts.

She raised her head, meeting his gaze. His eyes, so red and lacking the spark of joy and mischief which was solely Hudson, penetrated hers. "Please, Hudson, I beg you. Allow me to return to my family. They need me. You do not." It ripped her spirit in two to admit it, but she must acknowledge the truth of the matter and move on.

He reached out and clasped her hand. "You are wrong. I have never needed someone more than I need you." He swallowed and sniffed. "What can I do to convince you?"

Sarah viewed his hand holding hers and wished away the electricity shooting up her arm. To let her emotions rule her now would be foolish. She tried but failed to summon the words to express her thoughts and feelings. Closing her eyes for a moment, she shook her head.

His countenance dulled further. "You need sleep. The journey was long. Allow me to escort you to your room."

Her room. He spoke it as if they had been residing in the manor for years, not mere minutes. Perhaps he was correct about sleep, however; fatigue clouded her thought process. "Very well. But I do not believe I shall change my mind." Her head told her to yank her hand from his. Her heart urged her to leave it where it fit well and felt so right as he guided her up the grand staircase. Her heart won.

A maid motioned him to a large bedroom. "We prepared your bedchamber, m'lord. 'Tis the grandest. Lady Alleyne is settling at the far end of the hall."

"And Sarah?" Hudson drew her arm through his in a possessive manner.

"Oh, yes. Your maiden's bedchamber adjoins yours, m'lord." She pointed to the room next to Hudson's. Too close to Hudson's. An awkward pause ensued. The maid's face transformed from tired and pale to alert and rosy. She turned to Sarah. "Unless, of course, you would prefer another chamber. I—I assumed…"

Heat rose to Sarah's own cheeks. She wished to demand a room far from Hudson's but didn't want to keep the servants up any longer than necessary. The light of dawn filtered through the high windows, and no one had slept enough.

Hudson turned to her, a question in his eyes. "They can prepare a room near Mother's if you prefer," he said in a low tone.

Sarah exhaled a tired breath. "I do not plan on remaining here long enough for it to matter." She nodded to the maid. "Thank you." Without another word, she entered the room prepared for her, kicked off her shoes, climbed under the covers, and closed her eyes.

****

The sun blazed through her window at midday. Even with the bright rays streaming in, Sarah struggled to clear the cobwebs from her brain. New surroundings—a strange bed with poster boards and curtains—ahh, yes, she was once again in the nineteenth century. She sprang from her bed to find the bathroom—"No!" She groaned at the realization and located the chamber pot. Why had she missed the nineteenth century? … Oh, yes, because she'd left the man she'd loved there.

Within minutes a maid appeared from thin air to help her dress. "Here is a day dress Lady Alleyne wishes you to wear. She said it is a bit old fashioned, as you are much younger than she, but she believes you'll be more comfortable in it than that." She pointed to Sarah's wrinkled clothing."

Sarah took the gown, wondering what Lady Alleyne had thought of her modern attire, in which she hadn't bothered to remove to sleep. "Thank you. 'Tis a lovely shade of yellow." The sunny-colored dress, cut for a more mature female, was at least a favorable color.

"Shall I help you into the day dress, then?"

Sarah stole a glance at her abandoned backpack and sighed. She longed to pull on a pair of jeans and a T-shirt. Perhaps she had conformed more to the twenty-first century than she'd realized. "No, thank you. I will dress myself." The maid would be aghast to see her underwear.

Once dressed, and hair piled atop her head—proper for the time—Sarah entered the dining room, hungry for breakfast, lunch, or whatever food was available at two o'clock in the afternoon. Hudson and his mother were deep in conversation at the far end of the long table. Not wishing to interrupt, she crept to the sideboard loaded with delicacies from a forgotten world and filled a plate. She wondered how the cook had transported so much food from London, then remembered the hour. There had been plenty of time for Cook to shop in the nearby village this morning.

"Sarah." Hudson stood and bowed. "How did you sleep?" His profile was strong and rigid.

She placed her plate on the table, trying to remember if she should curtsy in return.

Lady Alleyne's eyes sparkled with amusement. "Come closer, child. No need to eat so far away."

"I don't wish to disturb you." Nor did she want to fake kindness toward Hudson.

Hudson pulled a chair out next to his. "I have been explaining time travel to Mother. You should be part of the conversation. Please."

Hesitant, Sarah resigned herself to the situation and sat in the proffered seat. "Lady Alleyne, thank you for the use of your dresses."

Lady Alleyne nodded in the same regal manner Sarah recalled from her youth. Then she patted

Hudson's hand. "That is quite enough about this strange fairytale travel, Hudson. I do believe I shall take a turn about the garden—assess the state of things in this neglected part of the country."

Hudson helped her to her feet.

How dare she? Sarah simmered as she speared a piece of minced meat pastry.

"I—I'm sorry, Sarah." Hudson reclaimed his chair. "I did not know she would leave. I truly wished you to be part of the conversation. If you'd prefer, I shall retire to the bookroom."

Sarah met Hudson's gaze. His eyes were still bloodshot. "Did you not sleep? You look exhausted."

Hudson ran a hand through his hair. "How could I sleep knowing the distress I have caused you?"

The sincerity in his voice almost convinced her of his contrition. *Almost.* Then Eddie's poisonous words rushed through her mind like a flood of sewage water. She turned away. "Perhaps we should discuss your mother. Does she at all believe you traveled through time?"

"I am uncertain. I did my best to explain my encounter—and yours—with time travel, but as you can imagine, until one experiences it, such a thing sounds beyond plausible."

Sarah focused on her plate of food. "Did you let her examine the vest? I hope you're still wearing it. Should your servants come upon it—" She looked up to see tears hovering in Hudson's eyes.

"Sarah, what will it take to prove I cherish you above all others? That I am the man you fell in love with? Still. I shall do anything. Just speak the words."

"You can give me the vest, so I can return home."

Chapter Twenty-Six

Hudson's heart bruised anew at Sarah's demand. But cold as her words were, they didn't sync with her beauty. Her ivory face had a musk-rose flush on the cheekbones. He wished to see her eyes—Sarah's eyes never lied. But she kept her gaze lowered. "Sarah, please…just give me a chance. Give us a chance."

"For what?" She raised her gaze to meet his. The clear blueness lacked its usual luster, speaking volumes—he saw in them anguish and an earnest desire to distance herself from him.

"We are in need of an opportunity to work things out. We did not find each other just to give up—at least I didn't."

She swallowed, and her eyes welled. Blinking back tears, she stood abruptly, her willowy body rigid. "We are in the country, Hudson. It is easy to give up your vices when you are away from the gaming halls, public houses and"—she swallowed—"brothels. It is easy to prove your love to only me when there is no one else to lavish it on. But how will you act when I become an everyday fixture in your life?"

"I shall be different—I vow it!"

"No, Hudson. After a time, you will become bored. I have no experience of worldly matters. The kisses we shared in my home were my first." The blush on her face became rosier. But her voice never faltered. "And lest you think I've not had the opportunity to experience men with a lust, I have. Josh attempted matching me with many of his acquaintances. Most of them were kind, but their advances repulsed me." She expelled a slow breath. "I suppose I have been in denial about you—denial about me, as well. Men and women are different in the future—equal in love. I have only ever desired your touch—your kiss. You."

His face burned, as if he'd been slapped. And her remarks, though clear, made little sense. Were men and women so unequal? Her words took his mind on an unexpected journey—thoughts of Sarah embracing other men crashed through his brain like a boulder through a windowpane. Revolting. No. He must admit, they were not equal. The men he kept company with used women as it pleased them—some for a meaningless thrill, while those women of a higher station were expected to remain pure, unruined, so men like him could marry, and the females provide them heirs. It was the way of things. Had life changed so much in two hundred years?

Sarah gentled her voice. "Hudson, you know I prefer attending to those I love rather than engaging in frivolity—wasting time with inconsequential activities such as gaming. We are different. Too different." She turned and exited the dining area before he had a chance to respond. Perhaps he didn't deserve that chance. But women gambling, drinking, and... No. He couldn't enfold his mind around the thought. Women were happy in their roles as mothers and homemakers. They were born to it. He had overindulged—earned a repugnant reputation—but he was a man.

Her words continued to torment him. He was unable to fathom a society other than his own. One thing was certain, however; no matter the time or place, only one woman could make him his best self—Sarah Somerset.

With an undeniable intensity, Hudson was drawn to her. Perhaps it was her mild, nurturing character that drew him in. No one he had spent any quality time with had measured up to Sarah. And not only her beauty enchanted him, but her character—reserved, yet humorous at times; intelligent, but innocent; compassionate, like a mother bear coddling her cubs, but equally ferocious when her cubs were threatened. The very differences Sarah had claimed made them an unsuitable match, had also claimed his heart.

He would not give her up.

Through the window he watched as she trod the path to the gardens, the wind whipping more color into her cheeks. The country estate had taken nearly seven hours to locate, traveling due north. The climate, cloudy today, had a nip in the air. He'd worried about her catching a chill the previous night, sitting on the cold, stone bench. He'd noticed her sniff several times in the course of their brief interaction moments ago but knew her emotions had played a role. He sat riveted, his eyes taking in her every move. Sarah was alive; she was real; she was here. Yet she was slipping through his grip, and he was helpless to stop her.

She rubbed her arms with delicate bare fingers, as if to encourage circulation. Leaping from his seat, he called for his cloak.

The butler bounded in, nearly bowling him over. "Forgive me, m'lord. Here is your coat…and a cloak for the lady."

"Thank you, Jameson." He donned his coat and rushed to catch up with the woman he loved. "Sarah"—he panted—"you will catch a chill out here. Take this cloak."

"I—I…thank you." She sniffed, then pulled the wrap tightly around her, keeping her eyes averted, but slowed down as he stepped beside her.

Hudson could see the tears glistening on her cheeks. "Please, talk to me."

She stopped and turned to fully face him. "I need time, Hudson. Will you allow me that? My dreams—visions of you—have been shattered. I need time and space—apart—to examine my feelings and know my heart." Her tone was gentle, without guile or aggression. The Sarah he loved.

Without thought, he clasped her hand. Ice cold. She needed to be deliberating their fate next to a fire, not wading through northern winds in this neglected garden. "I shall give you the time and space you require. But I shan't be whole until we are together as one—husband and wife. I've not been complete, or even myself, since you vanished from my life. Please consider this as you measure my repellent behavior." He rubbed her hand with both of his. "You are freezing. If you would like to occupy the bookroom, sitting near the fire, I vow I shall leave you to your thoughts." The vulnerability mingled with stubbornness in her eyes nearly undid him. She needed him. He needed her. Could she not see it? He restrained himself from pulling her into his arms, though it took every ounce of control he could summon.

She stood still, perhaps pondering his offer, then reclaimed her hand and tugged the cloak firmer around her. Fragrance of roses wafted through the breeze. Beautiful, like Sarah. But at this moment, the smell of roses cut like their thorny stems. "Thank you," she said. "Perhaps I shall come in…after a few more minutes. The garden, no matter how unkempt, brings me a degree of peace." She pivoted and plodded on.

Hudson retreated to the house, his heart heavy as sarsens. When he entered, he found Mother waiting near the door.

"You look troubled, son. She has not forgiven you, then?" She laid a gentle arm around him and led him to the parlor—scrubbed pristine now. They seated themselves on a pair of mahogany tub armchairs. The burgundy velvet backrests and seat pads, soft and comforting, hugged him.

Gratitude for Mother—someone…the only person with whom he could share his burden concerning Sarah—calmed him. He shook his head. "She may never forgive me. Have my actions been so repulsive? Have they been any different from those of my peers?"

Mother looked into his eyes with a searching gaze.

Is she trying to see my soul?

Finally, she spoke. "Hudson, your behavior, while not so unique from others of your age and rank, have not been the actions of the boy I reared. The boy Sarah fell in love with." She placed a hand over his. "You know I shall love you until my dying day, no matter your behavior—I am your mother. But Sarah…Sarah has a choice."

Mother's words sliced through his soul like a saber. She was correct—Sarah had a choice, and he must find a way to influence her to choose him.

A clamor in another room drew Hudson's attention to the foyer.

"M'lord"—Jameson wheezed—"'tis your lady."

Hudson jumped from his seat. "What is it? What has happened?"

"Amos, the gardener, came upon her collapsed outside." He waved his arms as he spoke. "I rushed out and attempted rousting her, but she would not—"

Before Jameson had finished his sentence, Hudson sprinted from the parlor and out the door. His heart pounded erratically. He should have insisted she come in at once.

He spotted the yellow of her dress strewn across rocks and brambles. She had wandered a great distance since he'd left her. He hurried to her side. Jameson and Amos hovered near Hudson as he bent to lift her.

"Do you need help, m'lord?" asked Jameson.

"No." Sarah was light in his arms. He held her face next to his cheek. "She's burning up. She needs a doctor."

Jameson's face wrinkled. "I am unfamiliar with the area, and the nearest neighbor is a distance away."

Hudson didn't stop to talk about the area. He kept moving, entering the manor, then rushed up the stairs. "There is a village nearby." He panted. "Surely they have a physician. Go—now." Throwing back the covers, he laid Sarah atop her bed, then placed a kiss on her forehead. Heat beneath his lips panicked him.

Mother appeared with a damp cloth. She laid it on Sarah's head, then took the shoes from Sarah's feet and pulled the blanket to her chin. "She was a beautiful child, and has become a beautiful woman."

Sarah began to cough and thrash about. Where had that come from? Only an hour before she'd seemed fine—had this turmoil been too much for her?

Her eyes opened. "Where am I?" Her voice, gravelly and hoarse, barely reached his ears.

"You are with me, love. You've taken ill. I have sent for a doctor."

She coughed again and tried to sit up. "I am fine. I just need some water, is all." Her hacking turned into a fit.

"Here, Sarah, drink this." Mother handed her a cup of water.

With shaky hands, she sipped it. Her eyelids looked heavy. Once the fit of coughing abated, she lay back down, and her eyes closed again.

A grandfather clock nearby ticked to the rhythm of Hudson's heartbeat. Time was slipping by. He strode to the window and stared out at the empty lane that led to the road. His eyes burned, and his heart raced. Hours had passed and still no Jameson.

"Hudson." Mother's voice startled him. "In the event Jameson can find no doctor, what shall we do?"

Why did she ask him? Mother was the person he took all his concerns to. She had the answers, not him. He wrinkled his brow and lifted his shoulders. "What do you think, Mother? Father was often sick. You've much more experience than I in matters such as this."

"Hudson, if Sarah were your wife and if I were not here, *what would you do*?" She drew the words out. "Think, son. You wish this woman to love and forgive you, but you must take yourself out of the equation. If you truly love her, what would you do?"

Her question rambled in circles through his mind until the door crashed open. He looked up to see Jameson—red faced and huffing.

"I have not found a doctor, but a woman—a healer from the nearby hamlet." He wheezed some more, then turned and motioned someone in.

A middle-aged woman with dark hair and a sturdy frame entered the room. A pungent smell of herbs followed her. Hudson moved from his seat beside Sarah to allow the woman room for her examination.

The healer glanced at her audience. "I think it best if I study the patient alone. It in't proper for you ta all be watchin'. Hie now and fetch hot water." The woman spoke as any hamlet woman would. Hudson only hoped her knowledge exceeded her grammar.

"Yes, yes. But I am her..." Hudson let the words die on his tongue. He wished to proclaim himself Sarah's husband so he could stay. He was not her husband—and may never be. His heart spasmed. Instead, he ushered Mother and Jameson from the room, closed the door behind him, and paced the hallway.

Waiting wasn't one of Hudson's fortes. He was a man of action. Several times he approached the door, ready to burst through and demand answers. But Mother, knowing his nature, would place a gentle hand on his arm, soothing him. She had a way about her—a calming demeanor. As did Sarah. He needed Sarah as much as he needed air.

After many long minutes, the door opened. The woman's pale face didn't give Hudson the reassurance he longed for. They entered the room and awaited the prognosis.

"I have examint her and gave her healin' oils and herbs. But in the time I 'ave been here, her cough grew from shalla and dry ta deep and throaty." She shook her head. "I thought the lass might 'ave putrid throat or ague, then she started hackin'." She lowered her ear to Sarah's chest. "Them rumblin's arn't good. 'Tis spring, but I think your lass has winter fever."

Winter fever. More people died of winter fever than any other illness. Hudson's insides roiled.

The woman stood erect again. "There in't a cure fer it. Me remedies will help, but I canna promise they'll save the lass."

Hudson wished to shake the woman for acting casual about something so dire. This was Sarah they were talking about. "What do you recommend, then?"

"Cool cloths on her head fer the fever. Dun't leave her. When she wakes, get water in her. Plenty a water. And use these herbs to brew her a healin' tea." She handed Mother a potent-smelling pouch. "Sheel be orf chump."

Hudson looked to Jameson for clarification.

"She means Sarah will have no appetite," Jameson said.

"And rub this poultice I have made on her throat and bosom ever coupla hours."

"Right." Hudson took the bowl of salve from the woman. "Will you be staying?"

She shook her head. "I left a lass preparin' ta give birth. It wern't right I went, but yer man urged me ta come."

"I thank you." Hudson handed the woman a pouch of coins.

Sarah should be in a hospital. He thought of the large building bustling with medical professionals in which Beatrice Somerset lay asleep. A twenty-first century hospital. *I was a selfish fool to keep Sarah from returning to her new home. It would have saved her life.* Now, however, it was too late for him to make it right. Should he give her the vest and send her home in such a dire condition, she'd surely not get to the hospital on her own.

Chapter Twenty-Seven

"What are you doing?" Mother tapped her foot.

Hudson looked up, his fingers in the bowl of poultice. "You heard the woman—we must apply this. Sarah's in trouble!" He began to rub it on her throat, praying with each stroke.

"Stop, Hudson. I or my maid shall take charge of the application. Where is her clothing? She should be in a nightdress, not that uncomfortable day dress."

He paid her no mind but kept applying the healing ointment. Sarah might die.

"She brought this with her, m'lady." The maid handed something to Mother.

"The girl needs to be attired properly. She must have—what is this?"

Hudson glanced up to see Sarah's backpack on Mother's lap. She'd pulled out Sarah's phone. It lit up at her touch and Mother gasped.

Hudson recalled having the same reaction when he first saw the device. "They call them cell phones. People talk to each other with them. I wonder why Sarah brought hers here." The tale of Arianna taking her phone back through time and its usefulness in freeing Christopher came to mind. And Christopher showing his uncle the picture of the article of his impending hanging at Newgate Prison. Hudson supposed there were a few compelling reasons to have a cell phone on board.

"How does it work?" Mother turned the phone around in her hand.

"It doesn't in this century. And I did not dwell in the twenty-first century long enough to learn much about it."

"Twenty-first century—pish." Mother replaced the phone and kept digging. "I cannot find a solitary item in here that resembles a nightdress—or even proper clothing."

"You finish applying the salve, Mother, I shall find her nightclothes." He wiped the ointment from his hands and took the bag from her. "I believe she sleeps in these," he said, holding up silky trousers and a matching top. Visions of finding Sarah in her hallway, dressed in the crimson nightclothes, temporarily stunned him. Her full lips had parted in surprise. He'd wished to kiss them on the spot.

Mother let out a huff, ruining his sweet ruminations. "Emma," she addressed her maid, "locate one of my sleeping gowns for Sarah."

The maid dropped a curtsy and left the room.

Hudson rolled his eyes. "Will you never believe what I have told you about Benjamin Somerset and his invention to move through time? I have *been* to the future, Mother. I am not speaking rubbish. I never do. You know I am honest with you. 'Tis all true— everything I have told you."

Mother finished with the salve, then busied herself arranging the ewer next to the basin, fanning out cloths to wet for Sarah's forehead…anything but acknowledging Hudson's questions.

The maid returned with a nightdress. "Shall I help you dress her, m'lady?"

Mother took the gown from her. "Yes, Emma." She turned to Hudson. "You can wait outside."

"Very well." He'd been dismissed. He closed the door behind him but refused to go far. His concern for Sarah growing with each passing minute.

Finally, Emma opened the door. "Lady Alleyne said to tell you we have finished dressing your maiden."

Hudson brushed past her and reclaimed the chair next to Sarah's bed. He gazed down at her. Beautiful. Freed from pins, her glossy, dark hair hung in long graceful curves over the bedding. Her black lashes—such a contrast against her fair skin—were still closed tight. "Did she stir while you dressed her, Mother?"

"She did. She even asked where her mother was. I fear the fever has made her delirious."

Hudson's heart rattled in his chest. "Delirious or not, she is no doubt worried for her mother, who is in much the same state." He pushed his fingers through his hair. Deep down he'd hoped Sarah had asked for him. "We should have remained in the twenty-first century. Then none of this would have happened. At least we'd have the proper medicine to cure Sarah."

"But did you not say *my* life was in danger?" Mother stood a few paces from the bed, her hands on her hips.

"Yes. Forgive me, Mother. Coming here was necessary—however, I should have made the trip alone." He recalled Sarah's insistence to accompany him. But so much pain could have been spared her had he refused. However, he'd be living a lie... None of it signified now—the truth came to light, and he must face the consequences.

Mother arched a brow. "Why don't you don your magical vest and soar off to the future and obtain the healing medicine for her, then?" Mother's voice rang with a combination of sarcasm and sincerity. But her idea was not altogether ill-conceived.

"Yes! What a splendid idea. I shall do it." He jumped to his feet and paced, thinking through the scenario. "I should take Sarah." Or would that endanger her further? Without much experience with the device, he didn't have sufficient information to know.

Mother's mouth gaped open.

"Perhaps it's better I leave her with you." Though the notion of abandoning Sarah—even for a few hours—tore him apart, it might also save her life. He halted in front of Mother. "Will you stay with her? I cannot leave unless I know she will be well-cared for."

"You are going to do this"—she flung her hands in the air—"...magical thing, then?"

Hudson opened his shirt to reveal the vest he wore beneath it. "Yes. But first you must promise to stay with her."

Mother's astonishment showed in the wrinkles of her forehead and squint of her eyes. "What... Of course I shall care for her, but—"

"And I shall need Sarah's phone." He grabbed her bag and located it. "Once I am in the twenty-first century, I shall use this to call her brother and ask him for help." He held the phone aloft. "You shall see, Mother. Everything I have shared with you is true. You shall see."

"But—"

"Take care of her, Mother. Do not let anyone know of your whereabouts." He bent and kissed Sarah's warm cheek, then kissed Mother's cheek, as well.

With perfect clarity he recalled Joshua's instructions. Setting the dial, he pushed the button, sending him back to the future. Perhaps Mother would believe his story now.

Like a magnet's pull to metal, Hudson felt the vest hug him as he traveled through time. A sensation he shan't have words to describe if ever asked. Impatient to arrive and accomplish what he'd set forth to do, the minutes seemed endless. When his feet finally landed on the firm floor of the Somersets' secret laboratory, the familiar stench of chemicals filled his nostrils.

He hiked the ladder and opened the trapdoor, needing to push hard because of the heavy rug hiding it. *Why do the Somersets keep the door hidden?* According to Sarah, no one ever came to the home but family. As he exited the bookroom, he heard men's voices, stopping him in his tracks. The sounds emerged from the kitchen.

"Get out of my way! This house belongs to me—as do all the contents within it. If your mother is hiding something from me, I shall find it. Now move!"

Hudson crept into the hallway, nearer the voices.

"You are nothing but a bully. What are you looking for, anyway? Do you not have enough wealth from the many things you have stolen?"

It sounded like Josh, but to whom was he speaking? *Ah!* No doubt his heinous father. Hudson had never heard Mr. Somerset growl at his children. The harsh tone unnerved him. He had hoped the horrid words Sarah had claimed he'd spoken to her were exaggerations. He now heard the truth of it himself.

"How dare you speak to me in such a way? I am your father, Joshua!" He paused, then lowered his voice. "Work with me, son—side by side. You and I are likeminded. You have my keen intelligence for science and math. Think of it. Together we could conquer the world."

Josh grunted.

"Do you know your mother inherited some of the rarest and most valuable vases in existence? I thought they had been seized by creditors years ago, but through investigating, I found the vases had not been confiscated."

Hudson moved closer until he could observe Benjamin's profile without being seen. However, Joshua remained out of his view.

"How do you know the vases weren't sold and scattered about London? Or anywhere else in the world?"

"I know because, at great risk, I traveled through time to our country estate to the very day we were evicted. I remained in the shadows whilst our belongings were crated and taken away. The vases were nowhere to be found."

"Great risk?" Josh snorted.

Benjamin stomped. "Yes! Traveling to a time before I had every component available for the machine is dangerous for a host of reasons. I shan't do it again."

Hudson wondered what had spooked Benjamin enough to keep him from returning to an earlier time to fetch the vases. Perhaps a malfunction of the device occurring before all components and chemicals had become available would leave him stranded there.

Josh cleared his throat. "If you were at the estate, you must have observed Mother's silent tears. Tears shed for her husband, her protector, who sat foxed at a public house, unfeeling, uncaring."

Hudson stiffened. Josh was either brave or foolish.

Benjamin snarled but didn't otherwise react. Hudson doubted the truth affected him. Everything Sarah and Josh had said about the brute rang true—loud and clear.

"I do not know where the vases are. I scarcely remember them at all," said Josh.

"No, but your mother does," Benjamin ground out. "Long before the eviction, she must have hidden them somewhere."

"Hidden them?" Josh emitted a scoffing sound.

"Yes! She knew they were valuable—the woman isn't dimwitted. She betrayed my trust! Either they are here, or with someone she trusted—Gwenillen Drake, perhaps. If so, I shall shake the truth from her."

Hudson's hackles stood on end. *The man is a monster*. He hadn't moved Mother from London a minute too soon.

"The vases belonged to her! She had every right to hide them"—Josh gulped loudly—"if that is what she did."

"I am the man! What is hers is mine. Now either help me search or get out of the way!"

Bile rose in Hudson's throat. Had he sounded like that when he'd spoken to Sarah?

"I won't help. And you are wrong about me, Father. We are not likeminded. I would never hurt my family the way you have hurt us. Mother is in the hospital with life-threatening injuries caused by your hand. And Sarah…she may never recover from the emotional damage you've inflicted on her. Your physical attacks may have healed, but beating her down as you did…why? She loved you, she trusted you. Everything you heaped upon her she took to heart. Was it not torture enough you forced her from her London home, her friends?"

Hudson was ill-prepared for the emotional oration from Josh about the woman he loved. Tears welled in his eyes. Benjamin was more of a fiend than he'd ever imagined. And Sarah…no wonder she wanted nothing to do with a man who shared so many vices with her wicked father. He vowed anew to give up everything and anything that would remind her of the brute, then prayed it wasn't too late to prove his worthiness.

Benjamin's voice roared, grabbing his attention once again. "*I do not answer to you.*" He drew out each word long and loud. "Your sister has been a thorn in my side. She stabbed me!" He lifted a hand to his shoulder. "That shan't happen again. I came prepared for a fight. If you aren't with me, you are against me." He pulled a gun from his coat and cocked it. "Get out of my way!"

Chapter Twenty-Eight

Without any forethought, Hudson sprang from his position in the shadows, pouncing on Benjamin. The gun flew from his grip. "Grab the pistol, Josh!"

Josh moved to action, but only kicked the gun out of reach. "Disable the vest, or he'll blast away, as he always does," he hollered.

Temporarily stunned, Benjamin took only seconds to fight Hudson for the mechanism in his vest pocket. "Scoundrel! Get away from me!" He swung an arm at Hudson, while using the other to grapple for the controls.

Josh pounced into the fray, tumbling the men to the ground. "I've got his arm! Secure the other, and I shall break the circuits."

Benjamin struggled with more strength than Hudson thought a man his age possessed. Dots of blood appeared near his shoulder, and one arm fell lifeless. "Get"—he huffed—"off"—more panting—"of me!" But it did no good against two younger, stronger men. Blood now oozed through his fabric. The wound from Sarah's blade, no doubt.

Hudson spotted a cast iron skillet on the stove. "His arm is lifeless." *If only Benjamin were.* Hudson lunged for the pan's handle, but Benjamin clutched Hudson's ankle with his freed arm, tripping him up. Hudson had the handle in his fingertips, and the pan came down with him, landing on Benjamin's head with a thunk.

Benjamin's body went limp, allowing Josh to sever the control instrument. He felt for a pulse. "He's still alive. We must shackle him before he wakes." His eyes darted around the room. "And I need to call the police. Perhaps he'll finally pay for a small portion of his crimes."

The adrenaline coursing through Hudson slowed enough for him to recall his motivation for being back in the twenty-first century. He panted several times, still winded from the skirmish. "Sarah is sick. I must get medicine for her at once."

Josh dropped his father's arm, and his brows drew together. "What? Where is she?"

"She's safe. Mother is with her in the country." He glanced down at Benjamin's still form. "We shan't need to worry about him tormenting Mother now. But if I do not return with medicine soon, I fear Sarah will die."

A shadow of indecision fell over Josh. Hudson understood—Benjamin must be dealt with. And Sarah needed medicine.

"What is ailing Sarah?" Josh asked.

"Fever, coughing, delirium—" Hudson paused, needing to swallow rising emotion. If it hadn't been for him, she wouldn't have exposed herself to the night air or the chilly country breeze. "We only have it from the word of a country healer, but she thinks Sarah is suffering from winter fever. Is there a cure?"

"Yes, yes! We have antibiotics. It is called pneumonia now and still takes many lives, but Sarah is young and in general good health. The medicine should cure her—assuming you return with it soon enough." Josh's eyes shot from Hudson's to his unconscious father, then to Hudson's again.

Hudson knew Josh was puzzling out the situation. "Can you use your new phone to speak with Christopher? Perhaps he can bring medicine from the hospital as well as call on his constable friends."

Josh blew out a breath. "I shall call him, but powerful antibiotics aren't just doled out without the patient being seen." He located his satellite phone on the kitchen counter and began dialing. "Chris will know what to do."

In moments, Hudson heard, "Sarah's ill?" Christopher's voiced boomed out of the device Josh held. "In the nineteenth century?"

"Yes, and Hudson and I have rendered Father unconscious on the kitchen floor. But I don't know how long he will remain asleep. We need medicine and a police officer here now! Can you help?" At the same time, Josh sounded both a commander and a younger brother.

Christopher's voice had lowered. Hudson could no longer hear him.

After a couple more exchanges, Josh pushed a button, ending the conversation. "He said to give him a few minutes to see what he could manage. He'll come up with something. In the meantime, we should lash Father's arms and legs to something. He's bound to wake up before long. I'll check the garage for rope."

Hudson followed Josh. "There is another problem."

Josh stopped. "What is it?"

"Once I acquire the necessary medicine for Sarah, I do not believe this vest I am wearing has a setting for the country estate in which we are residing." If he understood the working of these time-traveling devices, one could leave from anywhere, but must have a destination programmed for arrival. "It will take far longer to travel from London by coach to the estate than it will to travel through time two hundred years."

"I can reprogram the settings, but that will take precious time, as well—especially since I don't have the exact location." He turned back toward the garage. "Let me think on it while I search for something to restrain Father."

The door closed behind Josh and Hudson made his way back to the kitchen to watch over Ben—

He froze. Benjamin was gone. He scuttled to where Josh had kicked the gun. Gone, as well. Josh had damaged his vest controls—Hudson didn't know if they'd been broken beyond repair—but there were other types of traveling devices in the lab. Perhaps he'd fled to the basement. Faced with another bout of indecision, he settled on finding Josh before searching out Benjamin—especially unarmed.

Twenty silent steps later he twisted the knob to the garage. As he opened it, the door whined. He winced and held his breath. He still wore the more modern vest and could easily blast away from the situation—be done with Benjamin Somerset and his fervor to rule the universe—at least until the rogue showed up in London, searching for the Drakes and Beatrice's hidden vases. As tempting as it seemed, Hudson would not leave without the medication he'd come for. Nor would he desert Josh to face his father alone.

A gun cocked behind him. "Who are you? And what business do you have meddling in my affairs?" The voice was undeniably Benjamin's.

"I am Hudson Drake, Earl of Alleyne."

"Ahh. I thought I knew you. How did you get here?"

Hudson turned slowly, pushing the gun from his face. "I am here to collect healing medicine for Sarah. Nothing more." He wanted to rail on the man and blame Sarah's dreadful condition on him, but he couldn't. The blame lay with Hudson and Hudson alone. Now he had dug a grave of his own—metaphorically and perhaps literally. With a madman before him, gun in hand, and no medicine to return home with, perhaps it was best he die. The odds were better Sarah would forgive his misdeeds in the next life than in this. Were not all sins forgiven in the afterlife?

He peered into Benjamin's black eyes, daring him to shoot. Blood trickled down the man's neck from the head wound, and his left arm hung limply at his side. Yet his rigid countenance fairly shouted "I shall not fail!"

Benjamin narrowed his gaze and looked Hudson up and down. "Sarah. Where is she? And how did you get—" His eyes landed on an exposed section of the time-traveling vest Hudson wore beneath his clothing. Benjamin growled, his very being sparked, morphing into a volcano ready to erupt.

Hudson had little time to react. He charged through the door and into the garage. "Run, Josh! Your father has awakened and has a gun."

Josh jerked from the closet his head was buried in. "Open the garage!"

A bullet whistled past Hudson's head. Even if he knew how to raise the garage gate, it was too late. Opening the door to a large, black vehicle, he slid in and ducked below the window. He heard another door being opened adjacent to his. Josh. He exhaled in relief. Still, there was the madman with a gun, and Hudson knew what he wanted. Balls pelted the car. Glass shattered.

"Josh, what happens if I"—he clutched Joshua's arm, then pushed the controls on his vest—

Before he finished the question, the large vehicle began to hum, then it—along with its passengers— evaporated into the realm of time travel.

Chapter Twenty-Nine

"Where are we, Mother?" Between fits of pain and coughing, Sarah found moments of solace in the presence of her mother. How she longed to remain with her. In this realm, no discomfort existed—physical or emotional.

"I believe we have found each other in a void—somewhere between life and death. But you must return." Her mother's voice, gentle but adamant, both soothed and confused Sarah.

"Return?"

"Yes, return. To Joshua, Christopher, Arianna…and Hudson."

Her illusion of a safe-haven—a refuge from pain and anguish—shattered with Mother's final word. "You are mistaken, Mother. Hudson is like Father. He drinks too much, he trifles with other people's lives in gaming halls, he—"

"He is broken. Without you he cannot heal."

"His dearest friend called him a rake!" The word sizzled on her tongue, and the hurt and fear returned. She coughed, and her lungs burned.

"My dear girl"—Mother stroked her hair—"you mustn't stay here with me. You are young and have much to live for."

"No, Mother, you're wrong. I do not belong in the future or the past. I shall stay with you."

"Sarah, your father…"

"What about Father? If you are here to tell me he is evil, surely you know I am well acquainted with his wickedness."

Mother nodded, and her faced drooped, causing Sarah's soul to mourn for her. Mother had suffered from Father's abuse more than anyone. She imagined what it would be like to have pledged her life to a man as vile as he. She shuddered at the notion. Once a man of kindness and integrity. Now a criminal of the worst sort.

"Sarah, I am not here to rehearse your father's sins. You know them; you have lived through them nearly as oft as I. You, my girl, have a choice to make."

"A choice?"

"Yes. You can escape the world of worry and strife; you can return to your family—our family—and hide from it; or you can find your inner strength—strength I lost along the way—stand up for yourself and live a life of happiness with the man you love."

Sarah had never heard her mother speak with such conviction. However, her words baffled her. What could she mean? She writhed in her sheets, and a bout of coughing overtook her.

"Shh." A warm hand patted hers.

"Mother, are you here?" she choked out the words, her voice low and raspy.

"I am here, child."

"Hudson will hurt me. Just as Father has hurt you." More coughing ensued. Her need for water overpowered her desire to continue conversing with Mother.

She forced her eyes open to find herself tucked in a strange bed. Her lungs and throat burned. Someone placed a cool cloth on her head.

"Mum," she croaked.

"'Tis I, Gwenillen Drake. You've a fever."

If I am ill, should Mum not be at my bedside? Flashes and snippets of memories and conversations wormed through the gossamer threads, tangling her thoughts. Hudson—she'd transported through time with him to protect Lady Alleyne. Then…where was he? Her brain scrambled to solve the puzzle, but her thought process moved as slowly as a slumbering bear waking from hibernation. After several long moments, a recollection flashed in her mind like a bolt of lightning, and the cobwebs cleared. Lunchtime—that's when she'd last seen Hudson… No, the garden. She'd been stewing over her situation in the breezy country air— too cold for a walk without a wrap, yet her stubborn refusal to abandon the trek had kept her moving. Hudson had found her, had given her a cloak and begged her to come inside. She should have. But her fragile heart refused to listen to reason—especially from the man who'd broken it.

Her lids heavy, she moved her head from side to side to see who else occupied the room. Pain sliced through her skull and settled in her chest, triggering another fit of coughing.

"Emma, bring water." Lady Alleyne pulled Sarah to a sitting position and held a cup for her.

The cool water rendered her a measure of relief. But where was Hudson? She wished to believe he cared for her, but if he truly did, why was his mother nursing her instead of him? She peered down at her state of undress and wondered if he'd been sent from the room. Surely Gwenillen would allow him to remain by her side under such conditions.

"Where—" She tried to speak, but her throat, so full of mucus, choked off her words.

"Drink this broth, dear." Gwenillen held another mug to her lips.

Sarah clutched it, relishing its warmth in her shaking fingers. Gwenillen never relinquished her grip, and Sarah was happy to hold it and smell the savory aroma rising from the mug and wafting into her nose.

Gwenillen's lips tugged into a grin. "I do believe the broth will be of greatest benefit if you drink it."

Sarah obediently sipped the broth until the cup was empty. The taste tickled her tongue and slid down her raw throat. Painful as it was to swallow, the soup tasted wonderful. "I—" She cleared her throat and tried again. "I have never had such delicious broth. Thank you."

"In fact, you have. Several times." Gwenillen chuckled. "But I am happy you like it. Cook is famous for her soups." She placed a hand on Sarah's cheek. "You are still too hot. Lie back and let me apply more ointment."

Sarah hesitated, attempting to call up the question plaguing her before the soup had distracted her from it. If she were so ill, she'd possibly asked it before. She was a burden. The realization made the broth sour in her stomach.

Gwenillen opened the jar of the pungent smelling salve.

The distasteful odor awakened her even more than the warm soup had. "Hudson. Where is he?"

Gwenillen's brows knit together and her forehead wrinkled. "I do not know. He claimed to…"

Sarah's heart plummeted. Although Lady Alleyne continued speaking, she only saw the despair on Gwenillen's face and heard confusion in her words. Had he gone in search of the vases? Or worse, returned to London to carry on his riotous living? How long had she been confined to her bed? She hadn't a clue. But Hudson had abandoned her. Of that she was certain. A tear spilled down her cheek.

"He will return, Sarah. He vowed he would."

Her heart rent in two, Sarah no longer valued Hudson's promises. More tears dripped to her chin where someone dabbed them up. She hardly felt it—or anything—through the numbness enshrouding her like a cocoon. "I shan't have him even if he does return." She accepted a handkerchief from Lady Alleyne and blew her nose. *I cannot love a man who is anything like the father I once adored. I refuse to allow my soul to be torn apart again.* But she did love Hudson. She'd ached for him. *How do I stop?*

"I concede he has not behaved the way I've desired him to, but the same sweet boy still exists within the man. He loves you. He has pined for you all these years."

"Are you saying I am at fault for Hudson's actions?" Speaking brought on more hacking.

Gwenillen gave her more water, then put the cup down. "No, no. Not at all. He is a man, and as such makes his own choices." Lady Alleyne had a faraway look in her eyes.

"Why, then, do you believe he will not hurt me?"

She jerked her head toward Sarah. "Because he chooses you. He has always chosen you," she said, nudging Sarah to her pillow.

He chooses you. He chooses you. The words cycled through her mind.

"He loves you, Sarah." Gwenillen applied the odiferous salve to her chest and throat. "Please do not give up on him… He never gave up on you."

The words, though meant to be comforting, were untrue. If Hudson yearned for her the same way she had yearned for him, he would be holding her hand. Both mothers were wrong. They did not know Hudson—the true Hudson. Sarah willed her body to relinquish itself of consciousness—fall back into the void. To Mother. Or better, leave the cares of this pain-filled world behind.

Chapter Thirty

Thud! The large vehicle landed hard on the Drakes' London property. "What happened?" Hudson took in his surroundings—sure enough, he, Joshua and the futuristic carriage had all arrived in nineteenth century London. Nearing midday, the city was bustling with people—people who stopped to stare at the strange coach. "Why did the—"

"The car come with us?" Josh finished his sentence. He shrugged. "I'm guessing it's because the SUV…er…Escalade—the name of this car which Father once drove—is encased in metal, as all cars are." His eyes wide, Joshua peered through each window. The back right window had been blown out by bullets. "Huh! I cannot believe we turned this SUV into a time-traveling machine! Now what do we do?"

"We need to get to Sarah, but we don't have any medicine."

"Unless…" Josh opened a compartment on the passenger side and rummaged through it. Then he did the same thing in a box-like storage area between the seats. "Aha! Here's a first-aid kit."

"A what?" Hudson bent to get a closer look at the box Josh held.

"Father was fascinated with modern medicines." Josh dug through the tubes, wraps, and swabs until he found a bag of small bottles. "He'd store kits like these everywhere. He claimed it was for our family's health, but we knew he hoarded modern remedies—and future medicines—like he hoarded money. It is how he saved Christopher from prison fever. I believe Father thought they'd keep him alive forever." Josh smirked. He read each bottle, then replaced it in the bag. "This one might help Sarah." He held up a bottle with a word too long for Hudson to pronounce. "Father was prone to colds and fevers. This was what he took. He'd be cured nearly instantly. I believe it is from a century even more modern than the twenty-first."

"Excellent!" He clutched Joshua's arm. "Move over and I shall get us to Sarah in record time" He couldn't keep a grin from his face, imagining what English folk would think when they saw a motorized vehicle traveling through town.

"Uh, no. You have never driven a car."

"I am a fast learner." Hudson rubbed his hands together.

"Now's not the time. It will be difficult enough to drive this huge car on the narrow streets of London without mowing over pedestrians or running into carriages." Josh shook his head. "You can navigate."

Hudson frowned. Josh was right, but he still longed to play with this rig—give Londoners a show. Too bad they had no time to drive through Hyde Park during the fashionable hour. The notion caused his smile to widen.

"Before we go anywhere, you should check your home—see if there has been any foul play."

"Right." Hudson rushed from the car to the townhouse, ignoring the passersby collecting near the property. One look inside the home told him all he needed to know—cushions lay strewn about, drawers opened, paintings removed from walls—Benjamin had been there. His loathing for the man increased, as did his gratitude for Beatrice's forewarning to protect Mum. He had no time to tidy the place. Urgency to reach Sarah with the medicine had him sprinting back to the vehicle. He slid into the car. "Your father has been here. I am just glad we moved Mother out in time."

Josh's lips formed a straight line. After a moment he let out a breath. "I'm sorry Father involved your family."

Hudson was, too, but there were more urgent matters to attend to at present. "Never mind that. We must get to Sarah."

"Yes. Which direction?" Josh started the motor, and heads everywhere swiveled at the roaring of the engine.

Hudson rubbed his hands together again. "Go that direction." He pointed to the right.

The car moved backward at first, then Josh turned it in the direction Hudson had indicated. "Roll your window down. Warn everyone to move."

"Oh, I believe they know we are coming." Hudson laughed. "But how does one *roll* a window down?"

Josh pointed to a button on the door handle. "Push that."

The window moved down quickly, startling Hudson. One could hardly call it "rolling." Another thing to play with—later. Now he'd enjoy the gawking people who began trailing after the car. "Look at them." He barked a laugh. "They've never seen such a thing!"

"Until a few days ago, *you* hadn't seen such a thing." Josh shook his head, but his eyes sparked with mischief.

They crept through the crowded city streets, Josh constantly scanning the surrounding area. No one got in the way, but droves of people followed, and some called out to them. "'Tis a horseless coach!" said one man. A woman shrieked, "The end is near. Evil is upon us. Surely the devil is come." Amazement shone on several faces, while terror seemed to strike others as mothers clutched their children, dragging them away from the car.

"No need to fear. We are here from the future. In two hundred years, everyone will have a horseless carriage," Hudson hollered, smiling and nodding to their audience.

"That's Drake the Rake! Where's your gun?" a man yelled out.

Oh no. Hudson had all but forgotten there was still a bounty on his head. And here he was, parading through the streets of London for all to see. "We need to pick up the speed, Josh. There are a few men out there aiming to kill me, even in this fine vehicle."

Josh swerved hard, driving onto someone's property to miss an oncoming carriage. The horses reared, then bolted, galloping at an erratic speed. The coach swayed out of control—driver and passengers screamed, diverting the crowd's attention—including the thugs. Josh maneuvered the car back onto the road at a cautious pace. Other carriage drivers looked on in horror and made quick work of turning their conveyances onto side streets or into dirt paths leading to townhouses. The road now clear, Josh sped up and soon no one could keep pace with them.

"Hold up. Hold up." Hudson raised a hand as they approached the Palace of Westminster. Several men exited and were scattering from the building. "Looks like I missed a session." He smirked.

"But you said to hur—"

"I know, I know. Just slow down for a moment."

Josh shrugged, then let up on the pedal.

Hudson poked his head out the window. "Finley! You thought to scare me—nay, kill me in cold blood, did you? Well, try catching me now!"

Lord Finley's mouth gaped open like the whale that swallowed Jonah. And his eyebrows shot so high, they completely disappeared. Was it the vehicle or the fact Hudson still lived that astonished the man? Both, no doubt. He stood rooted in place, but if eyes could shoot daggers, Hudson would have caught his death.

The crowd trailing them had grown and were now gaining speed.

"We'd best get out of here. But can you make a noise with the car first?" asked Hudson. He waved his arm to the approaching onlookers. "Goodbye, London!"

Josh blasted on a horn, then sped away—faster than a carriage, but far from the pace the vehicle was capable. Hudson looked back to see Londoners throwing hands in the air or standing still as statues.

Both men burst into fits of laughter. Hudson hadn't had so much fun since watching old man Dumfery set his hounds on Eddie. "The look on Finley's face." He laughed some more. "Dumbfounded." The car bumped along the cobbled road much more smoothly than a well-sprung carriage.

"You might even call the bloke gobsmacked." Josh chortled.

"I haven't heard that word, but I like it." Hudson continued pointing directions, while carriages rushed to clear the way. Some horses pitched, rocking their coaches to and fro.

Josh kept a steady watch on the narrow road and its oncoming traffic. "The word is British. Just not from this century." They finally reached the city limits. Without so many coaches, Josh applied more pressure to the gas pedal.

Hudson sobered. "I hope we make it in time to save Sarah."

Joshua's lips turned down. "As do I." He shifted in his seat but kept his eyes on the dirt road. "About Sarah"—he paused—"did I hear that ruffian correctly? Are you called Drake the Rake?"

Hudson had hoped Josh hadn't heard that. No sense in pretending now. If Sarah lived, she'd surely tell Josh the rotten truth. "I earned the reputation at Oxford and I'm not proud of it. But I thought Sarah was dead." He threw his hands in the air. "I was grief-stricken. Then Father passed, leaving me with a large inheritance and a title."

Josh said nothing.

"Sarah knows. She is incensed."

"As she should be."

"I hoped I might garner sympathy from you, Josh. You are a man. We have needs. Why is she so angry? I am no different from most of the peerage."

"I have friends from work—good men—whom I have urged Sarah to court. I wouldn't classify any of them as a 'rake.' Yet she rebuffed them all, saving herself for you. Even though she knew she'd likely never see you again. She wouldn't so much as allow them a kiss."

"I should hope not. She's a lady. Allowing such behavior from your friends would cause her ruin."

Josh let out a huff and shook his head. "In the twenty-first century, men and women are on equal footing in these matters. And in the nineteenth century, if one is in a committed relationship, it should be no different."

"I have vowed to change. Less drinking, less gaming—"

"No philandering." Josh said emphatically.

"Of course."

"It might not matter. If she knows about your overindulgence in drinking, she may still turn you out. You have seen for yourself what our father has become. A brilliant failure turned drunk creates a lethal combination."

"I am nothing like your father. I know I can change, Josh. Those things that earned me a poor reputation—diversions. That is all. I love Sarah."

"It's not a matter of making simple changes in your behavior; you must alter your entire way of thinking. Diversions become addictions. No one in the nineteenth century speaks of such things, but it is well researched in the future. Sarah took a few university psychology classes. She knows plenty on the subject."

"Sarah went to university? Women don't attend universities."

"They do in Sarah's new world. She's intelligent— did well in her classes. But the social aspect of it overwhelmed her. Perhaps in a few years…"

"Surely she'll wish to stay in the nineteenth century, where she will be the wife of an earl—assuming she accepts my apologies." Hudson had never considered staying in the future. His life, his friends, his kingdom revolved around London.

"That may have been true a few years ago. Sarah has been the most stubborn of the Somerset clan about accepting the changes foisted upon us—of course now I know her reluctance had more to do with missing you than anything else. But she is growing accustomed to the positive views of women society has made over time. You must consider that while you are considering Sarah's heart."

"Are you implying I would hurt her? I shan't. Or are you saying a man from my century cannot get on with a woman from another?" Hudson didn't care for the direction this conversation had taken. Sarah's scrawny younger brother had grown up and now served as her protector. A role Hudson wished to fill.

"I'm saying neither. For instance, take Christopher and Arianna. I've not met two people better suited for each other. But they had to learn how to make it work. And then there is—" Josh clamped his mouth shut.

"There is what?"

"Never mind."

"Are you courting a lass, Joshua?"

Josh's face reddened. "We're coming up to a fork in the road. Which way do we go?"

Hudson chuckled. "You *are* courting someone. Keep to the right, by the way." He shook his head and punched Josh in the shoulder. "Tell me about her. Is she from your century or mine?"

"Neither. And I don't want to talk about her. No one in my family knows about her. I think Sarah fears I have been tinkering with the traveling machine because I am like Father. I am not."

"You have been improving upon your father's invention so you can visit a woman in a different century?" Talking about anything other than his own troubled relationship calmed the panic which had risen in Hudson's chest. "Wait. Make a turn here and the estate is just one league up the road." He marveled that they'd cut a seven hour carriage ride down to less than an hour. "Go on with your story." His nerves jittered, wondering the condition of Sarah. He sighed and rubbed his forehead.

"Later. Let's worry about Sarah now."

Chapter Thirty-One

Hudson directed Josh to pull into the gravel pathway leading to the carriage house. They rushed across the yard to the manor, glimpsing faces pressed against windows as they approached the entry. "The servants must have heard us arrive." He chuckled. Bursting through the door, he ignored curious glances thrown their way. "Come," he said to Josh, "we must see to Sarah." They took the stairs two at a time.

Without knocking, he threw the door open to Sarah's bedchamber. "How is she?" The room smelled of pungent herbs and ointments.

Mother startled and jerked her head up—her eyes puffy and red. A physician hovering over Sarah straightened and glared at him.

Hudson sprinted across the room, alarm constricting his chest. Sarah lay limp and lifeless. No, they couldn't be too late. Tears filled his eyes. "Is she…"

"Who are you?" The doctor's thick brows pulled down, forming a V-shape.

"I am Lord Alleyne, Sarah's betrothed." He didn't care if it wasn't the truth. It would be soon. "I demand to know her condition." He turned to Mother. "I thought there were no doctors in the village."

Mother sniffed and blew her nose. "Jameson located this physician in a town beyond the village.

227

Hudson, Sarah has teetered between life and death since you vanished."

A cloth hung from the doctor's hand. "She is not dead yet. I was preparing to drain the excess fluids from her." He began tying the cloth around her limp arm.

"No!" Josh pushed Hudson aside. "Bloodletting will not work and is a dangerous practice. I have antibiotics—medicine."

"Anti what?" the doctor stammered. "I beg your pardon!"

"No time to explain," said Hudson. He turned to Josh. "How will we administer the pills to her in this state?"

"We have to wake her. Crush the pills and put them in tea or broth. We must hurry, though. Lady Alleyne, has she taken broth?" Josh scanned the room, his eyes settling on a tray bearing a cup.

"When she wakes, but she hasn't woken for hours now. That is why I sent Jameson searching again for a physician."

The doctor's forehead wrinkled further. He glowered at Josh. "And who are you? Do you not see this girl is in distress? I must insist you both leave and allow me to attend to her."

"I'm her brother."

"He is a scholar of modern medicine," Hudson added. "*He* will now care for the girl. You may leave."

"I have been practicing medicine for over twenty years. And you think you know better than I?" the doctor blurted.

"I know I do." Josh nearly pushed the man out of his way to reach Sarah. He held up an oblong object that looked like a miniature piece of chalk. "Hudson, crush this and put it in a small amount of tea or broth."

The doctor stomped his foot. "But—"

"You are dismissed, doctor. Jameson will pay you for your services," said Hudson.

Turning to Lady Alleyne, the physician glared, apparently waiting for her to override Hudson's orders.

"Thank you for your help. You may go." She nodded to the angry man.

"I shall not budge. If you have a pharmaceutical remedy that will raise the dead, I wish to see it for myself." He grunted. "The girl's death will rest on your hands, not mine."

Hudson stopped listening to the blathering doctor and smashed the pill. "Is the broth warm at all?" he asked Mother.

Josh picked up the half-empty cup and held it out for him. "It doesn't need to be. We must get the pill in her."

"Mother, do you have any smelling salts? Anything that might wake her?"

"I do, but what she longs for most is you. She believes you have deserted her—returned to gambling and drink."

Hudson's heart cracked in two. "Did you tell her, Mum? Does she know I went for help?" His voice hitched, and a lump clogged his throat.

"It did not matter what I said. The dear girl hasn't been talking to me; she has been communing with her own mother. She wishes to let go—leave the troubles of this world. She mumbles words of betrayal and grief. Hudson, she has been tormented by your actions."

A chill raced down Hudson's spine. He moved past Josh, knelt next to Sarah and clasped her hand in his. "Sarah, my love, I am here." He kissed her pale fingers. "I never deserted you. How could I? You are everything to me." The room fell silent. Hudson knew everyone listened to his intimate words meant only for Sarah's ears, but he didn't care. He'd do anything to save her. "Please, my love, come back." Tears dripped from his eyes and landed on their intertwined fingers.

"She might have departed, son." Mother placed a soft hand on his shoulder.

He refused to accept it or even listen to anyone suggesting she had died. He must wake her. Through blurry eyes he took in her beauty. Her dark hair glistened like polished wood. The flush on her pale cheeks was like the flush of sunset on snow. Her rosy lips, full and sweet—*that's it.* Surely she would know him by a kiss.

He used one hand to lift her head and held it gently, while using the other to clear away errant strands of hair. "I love you, Sarah." He lowered his face and pressed his lips to hers, pouring every ounce of love he possessed into a slow kiss. In that moment, any disposition he'd had to gamble, drink, or ever hold another woman fled for good. He was Sarah's. She owned his heart—whether she wished to or not. Lowering her head, he held his breath, willing her to wake.

Her eyes fluttered. Gasps filled the room. "Hudson." Her voice, barely audible, melted through him like clotted cream.

"I am here, love." He motioned Josh over with the cup. "I have brought medicine for you, but you must drink this tea." He raised her just enough to pour out drops of the tepid drink.

She slumped back in his grip.

"Please, Sarah. I am here. I need you to live. Do not leave me." Tears poured from his eyes in earnest now. He couldn't remember the last time he'd cried in front of an audience, but he didn't care. His emotions, now exposed, could not be quelled.

Her mouth moved as if she were trying to speak, but nothing came out. Her eyes remained closed tight. He held the cup to her lips and tilted it just enough to wet them. It worked—she opened her mouth, allowing Hudson to pour the liquid in. She swallowed, then winced, but continued to drink until the cup was empty. He laid her back against the pillow and dabbed her wet lips with a cloth.

"Hmph!" said the doctor. "I hardly think a kiss and a spot of tea will help. Draining her of excess fluids is her only hope."

No one listened to the doctor. All eyes were riveted on Sarah and Hudson.

Mother cried into a handkerchief. "That was beautiful, my boy."

Hudson heard Josh sniff, as well.

Following his instincts, Hudson circled the bed to the opposite side and snuggled up beside Sarah, wrapping both arms around her. "Joshua, wake us when she is due for her next dose." Without any care of what his audience thought, he buried his head in her silky hair and closed his eyes. "I will never leave you again, love."

Chapter Thirty-Two

Sarah opened her eyes after a more restful sleep than she could remember. Her dreams, so vivid, replayed in her mind. Hudson had come to rescue her from the edge of a cliff—ready to plunge from this mortal existence. She remembered arguing with Mother about returning to life or letting her illness release her. Gloom drove her to the brink—she needed to depart this world of physical pain and mental anguish. Then a kiss—Hudson's kiss—had pulled her from the fog of hopelessness. In it she'd felt honesty, despair, torment, regret, and love.

The room, dark and quiet, still had an odor of the salve Gwenillen Drake had applied to her. Bits and pieces of conversation with Lady Alleyne pushed their way into her memory but made little sense. Warm arms were clasped around her waist. Whose? She turned to see who held her. Though fully nighttime, a sliver of moonlight illuminated the room enough for her to see a head of unruly hair. Hudson. Reflected light glimmered over his handsome face like beams of icy radiance. The shadow of a beard gave him a more manly aura than she thought possible. She didn't know why he lay beside her, but the heat from his body strengthened her beyond any ointments or teas could.

His eyes opened. "Sarah?" He caressed her cheek. "You are awake. How do you feel?"

"As if I am in a dream. Are you real?" She placed a hand over his fingers still holding her face.

"I am real. Your body has cooled and your coughing quelled." He smiled. "I believe you shall live."

"'Twas you who beckoned me back to life." Happiness warmed her heart until familiar memories and doubts pecked at her. Hadn't he deserted her in her darkest hour? "But you left me—"

"Only to collect some modern medicine. I would never desert you, love. Josh and I have been administering antibiotics from the future to you for a day and a half now. And I believe they are working."

"You traveled back to my home in the future? Josh is here?" So many questions bombarded her mind.

"Shh. I will explain everything in the morning. Do you wish for me to leave?"

Never. She wanted to remain in his arms for the rest of her life. But it wasn't proper. "What shall people think if they find you here?"

He chuckled. "I had an audience when I wept over you. The same audience witnessed me kissing you with an undeniable passion—a kiss I had hoped would raise the dead. Every servant, Mother, Josh, even a doctor watched me lie beside you and hold you to my heart. I care not what they shall say. I only care about you. What do you wish me to do?"

His tender words brought unexpected tears to her eyes. "Please, stay with me."

"As you wish. Now, roll over and go back to sleep. I believe your health will soon be restored, with proper rest." He brought her hand to his mouth and kissed her fingers.

Settled once again, enfolded in his arms, she closed her eyes, but sleep refused to come. Instead, she lay awake, wondering about other women he'd held in a similar fashion. Her head and heart seemed to be at odds often of late. Because of recent revelations, her mind had become suspicious of Hudson—every word he spoke, every action he took fell under scrutiny. Her heart countered with his promises to change and his recent chivalrous deeds. He had traveled to the twenty-first century to secure medicine for her; he had openly cried over her; and he'd stayed close, holding her when she needed it most; and that kiss—it had no doubt brought her back to life.

After battling these conflicting thoughts for what seemed an eternity, sweat beaded on her forehead, and her dry throat cried out for water. Careful not to wake him, she removed herself from his embrace and attempted to stand. The floor moved beneath her, or was it the entire room? Her legs, too weak to bear the weight, buckled. Before crashing to the floor, however, she caught the arm of a chair next to her bed and steadied herself. Relief.

Through filtering moonlight, she spied a cup on a tray nearby. With any luck it would contain water, broth, or tea. At this point, she didn't care which. She lifted it and smiled. The weight of the mug suggested there was indeed liquid inside. First, she sniffed it— broth—then gulped it down. Though not warm, the soup satisfied her thirst and after a time provided her limbs fortification. Eventually, she found the courage to stand again. This time she was successful. Dragging her heavy legs across the room, she cracked open a window and let the cool air clear her head.

She sat near the window, breathing in crisp air until the morning light turned the clouds pink, and the cobwebs crowding her mind were swept away. After pulling the pane shut, then latching it, she turned her attention to the man sleeping on her bed. He'd never crawled beneath the covers—had only held her in his comforting arms. How could she fault him? And how could she not forgive his past—a past filled with uncertainty and pain? "I forgive you, Hudson," she whispered.

"How long have you been awake?" Hudson sat up and rubbed his eyes.

She took a wobbly step toward the bed. "Did I wake you?"

His lips curved up to a lopsided grin. "No...well, perhaps the cool air did, but I am happy to see you standing. How do you feel?"

"Better than I have in days. Thank you for bringing me medicine." She longed to fall back in bed and into his arms, but now she'd confessed to feeling better, the innocence of sleeping in his arms might not be so innocent.

"You are still not well enough to be up. Your legs are weak." He patted the bed.

Without a second thought, Sarah walked on shaky legs and collapsed onto the bed, allowing his arms to close around her once more. The warmth heated more than her body—it healed her soul. This time she turned toward him, studying his features. His handsome face was kindled with a sort of passionate beauty and an inherent strength.

His lips parted in a dazzling display of straight, white teeth. "What are you thinking, love?"

"I am wondering how I became so lucky as to have such a gallant man lying beside me." She smiled.

He held her gaze, his eyes misting. "I—" His voice cracked. He cleared his throat. "I love you, Sarah. There is nothing I would not do for you. Thank you for returning to us—to me." He rose up on one knee and lowered his head to hers. A vaguely sensuous light passed between them before he moved his lips over hers.

His kiss left her burning, fire sizzling through her veins. Breathless, she paused, hoping for more, but Hudson reclaimed his pillow.

"I must leave you before I do something we shall both regret." He laughed, but it sounded strained.

She touched his cheek. "I long for the day we are wed and can be together always." Disappointed he was leaving her side, she admitted to herself that he was right. She had been brought up to remain pure for her husband, and she was determined to do so.

"As do I." He stood and brushed down his wrinkled clothing, chuckling at the futility of the effort. "Are you hungry, love?"

"Hungrier than I've ever been." She smiled, grateful he'd asked. Her stomach had been growling ever since she woke hours ago.

"Then I shall fetch you a tray of food to break your fast." He bent and placed a whisper of a kiss on her lips. "'Tis fully morning now. Cook will be filling the sideboard with delectable meats and breads. When you become my wife, you shall value Cook's talents in the kitchen." His eyes sparkled, then he slipped out the door.

Something in his words left her disconcerted. For so many years now, she'd longed to return to the nineteenth century—return to Hudson. But after just a short time in this era she had once called home, she now wondered if she truly belonged. Her family had firmly settled in the twenty-first century. Perhaps she could persuade Hudson to reside with her there. She imagined being the next Lady Alleyne. More doubt shivered through her. The *ton* would never accept her—Benjamin Somerset's daughter—posing as a countess. Not to mention facing Hudson's friends—Hudson's past. She nearly lost her appetite with her dizzying thoughts. One thing was certain—no matter the century, she would remain by Hudson's side, come what may.

Her door opened. Hudson must have found the sideboard empty. Surely he'd not had time to fill a plate for her.

A man who looked vaguely familiar entered. Lady Alleyne followed close behind. They carried on a conversation as though she weren't present.

"I need to examine the patient. I hope she is still alive after your son forced me, the trained physician, from the room, as if he knew medicine better than I." He grunted, then scanned the area. "He is not here now. If it is not too late, I shall drain her excess fluids."

"No!" Sarah sat up. "I am very much recovered."

The doctor froze. His eyes huge.

"Hudson has only gone in search of food. I am famished." She laughed, hoping to ease the tension in the room. The doctor had such an unfriendly demeanor, she didn't want him near her.

His face creased as he moved toward the bed. "How—"

"Medicine. Antibiotics. I'm certain Hudson and my brother told you." She stepped out of bed. "I have even been up and about this morning. I think I shall wash and dress now, if you would allow me some privacy." Above all, she wished the man to leave.

"'Tis impossible." The physician's eyes were still wide as saucers. "You were on the threshold of death, and now—"

"I am better. Thanks to my brother and my betrothed." Hudson had mentioned he had said he was her fiancé in order to remain in her room. She liked the way the word rang in her ears and would continue the ruse until it was official.

The doctor narrowed his eyes and put his hands on his hips. "This medicine. I must see it."

Lady Alleyne moved to intervene. "The girl asked for privacy. As you can see, she is doing much better." She turned to Sarah. "Sit down, child. You've been very ill. If you'd like to dress, I shall help you, but I do not think you should push yourself."

The doctor made no motion to leave.

"Dr. Brown, I do appreciate you coming here—though we did not call for you this morning—but I believe you can see we have things under control. Please see yourself out." Her firm voice left no question of her wish for him to depart.

He huffed, then gave an oh-so-slight bow before stalking from the room.

Sarah and Lady Alleyne waited for the door to close before they began to laugh.

"The look on the man's face," said Gwenillen. "He had some nerve storming in here like that. He was certain he'd find a corpse." She placed a hand on

238

Sarah's forehead. "No fever. But I do think you were putting on a show for the doctor when you sprang from your bed." She chortled. "Well done, my girl. Now, would you really like to dress or climb back into bed?"

"I believe I shall get bedsores if I spend another day lying about. I would like to freshen up and dress…at least for a short time. I promise to reclaim my bed when I tire."

"Very well. I shall return with a day dress. A fresh toilette is laid out on the washstand." Lady Alleyne left the room but returned promptly, carrying a cornflower blue muslin dress. "This will put the sparkle back in your beautiful eyes."

Sarah smiled. She'd barely had time to freshen up. "Thank you. I—I think I can dress myself. You are too kind."

"I have already seen your strange undergarments. Who do you think dressed you in that night dress?" Her eyes crinkled with amusement. "And you shan't be able to reach the stays. I shall help you."

"Oh…" Heat pulsed through Sarah, and she was certain it bloomed on her cheeks.

"Do not fret, dear. Hudson has explained where you and your family have been hiding. I did not believe it. Not at all. That is, until he showed me a strange looking vest with vials and knobs. Then he pushed a button and vanished before my eyes. Later he showed up in an unearthly conveyance. Not to mention the medicine, which apparently is a miracle cure for winter fever."

Sarah's stomach growled. "I wonder what is keeping Hudson. Perhaps once I am dressed, you could give me a hand down the stairs? I can surprise him, and we shall dine together at the table."

Lady Alleyne hummed while she helped Sarah dress. Sarah suspected she did so to distract her from being embarrassed. After all, undergarments in the twenty-first century scarcely covered anything compared to the uncomfortable layers she'd endured before being transported through time.

"There now, child." She ran a brush through Sarah's hair. I believe you are presentable. Let us go find your betrothed." She winked and took Sarah by the arm.

As they neared the bottom step, Sarah heard Hudson's voice rising up from the parlor. Strange. She and Gwenillen exchanged curious glances.

Once off the stairs, Sarah didn't wait to be escorted to the parlor. She let go of Lady Alleyne's arm and marched toward the arched entry, then stopped at the sound of a woman's voice.

"As I said before, I am delighted *you* are here, instead of Lord Finley. When I saw lights on, I knew I must call and welcome the Finleys back. They have sorely neglected this beautiful manor. Imagine my surprise to find Hudson Drake in their stead—someone with whom I've shared a lonely night or two. Have I ever told you how much your companionship meant to me?"

Sarah froze. Her insides roiling. She wished to run away—blast off to the twenty-first century. But hadn't she just pledged herself to Hudson? The old Sarah would flee. The new Sarah would wait for Hudson's response—give him the benefit of the doubt. Earlier he had declared her his betrothed. She had felt forgiveness in her heart. She peeked in just long enough to glimpse a beautiful blonde woman. A smile lighting her perfect face.

Hudson chuckled in that endearing way uniquely his. "Do not forget, I was lonely, as well."

An invisible knife plunged into Sarah's back. Still, she waited.

The woman trilled a flirtatious laugh. "I had plans to leave for London tomorrow. I've missed you so. How convenient you have come to me."

"Indeed. I hope now you shall change your travel plans and remain here in the country." His tone was infused with charm.

The blade in her back turned, as did her stomach, sending bile up her throat. This woman was clearly not just a diversion. Sarah covered her mouth and turned to find the nearest basin.

Chapter Thirty-Three

Anxiety whisked through Hudson's veins. Mrs. Barlow needed to leave so he could fill a plate of food and return to Sarah. Of all people to have found him at Finley's estate. He inwardly groaned. The young widow had sought him out on occasion in London. He thought himself safe in the country. But if he turned her away—told her about Sarah—she would no doubt rush to London and spread the word, revealing his location in the process. He needed to keep her in the country without giving her hopes of ever meeting up. An impossible task.

She scooted closer to him on the sofa they shared.

The physician who'd been with Sarah previously sauntered past the entryway to the parlor, a half-eaten pastry in his hand. The man must have returned to check on his patient—then stayed for breakfast. A brilliant idea sprang to Hudson's mind.

He coughed. Fake and hard. "Forgive me, Mrs. Barlow"—he covered his mouth with a handkerchief—"there has been an infectious fever passing through the family." He scooted away. "I would not wish you to catch it."

Widow Barlow flinched—her brows furrowed together. "Oh, dear. 'Tis dreadful news."

The doctor stopped in his motion toward the front door and faced Hudson. "Are you ill now, as well?" His lips formed a straight line, and no emotion lit his expression.

Hudson continued to cough. "Yes, I believe I am. I shall take to my bed at once." He turned to Widow Barlow. "Tell me you shan't leave the country. If I am fortunate enough to survive the fever, I shall send word. For now"—he hacked a few more times—"I think it best if you stay in your manor for a time."

Doctor Brown tipped his hat to the lady. "Mrs. Barlow."

She nodded, then looked at Hudson, trembling. "My late husband died of winter fever. Doctor Brown attended to him. I—I think I should leave now. I promise to stay in the country, Hud…Lord Alleyne. Good day to you both." She called for her wrap and rushed from the manor.

Hudson breathed a sigh of relief, but the doctor's gaze still rested on him. "Do not trouble yourself, doctor. I have healing medicine. You may go."

"I may go? I have been shooed from every room of this house. I am a physician. Just because I bear no title does not mean I am an uneducated man. Show respect to your elders."

"Jameson," Hudson hollered.

The butler was at his side in a heartbeat.

"See the kind doctor out." His words came out with more force than necessary, but Hudson didn't care. He needed to fill a plate for Sarah. The widow had wasted too much of his time.

As Jameson ushered the blustering doctor from the manor, Hudson aimed for the dining room. His mother intercepted him, a peculiar look in her eye.

"I must get food for Sarah." He tried to sidestep Mother, but she moved into his path once more.

"Hudson—"

"Mother, I have been detained long enough. Sarah is waiting for me."

"She is not waiting for you. She came in search of you, and—"

"No." He gulped. "Did she—"

"Yes. She heard enough. You spoke to that woman as if you were involved with her, not betrothed to Sarah." Mother's eyes narrowed. "Why? I am certain you have a reason."

"Because she planned to leave for London tomorrow. The woman is well-acquainted with Charles Finley. She would have told him of our whereabouts. I would be a dead man in a matter of hours once news hit the *ton*. I have no affection for Widow Barlow. Sarah is the only woman I care to be with—ever."

"I fear Sarah won't see it so matter-of-factly. She stood by the door, as if waiting to hear you enlighten the woman of your betrothal to another. Imagine her shock when you returned the woman's cooing tones and words of adoration."

Hudson didn't want to imagine it. He had hurt Sarah enough. She had just begun to trust him again, and now this. "I must find her. Where is she?"

Mother shrugged. "Most likely back abed. She cast up her accounts—what little she had in her stomach after being fed only liquids—and rushed from the washroom. I felt I should warn you. Hudson, that girl deserves better. Her mother, teetering on death's doorstep, an abusive father…" Mother shook her head. "See that she receives the joy and happiness she is due.

And, my son, be prepared if you find you are not the man to provide it."

A punch to the gut would have hurt less than Mother's words. But she was wise—always had been. He took a few fortifying breaths, then climbed the stairs leading to Sarah. Nerves rattled his body like the tail of a venomous snake.

He pushed open the bedchamber door and saw Sarah sitting on a chair, her back to him. The sight of her shuddering, slumped shoulders caused him to loathe himself anew. Had he abstained from his diversions, distractions, or any other word he'd used to justify his behavior, none of this would have happened. Too many times he had blamed his broken heart, blamed Mr. Somerset, blamed his father for dying so young, blamed Sarah... No, the blame rested on him alone. Now he must bear the weight of it.

"Sarah, may I enter?"

She turned toward the door. Her swollen eyes pierced his soul.

He waited, but she said nothing, so he crossed the room to her. "Please, will you let me explain?"

A long moment passed in silence. She straightened her shoulders and slanted her head. "No. I do not believe so. Ever since we have been in this century, you have done nothing but *explain*. I confess I once believed I could not live without you, but I was wrong. What I cannot do is live with this—constant doubts, distrust, and listening to you *explain* your actions. I am certain you can tell me a story justifying what I heard in the parlor—perhaps even convince me to forgive you. But when will the next beautiful woman appear? And your drinking and gambling—how soon will you pick those habits up again?

"Just let me—"

"It has only been a few days, and I have seen more of my father in you than I ever thought possible. So, no. I do not wish to hear an explanation of why you told another woman you hoped she wouldn't leave the country for London and how she gave you comfort through your lonely nights. No explanation can erase the sting of your words or proof of your nature."

"Sarah, she would give up our loca—"

Sarah held a hand up, cutting him off. "It doesn't matter, Hudson. I cannot allow you to hurt me any longer. I thought coming to the nineteenth century would bring me joy. I was wrong. But remaining here might kill me. And what if I agreed to stay, then became your wife? Do you think I would be accepted? The daughter of Benjamin Somerset—the *ton* would likely string me up in his place, just as they attempted with Christopher."

"We could live in the country."

"It seems even the country has constant reminders of your past." She stood, but kept a hand clutching the chair. Her body needed nourishment—nourishment he'd failed to provide. "Honestly, Hudson, is there anywhere in England we could reside in peace? Any town or village you haven't gained some type of reputation that would not mock me, or bring up unwanted reminders of your past behavior?"

He didn't have a ready answer.

She took a step forward. "Besides that, you are an earl. You cannot hide from your peers. You have responsibilities." Her head dropped and she let out a ragged breath before meeting his gaze again. "So, you see, no amount of explaining will change my mind. Please, leave me." The tears once in her eyes had been replaced by a savage inner fire he'd never witnessed in her. She kept a steady gaze on him.

The tensing of her jaw betrayed her deep frustrations. She wished him to go.

He couldn't.

She must listen to reason. How many times had he said he would not give up without a fight? Dozens. "Sarah—"

"No, Hudson. I refuse to hear it."

The problem stared him in the face—she wouldn't fight.

He must think of something to keep her here—allow him to win her back. He reached for her hand, but she drew it away. "You…you must be famished. I shall get you some nourishment."

Her face creased, and he realized his misstep. Had he not been on an errand to fetch her food before both of their worlds had collapsed? Lud, he was a fool. She erased the pained expression and squared her shoulders, replacing sadness with firm lines of determination. "I shall find my way to the dining room—alone." With a steadiness he doubted she possessed, she brushed past him, leaving her rosy scent in her wake.

He closed his eyes and willed his heart to stop beating. Without Sarah there was no point in living. He moved to the chair she had vacated and breathed in her scent. She must have dabbed it on before descending the stairs in search of him. His heart bruised as he imagined her anticipation, wishing to surprise him by being up and dressed—in his favorite color, no less.

The color of Sarah. Since they'd been young, he'd developed a fondness for the color blue. Her azure eyes could set his heart aflame. Pair them with a blue dress and they could set the room aflame. Her beauty was unmatched, but that was not why he loved Sarah—she was his soulmate.

What should his next move be? Earlier conversations he'd had with Mother gnawed at him. She had never come out and said it; he suspected she loved Sarah nearly as much as he did. But did Mother think him unworthy of her? … Perhaps he was. He could argue his actions were no different from many of his peers. He listed several such members of the gentry in his head. But plenty of others were good, upstanding men—or buttoned up and boring, as he'd put it. He pictured Sarah with the men who were not—the dandies and rakes—and his stomach tensed. None of them were worthy to even look upon his Sarah, let alone marry her. No wonder she found his behavior repulsive. And what about her argument about living in the nineteenth century—where else would they live? The man ruled the family, and Hudson's kingdom was right here in his own century.

Being thrust into the twenty-first century had changed Sarah. She had a knowledge of futuristic objects, such as cars and cell phones. She loved to cook. He recalled the radiant smile lighting her face when she'd served up breakfast. And she had a job. His wife would never work. *Sarah shan't lift a finger when we—if we—are married.* But she had said she loved her job. And Josh had mentioned she was good at it. What if she resented him for taking her away from her family, home, and work?

Sadness enveloped him like a dark cloud. He loved Sarah. He would always love Sarah. No one could ever take her place—in his heart or by his side. He wished Widow Barlow were present right now so he could yell it in her face. *I am betrothed to Sarah!* There had never been another and there never would be.

His eyes welled, but he knew what he must do.

Slowly, he unfastened the time-traveling vest, made sure the dials were set correctly for Sarah to return home, and placed it on her bed.

Chapter Thirty-Four

Sarah clutched the banister and took one wobbly step down at a time. Resolve to reach the bottom before Hudson cornered her again urged her on. She must find Josh and only Josh. Either of the Drakes might try to persuade her to remain with Hudson. Her heart smarted. Again. How wrong she had been to assume finding him would mend her broken spirit. If anything, it had worsened her pain. How would she get back to the twenty-first century? Hudson had refused her request for the vest before. Now that she had shut him down without allowing him an explanation, she had little hope of him acquiescing.

Her foot landed on the marble floor at the bottom of the grand staircase. Now to locate Josh. Her search took her from the dining hall to the bookroom before she became too weak to continue. She paused in the hallway, steadying herself against the wall. Closing her eyes, she pondered her next move.

"Sarah, who are you looking for?" Hudson's mother pulled Sarah's arm through hers.

"Oh, I—Hudson said my brother is here somewhere. I have been searching but cannot locate him."

Lady Alleyne's kind eyes helped quell Sarah's anxiety. The woman had been nothing but loving. "I believe your brother is asleep. He helped Hudson medicate you for nearly two days and paced between doses. He is a good brother." She squeezed Sarah's arm. "Have you eaten anything, child? You are pale."

Sarah's heart ached at the notion of Hudson and Josh tending to her for so long. But her appetite had fled the minute she'd heard the horrible conversation in the parlor. Her energy flagged, in need of food. She shook her head.

"Let us allow your brother a few more minutes of sleep while you eat." With her arm still holding Sarah's, she led her to the dining hall.

A servant was clearing breakfast from the sideboard but stopped at their approach. "Can I bring you fresh victuals, m'lady?"

"Yes. A plate for Miss Somerset."

Sarah raised a hand. "Just tea and toast please."

The maid dipped a curtsy and retreated to the kitchen. She returned with a plate of toast with marmalade and a pot of tea.

Sarah's mouth watered, the aromas reviving her appetite. "Thank you." She scooted up to the long table and began to eat.

"Would you like company?" Lady Alleyne placed a gentle hand on Sarah's shoulder. "Or would you rather be alone?"

Sarah blinked back tears. Hudson's mother didn't wish to lecture her, she wanted to mother her. Her heart warmed. "I would dearly love your company."

The woman smiled and took the seat next to hers. After watching Sarah eat several bites, she cleared her throat. "Tell me, dear, what is the future like?"

The question caught Sarah off-guard. She had expected queries about her conversation with Hudson, not the future. "Lady Alleyne, do you truly wish to know about whence I came? If so, I am happy to tell you."

"Please, Sarah. Your mother was my dearest friend. Call me Gwenillen." She patted Sarah's shoulder. "Yes, sweet child. Tell me."

Sarah brightened. "In two hundred years in America—and I am sure it will be much the same here in England—we have electricity, which powers"—she shrugged—"everything. Kitchen appliances—such as instantly heating ovens, ice boxes that need no ice, microwaves—"

"Micro—"

"Sorry. Microwaves are small ovens that by just a touch of a button will heat your food."

Gwenillen's eyes widened.

"Then there are televisions—moving and talking pictures on a screen. Computers with internet." She shook her head, knowing the woman wouldn't understand most of what she spoke. "Cars instead of carriages. Even airplanes that fly large amounts of people through the sky." Words were spilling from her mouth so fast, she could hardly contain them. "Things change so dramatically between now and then—I do not have the words to describe it."

"What about the people. Are they so different?"

"They are. In many ways they have evolved—in other ways their impropriety continues to astonish me. I believe I have struggled adjusting to human changes most of all. But after spending time here, I find myself missing the open-minded attitudes of people in the future. In the twenty-first century, women are not expected to hold their tongues or their tempers when their men misbehave. I had nearly forgotten what would be expected of me should I stay—nor did I remember what male behaviors I must accept as a woman here." She paused, thinking about her next words. "Lady Alle—Gwenillen, I cannot do it." Sudden tears sprang to her eyes. She hadn't planned on speaking of her relationship with Hudson to his mother. Now she expected a reprimand for expressing herself. It was the way of things in Lady Alleyne's world—Hudson's world. "For—forgive me. I mean no disrespect." She blinked away her tears.

A sparkle lit Gwenillen's eyes. "You needn't apologize, child. I know my son. His heart is golden, but I understand your hesitation. He has much to learn." She took on a faraway look. "I fear this might be the only way he shall be taught." Her gaze met Sarah's once again. "You, on the other hand, have matured into a fine creature. All grace and beauty."

Heat rose to Sarah's cheeks. She'd expected a set-down, not compliments.

Hudson's mother warmed her heart. Gwenillen would be the perfect mother-in-law...to someone else. She bit her lip until it throbbed like her pulse.

"Finish your toast, Sarah, and I shall see about raising your slumbering brother. I am certain the two of you have much to discuss. If he does not come down, I shall send him to your room soon. You look as if you could use a nap—you cannot possibly be fully recovered."

Sarah's eyes grew heavy. Gwenillen was right, she needed a nap. She'd been awake since before dawn, and the emotions of the day alone were wearing. She ate a few more bites, then decided her stomach had stretched to its limit. Seeing no sign of Josh or Hudson, she climbed up the stairs.

She opened the door of her bedchamber as quietly as possible just in case Hudson was still there. A mixture of relief and sorrow enveloped her to find him gone. Although she knew giving him up was the right thing to do, it still ripped her soul in two. *It seems we are not meant to be. I love him, but I cannot be his.* The thought left her empty, hollow to the core.

With a stretch of her arms and a yawn, she approached her bed, but stopped short. The time-traveling vest lay on her pillow with a note.

My Dearest Sarah,

I cannot bear to see you so bereft. And if I share your father's foul nature—a man who has stripped you of so much happiness—then you are correct in pushing me away. I am unworthy of your love. I, however, shall never stop loving you. Nor shall I quit striving to reach your standards. Go home, Sarah. Go back to the twenty-first century and read the history books. Read about Lord Hudson Drake of Alleyne—rake turned philanthropist, a transformation he credits to a mysterious blue-eyed, raven-haired beauty, whom no one beheld, but he alone. I shall mend my ways and make you proud, my love.

Sarah dabbed at tears leaking from her eyes. The urge to quit reading and rush to his side nearly overtook her, but she forced herself to continue.

I have left for London. There is much to do there, as your father has plundered the townhouse in search of the mysterious vases. Mother will be safe here with Jameson and the staff looking after her. They are loyal servants. I have left a missive for her, as well.

Sarah's heart plunged to her feet at the same time a chill crept up her spine. She'd not even bid him farewell. The realization combined with news of Father's abhorrent behavior caused her body to quake.

I shall never see Hudson again. And I am doomed to spend my life running from my own Father.

The rest of the letter was the end of Lord Byron's poem.

"Where thoughts serenely sweet express,
How pure, how dear their dwelling place.
And on that cheek, and o'er that brow,
So soft, so calm, yet eloquent,
The smiles that win, the tints that glow,
But tell of days in goodness spent,
A mind at peace with all below,
A heart whose love is innocent!"

I hope you find your peace and happiness, Sarah. You deserve nothing less.
All my love, Hudson

Chapter Thirty-Five

Sarah fell into a chair and buried her head in her hands. Hudson was gone. He had completed the poem—without her. She didn't know why, but that in itself made his disappearance final. Wiping tears away, she shook her head. *This is for the best. I must put my hopes and dreams of sharing a life with him behind me.* She contemplated writing a note in return, but what could she say? The tears continued as she pondered.

A rap at the door pulled her from her contemplations.

"Sarah, it's Josh."

"Oh, Josh, come in." She wiped her face dry with the hem of her dress.

He entered and narrowed his eyes at her. "What has happened? I heard you were well, but you don't look—"

"He's gone, Josh. I overheard him talking to a woman in the parlor and I"—she shrugged—"I snapped."

"That would be Widow Barlow. He told me. Sarah, you do know he had to act as if he wished to be with her—keep up the ruse—so she wouldn't rush off to London and give up his location, do you not? I witnessed for myself, on more than one occasion, the thirst for his blood. His photographic memory has gotten him into heaps of trouble. He should stay in the country until he puzzles a way out of his fix."

She gasped, panting in terror. "No! He is headed back to London as we speak!" Fear knotted inside her.

Josh paced the room. "It will be dark when he arrives. The goons watching his place when I found him in a bind in the first place weren't there two days ago. But he made a show of parading through London in Father's Cadillac. A few men drew pistols."

"Father's Cadillac? What are you talking about?"

"'Tis a long story. I'll give you the highlights. We were being pursued by Father and hid in his car. As you know, automobiles are enclosed in metal. Hudson grabbed hold of my arm and hit the button on the vest for us to escape—return to you—and the entire car transported." He chuckled. "You should have seen their faces. Londoners followed us in herds until we could navigate our way around carriages and get out of town."

Joshua's retelling of the events which had transpired elicited a range of emotions and an ocean full of questions for Sarah. "The entire car came with you? I'd wondered what Lady Alleyne was talking about when she said she'd seen the mammoth of a conveyance you'd ridden in on. I thought she was referring to a large coach. And Father—"

"Had a gun. He would have shot me, if not for Hudson. He saved my life. I guess we're even." He smirked.

"But now he's headed back to the very place and people who wish to kill him." Her skin crawled with anxiety.

"Sarah, Hudson is brilliant. He will take care. He shan't leave his mother childless. And I dare say, he spoke of you constantly. He said he'd never give you up without a fight. Have you given him reason to quit the fight?"

Fresh tears rolled down her cheeks. "I cannot marry a man with such vices. And who's to say he will change? I know he wishes to, but words mean little."

"I understand. I had many of the same questions and fears. But I shall never forget his display of emotion toward you. His love for you was made clear to all who witnessed."

Sarah swallowed hard. She had never doubted Hudson's sincerity.

Josh motioned to the bed. "I see he left the vest. What shall we do, Sarah?"

She coiled her fingers together, tormented by confusing emotions—two lives were at stake. Whom could they rescue? "Mother came to me in my sickness. She is ready to give up and die. She said she has no purpose—nothing to live for."

"Mother! We must return with haste." His eyes darted to the vest. "I hope it isn't too late."

"But Hudson—"

"As I said, Sarah, Hudson is clever. He will be fine."

Unconvinced, she nodded anyway. After all, it was she who had shunned him.

"Shall I take the time to reprogram the vest to land somewhere near the house, or shall we leave the Cadillac here? We cannot land in the lab with the car."

"I think we must rush to Mother's side. I should have thought of it sooner." But she'd been too busy nursing her broken heart. Self-loathing pricked her.

"I left the keys inside and the tank is mostly full. I think we should leave the car. Hudson can have some fun with it."

"And we shan't see the reminder of Father in our garage again." Sarah scowled.

"Let's get going, then. Gather your belongings and say goodbye to Lady Alleyne. I'll meet you in the foyer in ten minutes. I'm anxious to get back to Mother."

Sarah nodded and went to work, changing back to her modern clothes and tidying the room. Then she located Gwenillen Drake. "I must return. My mother needs me." Emotion bubbled to the surface. She blinked back threatening tears. "Thank you for being so kind."

Lady Alleyne pulled her into an embrace. "If you ever change your mind, send word. I now understand why Hudson loves that old tree so much."

Josh joined the pair and nodded to Lady Alleyne. He and Sarah linked arms, then blasted forward to the twenty-first century.

Sarah was happy for the numbness the time-traveling device afforded—she neither wished to speak or feel.

When they landed in the chemical-saturated lab, she coughed—gagging at the strong odor.

"Shh." Josh put a finger to his lips. "We don't know if Father is here," he whispered.

Sarah's skin prickled.

"I disabled his vest, but he probably fixed it by now." He glanced around the room. "The disc has been moved. He must have used it. But I'm certain he prefers the vest, as it can be worn at all times."

The two crept up the ladder and into the study. "Stay here while I check the house." Josh kept his tone hushed.

Within ten minutes he was back. "He has rummaged through rooms again, but I see no sign of him now."

"Let's get to the hospital." A sudden urgency to see Mother had Sarah moving at a rapid pace to her car.

Thirty minutes later, they were in the hospital elevator. Josh pushed the button sending them upward. "Hudson's reaction to this—and everything else—was priceless." He chuckled. "It was difficult to convince him he wasn't dreaming."

A lump formed in Sarah's throat, and tears threatened once more. She blinked them away.

Josh wrapped an arm around her shoulders. "Sorry, sis. This must be hard for you."

She nodded and patted his hand.

The doors opened and they hustled to Mother's room. Christopher, Arianna, and Dr. Reed were huddled around her. Ari's tear-streaked face sent a shiver down Sarah's spine.

"Are we too late?" Sarah asked, startling the group.

"Sarah, Josh." Christopher stood and pulled Sarah into his arms. "Mother's breathing is irregular—rasping one minute, then nothing for several seconds. Dr. Reed referred to is as"—he turned to the doctor—

"Cheyne-Stokes breathing," said the doctor. "It's common before the patient passes. You two arrived with no time to spare. I will step out and allow you some privacy. There's nothing more I can do." He exited the room.

Chapter Thirty-Six

A full moon lit Hudson's way as he trotted by horse into London. He slipped through the back door of his townhouse, carrying only one lamp to find his bedchamber. Emotionally and physically spent, he crawled into bed and let sleep cloak his pain.

The endless night finally grayed into dawn. His sleep—fitful as it had been—removed neither the ache from his heart nor Sarah's sorrowful face from his mind. Gritting his teeth at the condition of his own room, he eased out of bed and began a tour of the house. Each room had been rummaged through—some more than others. Mother could never see the place so disheveled. He hoped Benjamin Somerset had been satisfied the vases weren't there and would never return.

After dressing, he set to work, finding a mindless solidity that helped camouflage the deep despair of loneliness. Thanks to his keen memory, he knew in precise detail where each picture, pillow, blanket, and basket had been assigned. As he straightened portraits on the parlor walls, the large window beckoned him. He opened the heavy velvet curtain just wide enough to peek outside. The plane tree stood in full view. His eyes leveled on it, and a new anguish seared his heart. "I should cut that tree down."

He pivoted from the window and crossed the room to the liquor cabinet. After pouring golden-brown liquid into a small glass, he stopped himself just short of drinking it. "Blast!" He set the cup down hard. "I promised her," he said, then sank onto the chaise lounge next to the glass of whiskey. How would he bear losing Sarah without alcohol to dull the pain? For the next thirty minutes he sneaked furtive glances at the cup. "Perhaps just one—" *No*. He must prove he could do this—if not for Sarah, then for himself. He refused to become like Benjamin Somerset.

He exhaled a deep breath, then gathered the liquor bottles and slipped out the back door. Unstopping each container, he poured the contents into the shrubs, willing it to disappear quickly and completely before he lost his nerve. Watching the liquid stream from the bottles caused a dismal ache in his body. No one lived without spirits—they were part of daily life. He paused more than once, rethinking his decision. Then the vision of a magnificent azure-eyed beauty floated through his mind, giving him the strength to complete the task. "I can do this, Sarah." He swallowed a knot in his throat, knowing she would never realize the effect she'd had on him.

A carriage approached along the north side of the outbuildings. He ducked to the shadows. It seemed most people traveling this road were innocent Londoners, but he'd noticed a few exceptions—men craning their necks at the Drakes' townhouse. Men who wished him dead for a few thousand pounds. Changing his circumstances—removing the bounty on his head—had been a constant puzzle buzzing through his brain.

His stomach growled. What he wouldn't give to have Cook here. At least Mother was being tended to. He lifted his mouth to a half-smile, then let it flatten. *I hope she understands why I had to leave.* He sighed, realizing she'd dropped hints of his unworthiness the entire time Sarah had been in the nineteenth century. Mother was wise. She had warned him for years about the consequences of his reckless lifestyle.

After a small repast of fish and potatoes, he took a break to write a list of tasks. The bookroom desk overflowed with papers. An assistant paid any bills incurred, and Mother accepted all invitations, but notices addressed to the Earl of Alleyne were his responsibility—one of several he often neglected. He'd include it on his list. Uncorking the inkwell, he dipped his pen in the black liquid and began.

1-Finish putting London townhouse in order and attend to official correspondence.

2-Travel to country estates to see if Benjamin has been there. He paused, tapping the feather quill on his chin. Traveling to each estate and thoroughly setting them to rights would take weeks. Perhaps he could allow the staff to do that.

3-Bring back the servants—and Mother.

4-Get a message to Eddie. That one suddenly seemed urgent. He longed for company.

5-Make things right with my peers who wish me dead. That should likely be his highest priority. But how?

6-Return to Parliament and become a respectable earl. Make Mother and Father—may God rest his soul—proud. He shook his head. But as far-fetched as it seemed, he must do it.

7-Stop drinking and gambling, and never look at another woman with whom I am not wed. Easier written than done. But he must not become a man like Benjamin Somerset.

8-Put Sarah behind me. Tears filled his eyes, blurring his vision. *No, I cannot do it.* His list ended there.

He ran his hands through his hair, exhausted and frustrated from thinking of his list of impossible tasks. His mind took him to the time-traveling vest. Pages of Benjamin's notes turned through his brain, just as they would if he were reading a book. Then Joshua's instructions as to how he had improved upon the original device echoed in his head. After reading and rereading, then listening and relistening, he realized, if he located the chemicals and metals necessary, he could attempt to duplicate the machine—for what reason, he knew not. Sarah had been clear about her wishes to move on without him, but still…

Also, he would need to complete the items on his list before he considered itching the temptation now hovering in his thoughts—there would be no visits to any London shops in his near future. His enemies held him captive…for now.

Chapter Thirty-Seven

"No!" Sarah knelt beside Mother and took her hand. "You urged me back from the grave. Now you must return as well. I need you. We all need you." Her voice cracked, and sobs shook her body. "Come back to us, Mum."

A few seconds passed in silence except for everyone's sniffles. Mother wasn't breathing at all. Sarah squeezed her hand and said a silent prayer. "I came back, Mother. I came back for you."

Mother's body jolted and she gasped for air, gulping long, deep breaths. Her eyes fluttered open. "Sarah?"

The dam burst and Sarah couldn't quell her emotions. "Mother, I am here. We are all here," she said between sobs.

Mother peered into each of her children's faces, a smile hovering on her dry lips. "You are all here— except, where is Hudson?" She coughed and someone handed Sarah a cup of water to offer her.

Christopher and Ari helped Mother to a sitting position.

"Here, drink this." Sarah held the glass while Mother took a few sips.

Mother looked at her, a question in her eye. "You haven't answered me. Hudson saved you as much or more than I. Where is he?"

"I left him in the nineteenth century. Right now, we must focus on you." Sarah glanced up at Christopher and Arianna. Wrinkled foreheads and furrowed brows indicated their confusion. "There is much I need to explain, but please, can we set that aside for another time? Our mother has come back from the dead."

"Sarah was in the void—" Mother coughed some more.

Christopher shook his head. "Josh told me you were sick, Sarah, and that he and Hudson had rendered Father unconscious. But by the time I arrived, nobody was at the mansion at all. I am happy you are both back with us." He bent and kissed Mother's cheek.

Mother shifted, peeking between the siblings. "Where is that kind man who regaled me with his stories?"

Sarah wrinkled her nose. "Huh?"

"Your boss, Sarah," said Christopher. "You were away longer than expected, so Mr. Carver often spelled Arianna and me off so we could grab a bite. I guess he told Mother stories." He chuckled. "Mother"—he squeezed her hand—"Mr. Carver was released this morning."

"How nice of him," said Sarah. It seemed a lifetime ago since they'd all returned from lunch to find Henry in Mother's room. So much had happened in such a short time. She warmed at the thought of Henry Carver spending time with her unconscious mother. What a kind man. Once certain Mother was out of the woods, Sarah must return to her job.

"Mother clutched Sarah's hand. "Did you warn Gwenillen about Benjamin?"

"Yes, Mother. She is in a safe place now, though we did not arrive too soon. Father ransacked the Drake's townhouse in London after we vacated it. I suspect he has visited their country estates, as well. Where are the vases? We know that's what Father is after. He has turned our own house up-side-down searching for them, and even threatened Josh with a gun."

Mother's face crumpled. "I had hoped Benjamin would never find out about the vases—that he would believe they'd been auctioned off with the rest of our belongings. I inherited them. They belong to me. As his drinking increased, I realized I must conceal them before he sold them, or creditors seized the vases. Gwenillen is the only person who knows where they are."

"She hasn't betrayed your trust, Mother." Sarah squeezed her hand. "She wouldn't even tell Hudson or me their whereabouts."

The door burst open. "I knew it!" thundered Benjamin as he charged into the room.

Without hesitation, Christopher drew his arm back and punched his father in the face. "That is for Mother!"

"Oomph!" Benjamin groaned and fell to the ground, his eyes bulging.

Christopher bent over him, his arm cocked to slug him again, but Josh pulled him off.

Panting, Christopher yanked himself from Joshua's grip. "Don't you see? We cannot contain him."

Benjamin grunted and began to stand, rubbing his bleeding nose.

"Oh, I am well aware of that. But you're not the only one here who wishes to punish the man." Josh swung and connected with Benjamin's jaw, sending him back to the ground.

Barely conscious now, Benjamin huffed and moaned. "How dare you! I am your father," he croaked.

"Secure him, Josh. I'll grab my handcuffs from the cruiser," said Christopher, poised to bolt.

Arianna rushed around the bed. "I'll go. You help Josh hold him down. We've seen him disappear too many times." She ran out the door.

Benjamin thrashed, but his head lolled from side to side until he closed his eyes.

Everything had happened so quickly, Sarah and Mother clutched each other, mouths agape. "Should we call the police?" asked Sarah.

"I am the police," said Christopher, keeping his eyes on Benjamin. "He'll only get a slap on the wrist for spousal abuse. His time-traveling exploits will never be believed. In this case, the justice system will not work."

"I vote we take him home and keep him shackled until we come up with plan." Josh had a death grip on Father, but with his free hand managed to once again break the circuits on his vest.

Christopher nodded, holding him on the opposite side. "Breaking the wires will only slow him down, Josh. We need to remove the vest."

Sarah rushed to their aid. With Josh and Christopher holding Father upright, she slid the vest down, her brothers only releasing each arm long enough to remove it.

Benjamin's eyes opened into slits, then closed again, making her wonder how aware he really was.

"What's going on here?" Mother's doctor had entered so quietly, the group hadn't noticed him.

Sarah dropped the vest and used her foot to nudge it beneath the bed. "Dr. Reed, I'm so glad you are here. Mother is awake!" She forced a smile.

The doctor took his eyes off Father and flinched when he saw Mother conscious and sitting up. His jaw dropped. "But she was so near death…" He glanced back at Father. "And who is—"

"This man is Benjamin Somers," said Christopher. "He is responsible for our mother's injuries."

"But why is he unconscious on the ground? He needs medical attention." The doctor's gaze darted from Father to Mother several times.

Sarah saw indecision in his eyes, needing to attend to both. "My brothers were attempting to restrain my father, so he wouldn't hurt Mother again. He's a dangerous criminal, wanted by the law. If you can examine our mother, Christopher and Josh can get Father to the authorities. Chris is a Denver police officer." *Please, just let us deal with Father before he escapes again.*

Dr. Reed turned to Christopher. "Then as a police officer, you know you cannot take him away unconscious. The man needs a doctor whether he's a criminal or not! I won't ask how he came to be in this condition, but I demand he be admitted to the hospital." He moved toward the unconscious man.

Sarah's heart sank. Father, so slippery, would never be contained if her brothers didn't have him in their custody. She clenched her fists.

"I've got the cuffs!" Arianna panted as she rounded the privacy curtain, then froze in place as she took in the situation.

The doctor narrowed his eyes at her, then hit a button, calling for assistance.

The nurse who arrived moments later wasted no time following the doctor's orders to admit Mr. Somers and call for security to guard his room.

Sarah cringed as he was whisked away on a gurney. "He's a criminal!" She didn't hold her anger back as she glared at the doctor.

"But you can't take the law into your own hands." He turned to Christopher. "And even if you're an officer, Pueblo is out of your jurisdiction. Hospital security will guard his room."

Christopher shook his head. "I really wish you hadn't done that, Dr. Reed. Sarah, Josh, I'm going to see if I can locate his room." He rushed out, grabbing the cuffs from Ari's hands as he left.

"Where do you expect him to go? The man was unconscious," said Dr. Reed.

"He'll find a way out of here. Mark my words," said Josh.

Dr. Reed mumbled something indiscernible, then turned his attention to Mother. "This is what you should all focus on. A true miracle." He took her vitals, shined a light in her eyes, and shook his head. "A true miracle, indeed." He jotted something on Mother's clipboard. "She'll need a few tests to make sure she's doing as well as she appears." He pushed the call button again. Then reexamined Mother.

A new nurse materialized, and he gave her orders for tests to be run.

"If everything comes back normal, I see no reason to keep her here." He looked at the group with a broad smile—but it soon flattened.

Mother spoke up. "'Tis difficult to share your enthusiasm when you let the man who nearly killed me slip away."

"I did no such thing. I—"

Christopher flung the curtain open, panting. "I've searched everywhere. Father is gone!"

Chapter Thirty-Eight

A rap at the door startled Hudson awake. In a frenzy, he strained to see his surroundings. Though darkness cloaked the room, plush velvet tickled his fingers beneath him—the Charles Percier sofa. He'd fallen asleep in the bookroom. Again. Attending to correspondence had tired him to no end. *That's thrice I have spent the night in here.*

More thumping on the door. He reached for a candle, then recalled the reason he'd kept the place dark—too many enemies about London. Slipping off his boots, he moved silently to the parlor window, where he could ascertain who his guest was—friend or foe.

Eddie. Relief washed over him. He'd been puzzling for days how to reach his friend.

"Come in!" He clasped Eddie's arm. "How did you know where to find me?"

"I sent a letter to Finley's…er…your…country estate. Your mum sent a reply. I thought it best to come during the night, lest the blackguards be watching."

Eddie followed Hudson to the drawing room, where they could light some candles without being seen from the front of the house.

Eddie went straight to the liquor decanter—now empty. Clutching a glass, he moved his search to the cabinet. "Where—"

"I no longer drink spirits."

Eddie raised the glass, his eyebrows furrowed. "Not even port?"

Hudson frowned. He should have kept some for his guests, but the temptation to drink it himself would have been overwhelming. The past few days had been trying enough without adding the temptation to drink away his troubles. So many times he'd wished to throw caution to the wind, sneak to a remote public house, and drink his cares away. But he hadn't. "Sorry, my friend, not even port."

As Eddie put the glass on the table, his expression turned from disbelief to worry. "Why? You never had a problem. I mean, there were a few times you conjured up a lark or two while in your cups, but they were mostly innocent."

How could Hudson explain his reasons? He glanced around the drawing room, noticing several items still askew. "Do you remember Benjamin Somerset?"

"Are you ill? Of course I remember him. For the past seven years you've spoken more of his daughter than anything else."

"He has paid my house a visit—turned it upside-down, looking for something that does not belong to him."

Eddie scanned the room. "So I see." His face was still screwed up in a question mark. "Go on."

"I found Sarah. I fear her father has done irreparable damage to her and her family. Through his drunkenness, and his genius, he has—" He couldn't very well say he'd created a time-traveling machine to purloin valuables in different centuries. "He has committed many crimes."

"Why haven't I heard of these crimes? London is big, but news travels fast through society."

"He wasn't in London. He has gone…abroad."

"And the law has not caught up with the brute?"

Hudson shook his head. "He has become proficient at evading authority." A considerable understatement.

"But why has he come to your home? What is he looking for?"

Hudson gave Eddie a brief explanation of the vases. But the vases were not the point. "In his desperate search, Mr. Somerset has harmed many people, including Beatrice, his wife. She may have even passed by now."

"What? Where is Mrs. Somerset? Where is Sarah?" Eddie growled. "We need to hunt that man down!"

"There isn't any way of finding him." Hudson side-stepped the questions of Sarah and Beatrice's whereabouts. "He has a hiding place no one has discovered all these years." He pushed his fingers through his hair. "But Sarah will never have me if I am anything like her father. She already knows of my roguish reputation"—he exhaled a breath—"and has left me again. I must change, Eddie." He'd omit the fact that Sarah would never know he'd changed. But his intentions and determination were real. He'd do it—not just for Sarah, but for Mother and for himself—be the man worthy of Sarah's love, whether he received it or not.

"She will come around. Especially if you are going to such desperate lengths to prove your love—and your worth."

Doubtful. "I've made a list of things that must be done. Will you look at it? I could use some help."

Eddie nodded, and Hudson groped his way back to the bookroom, where he retrieved the list he'd made days ago.

He plunked it down on a table near the sofa.

Eddie picked it up and his eyes roved over the words. "Well, you can check off number four—get a message to Eddie. I obviously read your mind." Reading on, he let out a soft whistle. "How will you make things right with your peers? Which, by the way, all know you are alive. London has been abuzz for days about your horseless coach. They bring their enquiries to me, but I haven't the faintest idea of what they are asking. Would you care to enlighten me?"

He would not. But he sure wished Eddie had been with him when he and Josh had paraded through London in that fancy vehicle. "It is something Sarah's brother—an inventor like his father—showed up in." He shrugged. "It has an engine that propels it forward."

Eddie's eyes popped. "So the rumors are true? I scarcely believed them. Where is it now?" He was halfway out of his seat before Hudson raised his hand, stopping him.

"I don't know. It doesn't belong to me. But if it is ever again in London, I shall find you and drive you through town," Hudson said, confident he'd never see the amazing, motorized vehicle again. "But it was unwise of me to flaunt it, thus disclosing my mortal condition."

Eddie reclaimed the list, his eyes perusing it. "Ha! Become a respectable earl."

Hudson nearly grabbed the list from Eddie's hand. Instead, he balled his fists. He could do it. He could achieve everything on that paper. "I shall become a respectable earl. I must," he snapped. With a painting of Father staring down at him, he made a silent oath to see it through. *Forgive me, Father. I have failed you in many ways, but that stops now.* He swallowed against a bulge swelling in his throat. Sarah's visit had evoked emotions he'd thought he'd buried—along with any hopes of finding her. So missish.

"Put Sarah behind you? But I thought you were doing all these things to regain her affection." Eddie placed the list back on the table and narrowed his eyes at Hudson.

Lud, he'd forgotten about that last one. Now he wished he were alone so he could properly grieve his loss. "I am, but I fear it won't be enough."

Pain must have been evident in Hudson's eyes, because Eddie moved on to the things he could speak of while still preserving his friend's dignity. "It sounds like you need to concentrate on cleaning this place up and getting your mum out of Finley's estate. Then you can give it back to him—not that he deserves it. He continues to gamble. I do not know what he's putting on the table, but I see him at White's near every night."

"The clean-up is mostly done. This room needs some attention, as well as a few of the bedchambers. Perhaps we should start there."

"I shall return tomorrow—through the back door—and we can finish up then." Eddie mock-bowed to Hudson. "Consider me your humble servant. And do not forget—you promised me a ride in that horseless coach."

"Bring food. I ate the last potato tonight." He'd not need to open the jars he'd found of pickled…everything, thank the stars above.

Hudson saw Eddie out, then climbed the grand staircase to his bedchamber. He'd spent too many nights sleeping on the sofa.

Not bothering to pull on a nightshirt, he collapsed on his bed, pondering his good fortune. With Eddie's help, he could get the townhouse back into shape in no time. Mum could return, and he'd send a few servants to check on the country estates.

His mind swirled with ideas of covert methods of returning so many things he'd won from his peers— large items, which had landed him in this bind. He neither needed nor wanted extra coaches, horses, or estates. But winning at cards came easy for him—too easy. *I shan't gamble anymore. It will be too difficult to lose on purpose, and I cannot turn off my brain.* Why he hadn't thought of that before, he didn't know. Perhaps in his boredom, tormenting the likes of Lords Finley and Burke had become his entertainment. Even when he'd been dumped on the side of the road, or kidnapped for ransom, he'd never truly cared—about himself, the other gamers…anything. Until now. Sarah had brought back meaning to his life.

A loud creak jolted him from his thoughts. A door on the main level had either opened or closed. Eddie must have forgotten something…but Hudson was certain he'd locked every door.

He crept to the top of the staircase. Peering down, he saw nothing. Either the noise had been his imagination, or whoever had made it was in a room he couldn't view from his vantage point. He took a few steps down. Then five more, straining to hear anything out of the ordinary. Something clattered—like glass breaking. Angry oaths floated up to him.

"I shall find those vases if I have to tear the place apart again!"

Benjamin Somerset.

"That's it," Hudson whispered. "I have had enough of you, Mr. Somerset!" As he prepared to charge down the remaining steps, the scoundrel stepped within his view.

Hudson froze.

Benjamin carried a bright lantern with a long handle in one hand and a strange pistol in the other—neither of which Hudson had seen the like. As he shined the light across the walls, pausing to remove portraits in search of something—no doubt a hollowed-out storage area—he scowled. Then he turned his search to the floor, perching the gun and the light within his grasp as he moved rugs and looked for loose floorboards.

Anger boiled in Hudson's veins. His mind scrambled to puzzle out what to do. The man had a gun—a futuristic gun. Even if Hudson could get to his pistol, it would be little protection against Benjamin's weapon. He tried to smother a grunt of disgust but was unsuccessful.

Benjamin jerked toward the staircase, then grabbed the gun and the lantern. "Who's there? Gwenillen? Hudson?" He shined the light at the stairs. "I am not here to hurt you, but you have something that belongs to me. I have thoroughly combed your country estates, as well as this one, but cannot locate them. You must return the vases."

The gall of the man. Hudson opened his mouth to reply—

"And while I do not wish to harm anyone, I will use force to get back my possessions." He cocked his gun and pointed it up the staircase.

Chapter Thirty-Nine

Sarah glanced across the dining table at Josh, then to Christopher and Arianna. Last of all, Mother. By their dull eyes and downturned lips, she knew no one was enjoying Sunday dinner. "I used a new recipe on this roast chicken. An apricot glaze." She smiled, hoping to lighten the mood.

A brief rumble of murmurs buzzed around the room. While she heard compliments jumbled in their slurry of words, she could see for herself the chicken had barely been touched.

Today was the first family meal they had come together for since Mother had been released. She'd improved by leaps and bounds over the past few days.

Since leaving the hospital, Sarah and Josh had returned to their jobs. Spending time with Henry Carver had become a blessed relief from Sarah's tortuous thoughts and aching heart. He knew nothing of her history, and she could live in the present—serving, nurturing, caring for someone who needed her. She'd not forget the sparkle that lit his eyes when she told him Mother had awakened and now convalesced at home. If only she could help him more—ease his pain.

Christopher and Ari had remained at the mansion to watch over Mother until they were certain she had improved enough to be left alone, as well as protect her—should Father reappear. In the evenings, Sarah had recounted the events she'd experienced while in the nineteenth century—though Mother somehow already knew many of the details.

"Mother and I shared time in that space between life and death," she'd told them. "And, I dare say, Mother is the one who urged me back to life." Hudson had played the biggest part in raising her from the dead. But thinking about his role in her healing hurt too much to mention.

"And Sarah urged me back, as well," Mother had said.

Though some routines had returned, no sense of normalcy existed—not with Father still on the loose. Always on the loose. Now the awkward aura in the dining room caused Sarah to long for the brief respite they'd had before Father had careened back into their lives—no fear, anger, or frustration.

Christopher let out a loud breath. "I just can't believe we lost Father again. I checked every nurses' station, as well as the front desk." He stabbed at the drumstick on his plate, then winced. "Forgive me, Mother. We promised not to speak of him around you."

"Whyever not? I am just as disconcerted that Benjamin escaped capture as the rest of you." Her brows knit together. "I am part of this family, and you are doing me no favors holding your tongues when I am present. 'Tis as bad as being in that hospital, trapped in a lifeless body, but still aware."

Sarah gasped. "You were aware of everything we said?"

"And the doctors and nurses poking and prodding you?" Josh's face creased.

Mother nodded. "But I was also aware that you, my loving children, were always nearby. Thank you for staying with me." She sniffed. "I am not so fragile as you seem to believe. We need to discuss a plan to find Benjamin, and now is a fine time to do so."

"Are you certain, Mum?" Sarah had seen Mother's strength increase each day, but she still worried about upsetting her.

"Yes. Quite certain."

The room finally breathed again, while everyone spouted their opinions. But as concerned as Sarah was about Father, her heart ached for a different man— Hudson. Ever since leaving the nineteenth century, she'd wondered if she had made the right choice. Hudson had saved her life. And though he had vices and a past, which she loathed, didn't everyone make mistakes? Yes. She knew it was so. But could he— would he—truly change? Therein lay her doubts.

"Isn't that right, Sarah?"

Sarah blanched "Sorry, what?" She swept away thoughts of Hudson and gave Josh her full attention.

"I was saying Father couldn't be wearing his vest because you kicked it under Mum's bed, then brought it home. Brilliantly done, by the way."

"I thought we had already established that," said Sarah.

Josh tilted his head toward Mother. "She didn't know. We're catching Mum up on everything, so we can form a plan. Even though she was aware, she doesn't know the details she couldn't hear or see." He speared a potato, but just held it on his fork. "So, Father had to have been more conscious than he let on after you woke up, Mum."

"And somehow got away when they wheeled him from Mother's room," said Christopher.

A cloud moved over Sarah again. She didn't know how to escape its darkness.

Arianna, seated next to Sarah, reached for her hand beneath the table and gave it a squeeze. In a low whisper Ari said, "We can do this without you, if you'd rather. I know what a broken heart feels like."

What Sarah truly wished was to have Arianna to herself for an hour or so. Nobody else understood how she felt. Ari had been through the same heart-wrenching pain—probably worse—with Christopher being trapped in the nineteenth century, leaving Ari to believe he had chosen to remain there to wed another woman. If it hadn't been for Arianna's fearless determination, Christopher would have hanged for a crime Father had committed. Sarah's heart overflowed with warmth toward her sister-in-law. She squeezed her hand in return. "I'm all right. It's better for me to talk about Father than to think of Hudson right now," she whispered back. "Thank you for understanding."

"...And the newer vests are still where I hid them in the lab." Josh smirked, then stuffed the forkful of potatoes in his mouth. After washing the food down with a gulp of water, he continued. "The disc is missing, however. And since he overheard Mum say she'd given the vases to Lady Alleyne, I'm certain Father has returned to the nineteenth century. I'm glad Hudson had a safe place to hide his mother."

Sarah shivered. "His mother is safe, but Hudson is in London." Just when she'd shaken thoughts of him from her mind, Josh had brought Hudson back up. "He will be in danger." Her voice quivered as she spoke.

"Josh, you acted as if he would be fine. 'He's clever,' you said. But cleverness cannot save him from a madman with a modern weapon." She broke into a sob and left the room. She needed air. Ari was right—they could do this without her. Fleeing out the back door, she rushed through the garden and sank down on a bench reminiscent of the one she'd fled to in London after learning of Hudson's reputation. Too reminiscent.

She wept silent tears.

"Sarah." Arianna had followed her and sat down beside her. "I know the situation seems impossible. But don't you see? Your family loves—"

"*Our* family," Sarah interrupted, wiping away tears that continued to fall. "Ari, you are every bit a member of our family as I am."

Ari blinked a few times, but her eyes welled anyway. "Thank you, Sarah. That means a lot." She dabbed at her own tears. "Then *our* family loves you, and we can do hard things. We have overcome so many obstacles we thought impossible. All to stay together. I lay awake last night thinking about everything you've shared—your experiences in the nineteenth century. My goodness, Sarah, you nearly died! What would I do without you—my sister?" Her voice wobbled and she cleared her throat. "And Hudson—"

Sarah buried her head in her hands, her body shuddering. Just hearing the name of the man she loved—but shouldn't—caused her to tremble.

Ari placed a gentle arm around her. "I just need to say that, from everything Josh has told me, Hudson sounds like a knight in shining armor—"

Sarah flinched and sat erect. "But—"

"I know he has done some things you feel you cannot forgive, but weigh the good against the bad. Does he really come up short?"

Every word Ari said rang true but also cut like a dagger to her heart. "It doesn't matter anymore. He left me before I even had a chance to tell him goodbye. I don't believe he wants me. I had been nothing more than a pleasant memory. I'm not like the sophisticated women he spends his time with…" She shrugged. "Why would he care?" But *she* cared and would always care about Hudson—her first and only true love.

"Now you are imagining things. Of course he cares. You allowed me to read his letters—that kind of love isn't like a light switch. You can't just turn it off. He searched for you for seven years, Sarah!"

"When he wasn't busy gambling, drinking, or being otherwise engaged. Don't you see, Ari? He could turn out to be just like Father."

"What? I don't speak from experience, so maybe I'm wrong, but aren't there scores of wealthy men in London who pass the time the same way Hudson did? And how many of them have turned out to be depraved criminals?"

She had a point. Still, Sarah didn't wish to learn the hard way that Hudson was one of the few members of the gentry to emulate Benjamin Somerset.

"When I first met you, Sarah, you were quiet and shy, Benjamin had stolen so much from you. But using your journal to communicate with me was ingenious. And since then, I have seen another side of you—a brave, courageous woman—"

"Ha! If I am so brave and courageous, why am I out here crying like a babe?"

"Can't you see how much courage it took to walk away from the man you love?"

Sarah had never thought of it that way. But hadn't Ari just said to weigh his strengths against his weaknesses? She closed her eyes and shook her head. "I'm so confused, Ari. Am I to conclude that Hudson is worth my love, and at the same time stand tall for my courage to walk away from him?"

Ari smiled. "You walked away from a life you knew would be hurtful. For that, you should be proud. Now that you are here—away from the situation—give yourself a chance to ponder. Not everything is black and white. The time traveling devices have been a curse. They've also been a blessing. They brought Christopher to me. Perhaps they can help with your situation, too."

Sarah nodded, then wrapped her arms around Arianna. "They did bring you and Chris together, and I am so happy for that."

After a moment, Ari broke the embrace and looked into Sarah's eyes. "Let yourself grieve and move on— or prepare to fight for Hudson. Either way, I am on your side."

"We all are."

Sarah startled at the sound of Christopher's voice. He, Mother and Josh now stood just feet away.

"We love you, Sarah," said Mother.

Josh spoke next. "And we will fight with you and for you."

Sarah didn't try to contain her emotion. Affection for her family overwhelmed her. Aside from her criminal father, they provided a powerful support system. For that she must ever be grateful. "Thank you," she managed through hiccupping sobs. She paused a moment to compose herself. "But first, we must stop Father. He cannot keep hurting the people we love."

"I say we track him down in the nineteenth century," said Josh.

Christopher shook his head. "And then what? Even if we find him there, I don't think any one of us is capable of murdering our father"—he glanced at Mother—"or husband. And turning him over to the authorities might get me, or one of you, thrown into prison. I don't wish that on anyone."

"And if he finds what he's after, I doubt he'll show his face here again," said Sarah. "Justice won't be served; Mother will lose her vases, and I will never know what happened to Hudson and Lady Alleyne."

Chapter Forty

Hudson clamped his mouth shut and ducked, narrowly escaping the beam of light aimed his way, the gun close behind it. He crept back up the stairs, not making a sound, and fled down the hallway to his bedchamber. Groping in the dark for his pistol, he remembered leaving it in the bookroom. Lud. Even he wasn't foolish enough to expose himself to a twenty-first century gun without a weapon of his own.

Heavy footsteps sounded on the stairs. Out of options, Hudson rolled under his bed. Though the counterpane hung nearly to the ground of his large four-poster bed, if the rogue lifted the blankets and shined his bright light beneath it, Hudson would be caught.

His surroundings, though black as pitch, were simple to recall. In his youth, he'd fled from a governess or two and had found the underside of Father's—now his—large mahogany bed to be the ideal hiding place. He closed his eyes and saw in detail the rope mesh, supporting both feather and down tick mattresses. With no time to spare, he began to pry the ropes apart. With any luck, Mr. Somerset would begin his search in one of the three bedchambers in the hallway before his. Even better, the madman would turn right instead of left at the top of the staircase and look through the guest wing first.

The ropes must not have been tightened recently. With ease, Hudson was able to pull them apart. If he could make a wide enough space, he'd attempt to squeeze between the mesh and the mattress. Though it wasn't an ideal plan—yellow-bellied, even—it was all he could come up with, under the circumstances. His hand hit something solid. Feeling around, he realized it was embedded in the feather mattress. He tapped on it. Yes, solid as a rock, putting a kink in his plan. He continued to touch it, puzzling out where it began and where it ended, when his fingers hit a soft spot. Puzzling. Probing further he found another hard object. And two more. He knew the down tick atop the feather mattress was thicker than most, but how in the world hadn't he known he'd been sleeping on such hard objects? Wait…could they be…?

"I shall find you—whoever you are and wherever you are hiding," bellowed Mr. Somerset. The voice came just paces from his room.

That monster could *never* find the vases. Hudson crawled from under the bed. He may not have a gun, but in his bedchamber there were several large, silver candlesticks. He groped through the room to his bureau, where the tallest, heaviest set perched. After removing the candle from one, he hefted the candlestick over his shoulder and stationed himself next to the door.

Heavy footfalls hit the ground, heading his direction. His heart beat so loud, he feared Benjamin would hear it. Tightening his grip on the candlestick, he thought of Sarah and Mother. They gave him strength. Benjamin threw the door open wide, wielding his lantern and gun. Hudson sprang from behind him and brought the candlestick down.

Benjamin dodged, sparing his head the brunt of the blow, but the heavy candlestick still knocked him to the ground, his fingers releasing the gun and the long-handled lantern. Hudson scrambled for the gun, sure Mr. Somerset was still conscious. He trained it on Benjamin while he nudged him with his foot.

Benjamin caught his breath then glared—one eye was blackened, and his jaw was bruised, as well. "How dare you?" he snarled.

"How dare *you*?" Hudson yelled back. "You come into my home, ransacking and destroying my property, and you question me?"

"You have something of mine. And I have every right to recover it." Benjamin, still on his back, tried to rise to his elbows, but Hudson used his foot to push him back down.

"And what, pray tell, is it you are accusing me of stealing?" Hudson sneered. He must play dumb while he formed a plan. *I should just shoot the man—put everyone out of their misery.* But he thought of Sarah and couldn't do it. She might wish the man dead, but Hudson wouldn't be the person who killed her father.

"Vases. Asian. Have you seen them? They are worthless, really. I only want them for sentimental reasons."

Hudson barked his derision. "You have torn apart my estates all for some worthless sentimental vases? I will have you arrested. I have worked all week setting this townhouse to rights, just to have you come in and spoil it again. And you expect me to believe it is because you are sentimental?" He put more pressure on Benjamin's chest. "You have tortured your family, perhaps even killed your wife, injured your daughter to the point she can no longer trust a man…" his words trailed off, along with thoughts of Sarah.

Benjamin's eyes bulged. "How would you—"

"The real question is, why shouldn't I put a hole in your head?" Hudson squelched thoughts of Sarah.

"You're a bright young man. Tell me where the vases are, and we can split the value."

"Are you daft? Even if I had your vases, what would I want with something so worthless?"

"But they aren't!" Benjamin's face became animated. "Recently, at Sotheby's in Paris one alone was auctioned for millions—an entire set is worth a fortune. You could purchase anything and everything you desire."

"The only thing I desire, you stole from me seven years ago."

Benjamin's forehead wrinkled.

"You stole Sarah." His heart seized anew.

Taking advantage of his split-second Sarah-induced trance, Benjamin jerked out from under Hudson's foot, toppling him off balance. He righted himself, but not before Mr. Somerset had scrambled to his feet. Hudson rushed through the door in time to see him lumbering down the stairs. Hudson fired the gun but missed. He sprinted after him, but tripped on the modern lantern in the hallway, flinging him to the ground. He pulled himself up and fired a few more shots, the old man flinched, but reached the door.

"I will have constables stationed at each of my estates, should you ever return," Hudson hollered.

Benjamin slammed the door behind him, and within seconds the townhouse began to vibrate. Gone from his home, and likely his century.

Hudson closed his eyes, defeated. He hadn't helped anyone.

The vases!

He jumped to his feet, and with the help of the modern lantern, fled to the kitchen and located a knife, then raced back to his bedchamber. He scooted under his bed and carefully sliced through the rope mesh. The weights he'd felt instantly dropped, thudding together, still within the feather mattress. He cringed. If his hunch was correct, he might have caused damage.

Beginning at the far end of the mattress, he cut a straight line just bigger than his hand. Reaching inside, his fingers touched one of the objects. With care, he eased it through the slot. It had been wrapped in a thick, protective cloth. "Thank the stars above." He unwound the fabric until a bright yellow vase emerged. Exotic birds and colorful flowers adorned all sides of the piece, and a red stripe circled the midsection. Beautiful. He turned the vase over to inspect the bottom. Sure enough, he found Chinese markings of authenticity. After setting it on his bureau, he extracted another vase. This one had identical colors but differed in shape and size. Two more vases followed, each similar, yet different. All beautiful. He couldn't tell if they were a set of four or two sets of two. Either way, he knew he'd found what Benjamin had been searching for.

Though the first rays of morning light were pinking the sky, exhaustion overcame Hudson. He climbed into bed, confident he'd not see Benjamin Somerset again for a while. Closing his eyes, he let fatigue take him away.

Loud banging on his back door woke him up too soon. Who would be—*ah, Eddie*. He wiped the sleep from his eyes and hurried down to let Eddie inside.

"I have been out here knocking for several minutes. Did you give in and get foxed last night? Is that why you"—Eddie looked Hudson up and down, then shook his head—"slept in until nearly noon?"

"It's a long story. We've got work to do." His stomach growled.

"Perhaps you should eat first." Eddie plunked a bundle on the table. He opened it, revealing breads, meat, cheeses, and berries.

Food had never tasted so good.

"You did not imbibe spirits, then?"

"No. I had a visitor," Hudson said between bites of meat and cheese. How much he should tell Eddie, he didn't know. No wonder Sarah had been so mysterious in her letters. He warmed recalling her blue ink.

"Who?"

"The same man responsible for the mess I'm in—Benjamin Somerset."

"Benjamin Somerset? Was he still looking for his vases—or his daughter?" Eddie chuckled. "One would think he'd stay far away from here. It wasn't too long ago every Runner in London was on the lookout for him."

Some of the food lost its savor, as Hudson thought of Sarah. "He came in search of the vases. Imagine his surprise finding me instead. Eddie, I found them. I found the vases! I must get them to Beatrice without her husband's knowledge. But how?"

"Where were they?"

"Mother is brilliant! She hid them in my mattress. Come see."

Eddie analyzed the vases. "Who would have thought vases would be something worth killing your wife over. That man needs to be put away." His eyes moved to something else on the bureau. Is that a pistol?"

"Uh…yes. It was Benjamin's." How would he explain such a complex weapon without explaining time travel?

"I've seen nothing like it." Eddie picked it up, turning it over to see every detail.

"Eddie, I need to tell you something, and you're not going to believe me. But I swear on my father's grave it is all true. And I wouldn't tell you if I didn't need your assistance."

Eddie put the gun down and gave Hudson his full attention. "With what? I am here to help you, am I not?"

"Yes, yes you are. But I need supplies—chemicals, metals—to create a machine that moves through time. I need to get to the twenty-first century—where Sarah is."

Eddie chuckled. "Well, that's a new one."

Hudson didn't smile. He must reach Sarah and her family—help rid them of the scourge that was Benjamin Somerset. "Beyond your wildest imaginings."

"You are serious?"

Hudson nodded. "I have been there. This gun came from there. The vehicle I drove through London I accidentally brought here from two hundred years in the future."

Eddie scanned the room, walking around the bed, the dressing area, the washstand. "Where is it? Where is the bottle of whiskey, brandy, rum—"

"I have not been drinking, Eddie." He threw his hands in the air. "I knew you wouldn't believe me. I don't blame you. I thought I was dreaming while in the twenty-first century. I wasn't. Benjamin is a genius and created a time-traveling machine so he could steal valuables from different times and places around the globe, then disappear. Ironically, some of the most priceless items belonged to his wife." He smirked. "But she was smart enough to hide them from him, and here they are."

"So you wish to return them to her? I am not saying I believe this time-travel fable, but do you not think Benjamin will find out? If he hasn't killed her yet, he will certainly kill her once the vases show up in her home."

"'Tis true enough." Hudson pushed out a loud breath and shoved his hand through his hair. A solution to his dilemma eluded him. "I shall think on the details. In the meantime, I believe I can duplicate his traveling device, but I need supplies."

"Ha!"

Hudson ignored Eddie's sarcasm, located a leaf of paper, ink, and pen and scribbled down the chemicals required for a new machine. He wasn't certain where to obtain any sort of metal alloy to create the vest. Perhaps he'd build a disc… More details to contemplate. He'd begin with the chemicals. "Will you purchase these?"

"You know how to—" Eddie shook his head. "Of course you do. You only need to see something once to recall every detail." He took the list. "I shall play along.

After all, am I not always up for adventure—no matter how preposterous?" He scanned the paper as they descended the stairs.

"Preposterous or not, you shall see. Thank you, my friend." Hudson clapped Eddie on the shoulder, then saw him out the back door.

Alone now, he paced. *What am I thinking? Even if I recreate the machine, how will I deliver the vases safely?* His usually organized thoughts were jumbled. *And how can I do it without seeing Sarah? She made it clear she doesn't want anything to do with me.* His heart weighed as heavy as the vases in his bedchamber. *Still, I must help her family.*

He wandered through the house until spotting blood on the floor. Perplexed, he followed it to the front door. "Ah, I must have wounded Benjamin."

A knock at the door startled him. Without thinking to surmise if it was friend or foe, he opened it. His eyes widened, and his jaw dropped at the sight of the person standing before him. An angel sent from heaven.

His sweet Sarah.

"I…I came to beg your forgiveness." A rosy blush bloomed on her cheeks.

Chapter Forty-One

Before she knew it, Sarah was wrapped in Hudson's arms.

"I feared I'd never see you again." He pulled her through the door and closed it. "'Tis not safe here. You risked your life. Why?"

"For that very reason. Because of my father, you are not safe. Hudson, I could never forgive myself if something happened to you." Her eyes landed on the bloody spots near their feet. She gasped. "What happened? Are you hurt?" She scanned him up and down.

Hudson chuckled. "'Tis your father's blood. He was here last night—"

"Not yours?" Relief washed over her. "But he was here. What happened?" The room spun. Father had been here.

He held her arms to steady her. "As you can see, I am unharmed. We had an altercation. Regrettably, he is likely fine, as well. I was only able to wound him."

She clutched him in a tight embrace. "Do you forgive me for leaving you? I should have let you explain. I have let my father skew my—"

Hudson's warm lips cut off her words as they covered her mouth. He kissed her tentatively at first, as if asking permission.

Yes, the answer is yes! She deepened the kiss, hungry for his love, his forgiveness, for him. Though still uncertain she could overcome her trust issues, she set them aside for the moment, allowing a delightful frisson to course through her body.

When they ended the kiss, he held her close. "There is nothing to forgive, love. I am the one in need of change. And I shall. I vow to you I shall." He touched the vest. "You came alone? Your brothers are quite protective of their sister."

She shrugged. "They are also supportive. I told them I must come to you. Hudson, I've been so worried. If only we could find the vases and get them to Mother—"

"She's alive, then?" Hudson brightened.

"Yes! And she asks about you repeatedly. She recalls that you were in the hospital room—she remembers everything."

Hudson twirled her around, lifting her off her feet.

Sarah laughed, her heart warm at how happy the news had made him, as well as how safe she felt in his strong arms.

"Sarah, I have found the vases!"

"You found them?" She jumped back and clapped her hands "How perfectly wonderful!"

"Yes. I will explain everything. I have sent my chum Eddie to buy some items necessary to duplicate the machine. I planned on returning the vases to your mum. But I cannot puzzle out how to create metal alloy. Now you are here with the vest." He paused. "But the vases are large. I do not think we can transport them with only the vest." His brows furrowed. "…Unless you do not wish me to come. But I'd like to see it thr—"

"Of course I want you to come. Hudson, I didn't return for the vases, I came back for…well…" She stammered, contemplating feelings she herself was still uncertain of. "What I mean to say"—she took a steadying breath—"while I am unsure of sharing a future with you, I will always love you, and I refuse to let my father hurt you in any way." Tears stung her eyes. "With all of my heart, Hudson, I am endeavoring to detach his actions from yours—praying your affection for me is—" A flush heated her cheeks. "Am I just another woman to you?" She peered up at him through blurry eyes.

"Never! Sarah, you are part of me—the missing part." His eyes had welled, too. "And I vow I am nothing like that monster. He has hurt you beyond belief. My heart is rent in two that you would ever doubt my love." He swallowed and squeezed her shoulders. "Please, allow me to help with the vases and your wicked father. Then if you find you cannot abide my presence, I shall set you free. I refuse to cause you pain." Tears wet his cheeks.

His sincerity both warmed her heart and crushed her soul. *My broken parts are breaking him, as well.* She walked back into his embrace and let his arms enfold her. She could feel his heart thudding against her own as he rubbed her back. Shivers of desire raced through her, but she refused to give into them. Not yet.

After a long moment, he released her. "Shall we design a plan, then?"

She nodded, though she longed to remain in his arms.

"I have been wracking my brain. Having you by my side gives me confidence that we can puzzle this out." He took her hand and led her to the parlor.

Even though the day was sunny, thick velvet curtains cloaking the large window made the room dim. Nostalgia once again enveloped her.

Seated on the sofa, she was entranced by the chocolate brown of his eyes and the firm set of his jaw.

"I'll start from the beginning." He placed a warm hand on hers.

After hearing a detailed explanation of his confrontation with Father, Sarah didn't know what to think or what Father's next move would be. He'd not give up. "I'm grateful we got your mother out of here." She shuddered. If anything happened to Gwenillen at the hands of her wretched father, she'd be devastated. "But now we must somehow get the vases back to Mother, bring your mum home, and—" She shrugged. "How?"

He exhaled. "Precisely. How? I will need time to come up with a metal disc and construct a new machine—"

An idea struck Sarah. She clutched his hand. "You won't need to do that. We must get to Finley's estate as soon as possible. Can you arrange that?"

Hudson narrowed his eyes, his face creased. "I believe I can. We shall leave tonight and be there by morning. But why?"

"I will explain. Can we leave now?" She wanted to get this over. The sooner the better.

"I fear there are still thugs out, hoping to send me to the afterlife."

She grimaced. "Still? I'm sorry, Hudson. You have risked your life in so many ways."

He placed a finger on her lips. "As a result of my own foolish actions." He moved his finger and replaced it with a sweet kiss. "So, why are we going to the country?"

She fought the urge to return and deepen the kiss, determined to keep a level head. "You and Joshua came here with the vest and Father's car, did you not?"

"Yes. Josh told me the vest—being surrounded by the metal vehicle—transformed the entire car into a time-traveling machine. It was spectacular." His eyes sparkled.

"We left the car in Finley's carriage house, imagining you might like to play around with it." She curved her lips to a sly smile.

"Ha!" Hudson beamed.

"We can return home the same way. Can you program the machine?"

"I read both your father's and Joshua's notes. I remember every word."

"Of course you do! I've never met another person with a memory like yours."

"You called it something before…photographic?"

"Yes. That's one word for it. I call it genius." She hugged him. Her heart raced with anticipation for their plan, and his nearness. "If you can program it to land near Christopher's home in Denver, we won't encounter Father. We can leave the vases hidden there, then drive to my home."

Hudson lifted a finger. "Instead of hiding the vases, I have a better idea. Let's get rid of them once and for all. Then your father might stop tormenting your family—and mine."

Sarah listened to Hudson's plan with rapt attention. He truly was a genius. Now to execute it. She bit her lip, thinking of everything that could go wrong. "We will need more chemicals to pull it off. Josh only gave me enough to come here and go back, along with strict instructions to do just that."

"Did someone say chemicals?" A man bounded into the parlor, a wide smile on his face. "You must be the beautiful Sarah Somerset." He bowed. "Edward Falwell at your service."

Sarah sucked in a breath. "Falwell, as in the Duke of Chamberlain?"

"Not yet, but soon, I fear." He chuckled. His gaze moved to Hudson. "I have brought the chemicals you requested." He placed a bundle on the parlor table. An odor rose up from its wrappings. So familiar—like Father's lab.

"Your timing is impeccable, Eddie." Hudson analyzed each tiny bottle. "They are all here. I have just a few more favors to beg of you. But I promise you will enjoy the benefit of the biggest one."

"Please, do not keep me in suspense."

"Ride with us to Finley's estate in the country, then see Mother safely home."

"And you will remain in the country? I thought you wished to return the estate to Finley the Fool."

"No, Sarah and I will depart from there to a different destination. And not only shall I return Finley's estate, but I'll drive his coach there, as well. You but need to inform him when all is finished, and we are safely away. I shall also leave keys and titles to

302

the other estates, thus removing the price on my head, and restoring my family's good name."

Eddie grunted. "They do not deserve it, but I shall do it. And my reward for all this…?"

"Will be beyond anything you can imagine." Hudson clapped Eddie on the back. "Thank you, my friend."

Sarah watched the men, enjoying their camaraderie. She didn't know Eddie, but what she witnessed today—a brotherhood of sorts—warmed her.

Eddie lowered his voice, but still spoke loudly enough for Sarah to hear. "Everything you said about Sarah is true. I've not seen such beauty in all of London. 'Tis worth giving up strong drinks and gambling." He nudged Hudson with his elbow, then turned to Sarah and winked.

Heat traveled up her neck in record time. Should she reply? … No. She had no response. But could Eddie be right? Had Hudson given up liquor and gambling for her? She wished with all her heart it was so.

Chapter Forty-Two

Hudson lit a carriage lamp and used the time on the road to program the vest—adding new destinations, according to Joshua's notes. Eddie sat opposite him, pelting him with questions about the fabled time travel. Sarah shared Hudson's bench, but nestled beneath his coat next to the window, her eyes fixed on the road.

She flinched and sat up straight.

"What is it, love?"

Fear, stark and vivid, glittered in her eyes. "Someone is out there."

"Highwaymen?" Hudson and Eddie said in unison.

Hudson laid the vest aside and scooted closer to Sarah and the window. "What did you see?"

"I have sensed someone in the distance since we left London." She pointed at the window. "But I thought I'd just imagined it. Then the foliage cleared, and I saw him."

"Him?"

"My father." She raised quivering fingers to her mouth. "He is following us, Hudson. He thinks you'll lead him to the vases."

A flicker of apprehension coursed through Hudson. He'd rather it be highway robbers. Reaching beneath the seat, he pulled out Benjamin's gun. "Trade me places, love." Once settled near the window, he kept a steady eye on the landscape. Trees and shrubs once again obstructed his view.

Sarah sidled next to him, also watching the road. He pulled her close, hoping to calm her. The vegetation thinned just enough to see a dark shadowed horseman in the distance, moving parallel to them.

"There!" She thrust her finger out. "Did you see him through the trees?"

Hudson nodded. "Are you certain it is your father? We are a great distance apart."

"I'd know him anywhere. And that round shadow hanging from the horse has to be the disc." Her body tensed.

"We can take him, Hud." Eddie held out his pistol.

"Not from so far away. And should we shoot and find it wasn't Benjamin"—he shook his head—"we cannot risk it."

"Then we must outpace him," said Eddie. "Though difficult in a coach."

"No." Sarah turned toward Eddie. "That will tip Father off. He'll know we've spotted him."

"Sarah's right. We must keep our pace but alter our plans once we arrive at the estate. Eddie, I'm afraid my parting gift of driving you in the horseless carriage will have to wait. I need you to create a diversion. Just don't get shot doing so. I shall move the vases to the car and make our escape."

Eddie frowned.

"Even more important, you must protect Mum. For now, Sarah, you keep watching him, and I shall finish programming the vest. I am close." The scheme was amateur at best. He needed to ensure the safety of Sarah, Mother, and the vases—Eddie's pistol would be no match to Benjamin's twenty-first century weapons, should it come to that.

Sarah shivered. "What about our stop for fresh horses? If Father approaches us, he might discover the vases in the storage compartment."

Too many variables made every move a gamble. Hudson thought he'd given up gambling. "He will need a fresh horse, as well. Since he turned the townhouse upside-down once and came up empty, I suspect he believes I am traveling toward the vases and not with them." He kept his voice firm, confident for Sarah's sake. "Benjamin will keep out of sight." Hudson hoped. He dropped the vest and gave Sarah a brief hug. He wished to hold her longer—soothe her fears but learning something so foreign to him required concentration.

As they rolled up to the staging post, Sarah clutched his arm, but her eyes never moved from the window. "Where is he?"

"I assume he stopped and is waiting for us to get back on the trail. He doesn't wish to be discovered until we arrive at our destination. Close the curtain just in case. I'll tell the driver to keep an eye out." He tapped on the driver's window, catching him before he went in search of fresh horses.

The driver gave a nod after Hudson's explanation. And before long they were back on the road.

Sarah sat on the edge of her seat—anxiety rolling off her in waves. "Perhaps…maybe it wasn't Father. He's not patient enough to wait until we arrive at the estate."

"Perhaps not," Hudson agreed aloud but knew Benjamin would not confront them until they'd led him to their destination—and the vases. Traveling by night from his townhouse no doubt rose Benjamin's suspicions. The foul man had been watching his home—the quick and disturbing notion caused Hudson to inwardly cringe. Had Benjamin seen Sarah? Hudson gathered her in his arms. "It will be all right, love," he whispered. He must protect her.

Sarah's breathing slowed after a time. "Do you suppose it is safe to open the curtain yet?"

Hudson nodded. Hesitant to release her, he felt cold the instant she left his arms.

She resumed her lookout.

Hudson finished programming the vest. "Sarah—"

She startled, then let out a breath.

He showed her the dials. "This one will get us very near Sotheby's"—he pointed to another setting—"this one will bring us back to Finley's estate." He swallowed down rising emotion. "This one will take you back to your home in Colorado."

"But you shall be with me—"

"I am explaining it in the event something goes awry. Do you still speak French?"

She shivered, then nodded and directed her concentration to the vest.

"When we arrive, slide into the driver's seat of the car while I transfer the cargo. You'll need to drive as soon as we land in twenty-first century Paris. Is the vehicle in view, or in the carriage house?"

"Hidden in the carriage house," she said.

"Paris!" Eddie wrinkled his brow and made a scoffing noise. "How will you get across the sea? Does your horseless carriage fly, too?"

"As a matter of fact, it does," said Sarah.

Eddie shook his head.

After studying the controls, Sarah turned back to the window. "If Father's out there, he's staying hidden... Perhaps I was mistaken."

"Perhaps, but we shall stick to the plan, regardless." Hudson was glad Sarah had calmed. He wouldn't tell her Benjamin had moved to his side of the trail. "Close your eyes. Get some sleep. I shall wake you when we arrive."

He hoped she would snuggle up to him to sleep, but she shut her curtain and curled against the side of the coach. Gazing at her long, silky hair, falling over her shoulders, his heart quivered. For the first time in his life, he was genuinely frightened—not just for their present condition, but for their future. If by some miracle they pulled through the situation unscathed and she found him unworthy—not the man for her—*I shan't bear it.*

Another hour passed. Hudson and Eddie kept a vigilant watch, each subtly motioning when they caught sight of movement. "Have you a diversion in place?" Hudson whispered.

Eddie nodded.

"And your leg—does it still ail you?" So much had happened since he and Eddie had been kidnapped, Hudson nearly forgot Eddie had been wounded.

"'Tis fine, Hud."

Chapter Forty-Three

Sarah closed her eyes, but knowing Father could appear at any time kept her nerves on high alert. Still, the gentle swaying of the carriage soothed her. She'd rather Hudson soothe her, but she must keep her wits about her, unsure of her feelings toward him. She loved him, but love might not be enough.

Something hit her window. She jerked to attention. The horses whinnied and bucked, throwing the carriage to and fro. "Hudson!" She reached for him, but he was gone. Icy fear twisted around her heart as she gripped the seat. The coach jostled violently until shuddering to a halt. Sheer black fright swept through her. Where was Hudson? Where was Eddie? The window crashed open, and coal-black eyes penetrated hers.

Father!

He sneered as he reached in, yanking her hair. "Why are you here, brat? You have never done anything but get in my way!"

She screamed and clawed at him, but her efforts were futile.

He dragged her through the broken window, glass slicing through her. Pain and fear tore at her, then she saw Hudson and shrieked. He lay lifeless on the ground below, blood oozing into the cracked dirt road. "What have you done? He can't be—"

"Dead?" Father snarled. "Why do you assume he—an earl—would ever wish to marry someone as weak, disrespectful, and insignificant as you? The boy and his harridan mother have caused me nothing but grief!"

She wrenched loose from Father's grip and knelt next to Hudson's body. Laying her head on his chest, she sobbed. "Hudson. You cannot leave me—"

"Sarah! Sarah!" Someone gripped her waist.

"Get away!" She struggled against him but couldn't break free.

"Love, 'tis I, Hudson. Wake up!"

"Hud—Hudson?" Father vanished. The carriage still moved steadily. "What…"

"You had a nightmare, love." He pulled her into his arms.

Her resistance crumbled, and a flood of emotion spilled from her quivering body. She wept, clutching him to her.

He held her tight. "I've got you." He kissed her head and massaged warmth into her chilled limbs.

She buried her head in his chest. Hudson was alive. More tears flowed, wetting his shirt. She never wished to release him.

After soaking in his strength for several long moments, her breathing steadied and her pulse slowed. She peered up at Hudson. His dark eyes brimmed with tenderness and passion. "I—I'm all right now."

He wiped away her tears. "We are getting close to the estate. Are you well enough?"

She jerked to attention. Had she a choice? Well or unwell, they must carry out the plan. She nodded. "I can do this, Hudson."

He squeezed her hand. "Prepare to run. Wear the vest, and if the plan gets muddled, disappear."

She narrowed her eyes. "But I was mistaken. Father isn't following—"

"No, you weren't." Hudson motioned to his window. "He just moved to my side of the road."

She gasped, and the icy fear returned. "Why didn't you tell me?"

"Would it have helped?"

She looked down and twisted her fingers together. "I suppose not."

He slid the vest over her shoulders and caressed her arms. "Vow you will vanish if Benjamin gets near you."

"I cannot leave if you are in trouble."

"Vow you will."

She hesitated, then gave a slight nod. The notion of Father hurting him smarted.

"I love you, Sarah." He slid his lips over hers, sealing her vow with a fiery kiss. Then he held her face in his hands and studied it.

Electricity sparked through her veins. She hadn't anticipated a kiss—especially a kiss so passionate. And all with Eddie watching. Now Hudson looked at her as if he were photographing her with his eyes. A sudden dread inched up her spine. Hudson feared he'd never see her again.

He broke the trance and tapped on the window three times. The carriage picked up its pace exponentially. As did Sarah's heart.

"Ready?" he asked as the coach wobbled nearly out of control.

No. But she'd have to be—thanks to her father. She nodded.

"Eddie, you're the distraction. Exit first. I'll go next, then hand Sarah down. Don't wait for the carriage to fully stop."

Eddied pulled his hat low on his head and leapt out the door.

Hudson paused for a moment. Watching through a slit in the curtains. "There's Benjamin. Get down, Sarah!"

Sarah's world spun, her adrenaline racing. She ducked out of sight and prayed.

Without warning, Hudson lifted her out. "Run," he whispered.

She didn't look back—just sprinted for the car, slid in, and watched through the window. Father had fallen for the trick and rode after Eddie, disappearing behind the estate. Hudson pulled out the vases at a frantic pace. She should have stayed to help him. It would have gone twice as fast.

Wait… Sarah gasped. Father had changed direction and now rode back within view, aiming for Hudson. She sprang from the car.

Hudson shoved the vases behind a stack of hay and now glared at her. His voice low and demanding, "I said disappear!"

She slipped into the carriage house.

"Where are they, Drake?" Father dismounted, his arm was in a sling and he sported a black eye. Good.

"Will you never give up? I do not know where the vases are."

Father scowled. "You know something. The vases are here." He jabbed a finger toward the manor.

312

"They're hidden in your chum's estate—that man who tried to divert my attention. You wish to keep the wealth—my wealth. You shan't do it." Without waiting for a response, he mounted his horse and fled back to the home.

"Wherever you are, Sarah, leave. You vowed to disappear." His voice cracked. He pushed out a loud breath, then raced toward the estate.

Shaking, she hid the vases in the back of the Escalade. Now what? Her heart wrenched at the thought of Father hurting Hudson. But if she removed the problem—the vases...

Chapter Forty-Four

As Hudson approached the estate, he paused at Benjamin's abandoned horse and freed the traveling disc from its lashings. Men's sharp voices hit his ears the minute he blasted through the doors of the manor. He skidded to a halt when he heard a crack in the air.

Eddie's pistol or Benjamin's weapon?

He crept through the hall leading to the drawing room where the voices originated, then reached for his gun. Empty. His coat pocket had nothing in it. Ah, he'd left it in the carriage. He exhaled a deep breath. Still, he must go in. His gut churned with anxiety and frustration as he neared the room.

"Now, where are they?" Benjamin's voice boomed.

"Why do you assume I know where your relics are?" Mother. Her voice firm, but uncharacteristically high spoke volumes. And where was Eddie?

Keeping out of sight, he craned to see inside the room. His chest tightened, and his gut knotted at the scene. Eddie lay motionless on the ground, blood pooling around his head, his pistol still in his limp fingers. Benjamin's back was to Hudson, his gun trained on Mother, who sat on a seat, hands clutching the chair's arms.

"Lower your gun," Hudson said from the entry.

Benjamin jerked toward the door. "You have no leverage, boy. Beatrice and your family have led me on a wild hunt. Tell me where the vases are."

"Ahh, but I do have leverage. I have this." Hudson lifted the disc he'd hidden behind him to his front like a shield. "I assume your bullets cannot penetrate the metal. And if I damage the modern controls, it shan't be easily repaired in this century. Drop your gun and I shall give you your device, and Mother will divulge the location of the vases. She is the only person who knows."

Benjamin sneered. "You fool. If you damage my creation, I shall shoot her." He turned his aim back to Mother. "Where are the vases?"

Hudson's heart quivered. "If you kill her, then no one shall know the location of your…er…Beatrice's vases." He examined the disc. "Let me see, I read your notes, and I believe if I sever—"

Benjamin jerked back to Hudson, his eyes wide. "Unhand my device!"

"Not until you drop the gun," said Mother as she walked toward Benjamin, Eddie's pistol in her trembling hands.

Benjamin's eyes darted from mother to son, then he lunged for the disc, dropping his gun and knocking Hudson to the ground. He grappled for the control tower and pressed a button.

"Oh no. You are not escaping again." Hudson jumped onto the disc and clung to the tower, swerving to avoid Benjamin's wild swings.

Sarah appeared in the doorway.

Hudson nearly let go. "W—why are you here?"

The vibrations began shaking the house.

"Go home Sarah."

Her face crumpled. "But—"

"Please. Go home now!" Hudson and Benjamin disappeared.

Chapter Forty-Five

"No!" Sarah stood, stunned. What had happened? Where had they gone? Something clanked on the marble floor. She looked up to see Gwenillen quivering, her eyes vacant. A pistol at her feet.

"I could not kill him—not with Hudson in the way," said Gwenillen.

Sarah rushed to her side. "What can I do?" She clutched the dear lady's arm.

"Just help me to a chair. See to Eddie."

Sarah helped Gwenillen get seated then turned her attention to Eddie. Blood pooled around his head. She gasped. "Is he dead?"

"I thought so, but he nudged my foot with the pistol when Benjamin turned his back."

"Eddie!" Sarah knelt at his side, examining him for a wound. Blood stained the floor around him. So much blood.

Eddie moaned, then his eyes slanted open to slits. "Am I dead? If I am not, then shoot me. My head—"

"Your head." Sarah's gaze landed on the side of Eddie's blood-matted hair. "You were shot." She peered closer. "But 'tis only a graze." Relief washed over her.

"It cannot simply be grazed. It hurts like the devil himself plunged his pitchfork into my skull." He groaned again.

"We must bandage him." She stood.

Gwenillen caught her hand. "Sarah, I am feeling stronger and can take care of Eddie. You must do as Hudson said. Go home."

"Hudson! But where is he? Did Father say nothing of their destination?" She couldn't help Hudson if she didn't know where they'd gone.

Gwenillen shook her head. "But Hudson did. He said to *go home*."

Sarah winced at the blatant rejection. She'd brought nothing but trouble to the Drakes—no wonder they wished her away. Fine. If they wanted her to leave, she would. Turning the dial in the vest pocket, she vanished into oblivion.

Joshua had made remarkable improvements to the vest. It not only purred instead of shook like an earthquake, it also moved through time much faster.

Before she had a chance to feel too sorry for herself for being sent away, she landed in the lab in her Pueblo home—exactly where the Drakes wished her away to. Without even shedding the vest, she headed to the ladder, her heart heavy. She'd gone to help Hudson but had only caused more problems. *I led Father straight to Gwenillen's hiding place. And now he has Hudson.*

The room shook. Sarah clutched the ladder as the disc clattered to the ground carrying both Hudson and Father. She gasped.

Father shoved Hudson out of his way in his haste to reach his arsenal cabinet. "You will tell me where the vases are or else—"

"Father!" Sarah diverted his attention from the cabinet. *Think, think, think.*

He snapped his head around and scowled.

"Please, Father." She swallowed. "Papa, what did I do to make you stop loving me?"

Father winced.

"You once bounced me on your knee—called me your little bluebell." Emotion burned in her heart. She'd only wished to distract him—get Hudson out of harm's way, but now she realized the question had plagued her for years.

For a split second, his face softened, and his eyes took on a flicker of remorse. "I…you…blue—" Shaking himself, he huffed, and the demonic glint returned to his eyes. "Get out of my way, girl."

"Stop right there, Father."

Sarah jerked her head up to the voice coming through the open trapdoor. Christopher had his gun trained on Father. Mother and Ari hovered behind him.

Father smirked. "How many times must you threaten me before you realize I am unstoppable?" He mounted the disc once more and tweaked the control knob then glanced at the chemical vial. Empty. Father was trapped.

Christopher cocked his gun. "As much as I do not wish to kill my own father, to protect my family, I will."

Father's eyes darted around until landing on the vial Sarah had filled the night she had determined to find Hudson on her own. The lethal mixture. He fastened it onto the device and looked up with an evil sneer. "*I am unstoppable.*" He drew out every word, then reached toward the transport button.

Oh, no! "Go!" Sarah shouted. "Everyone, get outside!"

Hudson furrowed his brow. "But—"

"Go! Go now!" Sarah screamed.

He shut his mouth and helped her up the ladder, following close behind.

"Don't stop! Get to a car! We need to get away from here!" Sarah waved her arms, panic growing in her chest.

"My car is unlocked," Christopher yelled, dashing from the porch and throwing open the door to his police cruiser parked in the mansion's driveway. "Everyone, get in!"

The group crowded in huffing and panting.

Christopher started the car, backed out, and slammed his foot on the accelerator. He exhaled a few heavy breaths. "Sarah, why are we—"

Loud rumbles built until a crack of light lit the night air and a deafening explosion made Sarah's heart lurch. She looked through the back window. "That's why."

Chapter Forty-Six

On their way down the dirt road, Hudson shielded his eyes against the brilliant lights of an oncoming car. "Who is that?"

"It must be Josh." Christopher pushed something, making the headlights of their vehicle flash bright, then dim, then bright again.

The approaching car stopped.

Joshua's eyes were fixed on the house in flames. "What happened?" he shouted. "Is Mum all right?" His face was etched with concern.

"Yes, she's with us."

"Has anyone called the fire department?"

Sarah tensed.

Christopher picked up his radio, paused, then replaced it. "Too many questions we cannot answer. But the fire department should know so they can prevent a brush fire." He scratched his head. "Go to the hotel just off the highway. We can place an anonymous call from there."

Josh nodded, then made a turn and followed behind them.

Sarah sat between Beatrice and Hudson. Her body trembled. Hudson clutched her hand, but she pulled it away.

"It will be all right. You did nothing wrong," he tried to reassure.

"I could have warned him the vial was filled with a lethal mixture." Her voice was flat—devoid of emotion.

"Would he have listened?" Even Hudson knew the answer to that.

"Listened?" Sarah repeated. She shook her head. "No. He never listened to me. In fact, had I warned him, he would have accused me of trying to trick him… And I didn't even think to check upstairs. It all happened so fast. If Josh had been up there…"

"But he wasn't."

Christopher parked the car, and Sarah leapt out. Hudson helped Beatrice into the hotel while keeping an eye on Sarah. Her ashen face worried him.

Christopher caught up and clutched Beatrice's arm. "See to Sarah."

Hudson rushed to her side. "Are you all right, love?" he said in a hushed tone. He blinked against the bright overhead lights where they waited to check in.

"I don't know. I've never seen anyone blow up." She twisted her hands and studied the ground. "Well, I guess I didn't see it—" She paused. "But, Hudson, why did you tell me to go ho—" She flinched and then faced him. "Wait, did you know Father was coming here?"

Ah, that was why she had recoiled at his touch. "Yes. I saw where the disc's dial was set." He peered into her eyes. "Forgive me if I was terse. I was only trying to tell you where we were headed."

She closed her eyes, folded her arms, and leaned against him. Her body still jittery next to his. "So you don't wish to be rid of me?"

He barked a laugh. "Never. And while I've not witnessed anyone blow up, I have seen people die—'tis always traumatizing, even when it is expected."

"Your father?"

"Yes… And you." He swallowed. "Sarah, you were not dead, but the doctor had all but declared you so." He blinked back rising emotion. "Mother said the only thing that would bring you back would be a kiss."

"That's why you kissed me? Just like a fairy tale." Her face broke into a timid smile.

"Yes. Fairy tale come to life. Only I am no prince."

"I beg to differ." She placed her soft hand in his. "You are my prince."

Sarah's words soothed his soul. He hoped she really meant it. He debated his next question but must ask. "Love, did you wait in the carriage house, or did you make it to Paris?"

Her face scrunched. "Are you being earnest? You made me *vow* to disappear. It was the hardest thing I've ever done—leaving you with my father—but I knew I must sell the vases. And aside from nearly landing on a few Parisians, then fumbling over the French language I haven't practiced in years, everything went as planned."

He pulled her into his arms. "Bravo, Sarah."

Arianna turned to the group. "We're all checked in."

Josh had arrived without Hudson noticing. "Is anyone going to tell me what happened?"

"We'll explain upstairs." Christopher led them to a set of those familiar silver doors. "I'll meet you up there. Suites 301 and 303—they're adjoining. I must find Mother something warm to drink. She's freezing—likely in shock."

As ashen as Sarah was, Beatrice Somerset was even more pale. Hudson's heart lurched. The poor woman had just lost her husband and her home. "I'm so sorry, Mrs. Somerset. This must be horrific for you."

She mumbled something, but Hudson couldn't understand, her tone so low.

Arianna narrowed her eyes. "Maybe she needs a hospital."

"No!" Beatrice finally said something coherent. "I shan't be put in the hospital again." She reached for the panel of numbered buttons. "My house just went up in flames. Where will we live? I do not even know if Benjamin insured it. Oh, Benjamin—"

"It's going to be okay, Mum." Sarah looked into her eyes. "I promise."

"Can someone tell me what happened?" said Josh again. "How did the fire start?"

No one said anything until they were settled in the family room connecting the suites. Then Sarah spoke up. "It's a long story, but after being stalked through England by Father, we—Hudson, Father, and I— eventually all ended up in the lab."

Christopher returned with a cup of hot chocolate for Beatrice. Her hands wrapped around it, and she let out a breath, her shoulders relaxing. Arianna covered her with a blanket.

Sarah continued the story, skipping from one detail to another in a jumbled fashion, completely forgetting about her time in Paris.

"Then Christopher was at the trapdoor with a revolver."

When she got to the part about Benjamin's vial being empty, Joshua's eyes widened. "Wait. Don't tell me…did he use the chemicals you mixed up back when you tried to time-travel, Sarah? The ones I said would blow up the entire house?"

"Yes. We barely got out in time."

"We are so blessed." Beatrice began to weep. "Just think of how much we could have lost but didn't. We are all still here."

"Mrs. Somerset, I know it isn't my place to ask," Hudson said, "but will you be all right without Mr. Somerset?"

The room fell quiet, all eyes on Beatrice.

"Hudson, Benjamin was a kind man when you knew him, but after listening to Sarah recount what he did to you, I'm certain you've discovered he had become greedy and depraved. I'm just happy he didn't get his hands on those vases."

Anxiety snaked through Hudson's nerves. Sarah had sold the vases without consulting with Beatrice. They were likely dear to her.

"I didn't even like the old things," she continued, "but they were worth something. And since Benjamin's drinking had increased, and he gambled away everything we owned, I knew I must hide them. Hudson, forgive me for putting your mother in such a dangerous situation. That was unfair of me."

He allowed himself to breathe again. "I believe you did the right thing, Mrs. Somerset." He steepled his fingers. "You really didn't like the vases?"

"I inherited them from my grandparents. They had been around my whole life. I suppose I should have appreciated them more than I did, but they just seemed old. My mother showed me the markings on the bottom when she and Father gave them to me and told me of their significance. Those vases are worth hundreds of dollars. But that's not so much for Benjamin. I cannot imagine why he wanted them so badly."

Christopher spoke up, "They weren't just worth hundreds, but thousands or more—if you can find the right buyer. I saw an article where someone found one in their attic and sold it for over a million dollars."

Beatrice sucked in a breath. "I could use that money right now. But how would I find a buyer for something like that?" She raised her hands, then dropped them.

"Mother," Sarah said in a gentle tone, "I did something I probably should have asked you about first."

"Did you get married?" Mrs. Somerset lit up.

"No." Sarah laughed. "With Hudson's help, I…sold your vases."

The room echoed with gasps.

"I'm sorry if we overstepped, but Father was torturing everyone in both centuries, and when Hudson found them, we decided to sell them and wire the money to your account."

"Sarah, are you serious?" Christopher's brows drew down. Hudson saw the protective older brother in him, but also the brother who took care of business for his mother and siblings. "How did you know where to sell them, and how much were you able to get?"

"It was a team effort. Father let a few things slip to Hudson, and I know a bit about modern banks, since I manage the family's finances. The money is in Mother's account accruing interest as we speak."

"How much?" Christopher and Josh both asked.

"Nine—"

"Nine thousand? They were worth far more than that!" Josh thumped a fist on his leg.

Sarah gave Josh a hard stare. "Nine…ty…million."

Silence.

Mrs. Somerset began to sway. Hudson jumped up to steady her.

"Ninety million?" Josh's eyes bulged.

Sarah nodded. "Mother can buy any house she wants now. But I suspect, even more than the money, Father was after this." She stretched out an old, curled piece of parchment.

Christopher narrowed his eyes. "Is that—it's proof of pedigree. Father's great grandfather was a duke. Do you supposed Father stored the document in a vase in the event he could travel back in time, covertly murder his great grandfather, and claim his dukedom?"

With a hand still clutching Hudson's arm, Beatrice peered down at the parchment. "Wealth, power, and a title. He would have finally acquired everything he'd longed for—at the expense of everything most precious." She turned watery eyes on her children.

A hush fell over the room.

Christopher shook his head. "We'll not have to worry about him now." He pulled Beatrice into his arms for a hug, then faced Sarah and Hudson. "Nicely done, you two." He smiled. "Mother, you are likely the wealthiest woman in Pueblo."

Beatrice swooned, but Christopher caught her.

Chapter Forty-Seven

Conversations carried on late into the night. Despite losing everything with the explosion of their house, Sarah was surprised that the biggest topic of discussion was her management of the vases' sales. No one shed so much as a tear for the demise of Father.

The following morning, Christopher burst through the door and dropped a sack of bagels on the kitchenette table in the hotel room. "I'm back with food."

"What else are you holding?" Sarah squinted at his closed fist.

"I drove out to the explosion site." He opened his hand, and a charred ring fell on the table.

"Benjamin's onyx ring." Mother turned it over in her hand.

"I found nothing else of Father's." Christopher wrapped an arm around Mother.

"He couldn't have survived the explosion"— Sarah's heart hammered—"could he?"

"Not a chance," said Josh, plucking a bagel from the bag.

"Mother, you can move anywhere in the world now. I suppose you can even return to the nineteenth century. Where do you wish to live?" asked Christopher.

Mother's face creased in concentration. "Are my gardens still intact?"

Of course…her gardens brought her solace.

Christopher nodded. "They are. Would you like to rebuild?"

"I know the location of our home was not convenient to, well, anything, but I have grown to love our spot in the outskirts of Pueblo." She looked at Josh, then Sarah. "Is that all right with you two?"

Sarah nodded. She'd also developed a fondness for the obscure location of their home.

"I suppose." Josh wasn't as enthusiastic. "As long as I can design the lab—above ground." He snorted. "I'm just glad Sarah saved my newest vest from the explosion, so I won't have to start completely from scratch."

"More than anything, I wish to be near my new grandchild, so another century is out of the question." Mother extended a hand to Ari, who was seated next to her. "Arianna, are you available to decorate another home?" A twinkle entered Mother's eye. "I hear the owner is a very wealthy, yet eccentric woman who will only be satisfied with her favorite designer. But she pays top dollar."

Laughter rumbled through the room.

Ari's smile spread from ear to ear as she took her mother-in-law's hand. "There's nothing I would love more. Of course, it means I'd have to work on location." She turned to Christopher. "How would you feel about transferring back to the Pueblo Police Department? I have a feeling this project is going to be a lengthy one. We'll even have our baby here."

Christopher put an arm around his wife. "I think that could be arranged. I've missed Joe and the other officers at the precinct." He kissed Ari's forehead.

The room buzzed as everyone chatted about plans for the future.

Everyone but Sarah and Hudson.

The elation over selling the vases and ridding the world of Father had dwindled, and Sarah wondered how she and Hudson could move forward. She longed to be with her family. But Hudson's life—his earldom and family—remained long ago and far away.

"Are you well, love?" Hudson's voice was low, meant for only Sarah's ears. He pulled her close on the sofa they shared.

She realized she was the only person in the room not enjoying the conversation, so uncertain was her future. Forcing her lips into what she hoped resembled a sincere smile, she wove her arm through his. "Yes, I'm fine—" Her voice hitched, and she could no longer disguise her fears. "Sorry, Hudson. I'm not fine. Everyone is making plans for a new beginning, but—"

"You do not know where you fit in the plan?"

She blinked back tears. "Yes."

"Perhaps I can help." Hudson let go of her arm, leaving a cold emptiness in its absence. He rose, walked to the center of the room, and cleared his throat. "May I have your attention for a moment?"

The room became still, all eyes on Hudson.

"I realize now is not the most romantic time for this; however, we are with the people Sarah most loves and cherishes. I have grown to love and cherish you, as well." He tugged something from his pocket. A pouch. "Before leaving the country for London, my mother— once I convinced her time travel was real—gave me two things: some sound advice about choosing to marry for love, and this ring. She said its color suited perfectly the woman I love perfectly." He held up a the most exquisite sapphire and diamond ring Sarah had ever seen. He dropped to one knee. "Sarah Somerset, will you marry me?"

Tears poured down Sarah's cheeks as she rushed to Hudson. "Yes…but—"

"And, I have another proposal." He turned to Mother. "Mrs. Somerset, would you find it acceptable to have neighbors, who might seem a bit stuffy—since they insist on employing a butler and a cook—but who will also be wonderful friends for you?"

Sarah sucked in a breath. "What are you saying?"

"Mother has agreed to come to this century, as long as she can live near her dearest friend. She also wishes to bring Cook and Jameson, if they're willing, and perhaps her lady's maid. Sarah, if you agree to marry me, we can build a home next to your mother's, plus a dower house for mine." He winced. "Is that too much?"

Sarah sprang into his arms. "You would do that for me? You are giving up so much!" She wept openly, caring little about her audience. She couldn't contain the happiness bursting from her heart if she tried.

Hudson pulled back and placed both hands on her cheeks. "Sarah, my raven-haired, azure-eyed beauty, I would do *anything* for you." He wiped her tears away, then pressed his lips against hers, leaving her mouth burning.

When they ended the kiss, she looked around the quiet room, embarrassed at the intimacy of the moment. All eyes were wet—even Joshua's. She smiled, realizing her family—the people with whom she'd been through so much—were perfect to share this moment with. She rose on tiptoes and kissed Hudson again.

Whoops and cheering ensued. Mother wrapped her arms around them both. "I've longed for a friend—for Gwenillen—ever since we moved from the country estate. Hudson, I cannot thank you enough."

Hudson bent and kissed Mother's cheek. "My mum feels the same way about you."

****

A few weeks later, Sarah entered Henry Carver's residence, she called out to him, not wishing to startle the dear man.

"I'm in my study, Sarah."

She walked in holding a wedding invitation and a sack. After opening the sack, she put a small bottle on his desk beside him. "I happened on a doctor, of sorts, who claimed to have a cure for Multiple Sclerosis. Are you willing to take a few pills?" Sarah wouldn't mention a cure for MS had been found by the twenty-second century. Time travel must remain a secret even from her dear friend Henry. But since his topple down the stairs months ago, his condition had severely declined. Sarah had become proficient at mixing chemicals, and now owning a custom-made vest, visited the future to purchase the product.

"It never hurts to try." Henry took the bag and popped a pill without question. "And what's this?" His eyes roved over the wedding invitation she'd placed beside the pills. "You're getting married? That's wonderful, Sarah. I've always regretted not marrying."

"If you need a date to the wedding, my mother will be there." She couldn't keep a smile from spreading across her face.

"Your mother is grace and beauty combined. But she won't want to be seen with someone in a wheelchair. I can scarcely lift an arm—good for nothing."

"I don't believe you know Mother as well as you think. She adores you, Henry. And if you take those pills every day for a week, who knows? You might not need that chair."

Henry scoffed. "I've tried every 'miracle cure' money can buy. But for you, I will do it. Thank you, Sarah. Now, since I can no longer read even the largest print, shall we start with our book, or would you rather play the piano for me this morning?"

Sarah smiled and picked up the book.

Chapter Forty-Eight

Hudson returned for the last time from the nineteenth century just days before the wedding. He plunked the list he'd written—what seemed an eternity ago—on the kitchen table. A savory aroma filled the air. He glanced at the clock. Nearly six. Soon the kitchen would fill with hungry Somersets and a squalling newborn baby girl with hair as dark Sarah's. Everyone lodged at Christopher and Arianna's newly-purchased home while their new house was being constructed.

Sarah appeared at his side. "Were you successful? Did you complete your list?" She wrapped her arms around his waist and peered up at him. Her intense blue eyes sparkled. Those azure orbs continued to mesmerize him whenever he gazed into them.

Lifting her weightless off her feet, he twirled her around. "Yes. My bill passed. I stepped down from my seat in Parliament and finished all other matters of business. I have also returned every estate, landau, even the gold pocket-watches I won. No one wishes to kill me now—I hope." He chuckled. "All Londoners—apart from Eddie—think I have gone abroad and am now residing on the continent."

"Hudson, you are giving up far too much for me." She looked up at him with glistening eyes.

"Do you not see, love, that without you, my life has no meaning. I have never cared for title or position. I was born into privilege; I didn't earn it. The only thing I ever desired was a life with you. And if giving up a few things from my cosseted existence is all I must do to make it so, so be it." He showered kisses around her lips and along her neck, then crushing her to him, he pressed his mouth to hers. His heart raced as sparks ignited a fire in his veins. Sarah and only Sarah stirred such passion in him.

****

Sarah said she thought two days would fly by, but to Hudson they moved so slowly, he considered taking another trip to the nineteenth century just to literally watch time fly.

When the day finally arrived, Arianna and Beatrice kept Sarah hidden from him until the ceremony. Hudson ached to see her.

He waited not so patiently for his future bride to enter the beautifully bedecked—thanks to Arianna—church, and walk down the aisle. Standing next to him were his groomsmen, Christopher, Joshua, and Eddie—happily, he'd brought his best chum to the twenty-first century for his wedding. Mother sat next to Beatrice, both radiant.

"All rise," the priest said. Organ music began to hum.

The chapel doors opened, and the most beautiful woman he'd ever seen strolled in, accompanied by her employer, Henry Carver, who now walked with a spring in his step—thanks to his bride. Unbidden tears gathered in Hudson's eyes. How he loved Sarah.

So smitten by her graceful beauty was Hudson that he failed to listen to what the pastor was saying until he received a gentle nudge from Eddie.

"Your vows? You said you were writing your own vows?" The priest looked at him expectantly.

"Oh, yes." His head still flustered, he motioned to Sarah. "Can she go first?"

"If it is all right with the bride." The pastor tipped his head toward Sarah.

Sarah nodded.

Arianna handed her a slip of paper.

"Hudson—" Her hands trembled, and she dropped them to her sides, hiding them in the folds of her gown.

They had kept the list of congregants short, yet she was still fearful. Reaching out, he clasped her hand. He prayed she'd remember her vows so she wouldn't need the paper. His heart reached out to her.

"I lost you once, and it nearly killed me." Her voice was so quiet, only Hudson could hear, which was fine with him.

He gave her hand a gentle squeeze and captured her eyes with his.

She cleared her throat and started over. "Hudson"—her voice rang loud and clear now—"I lost you once, and it nearly killed me. I set you free, and you returned. From now to eternity, I vow to hold you close to my heart and never let you go again. You are bold; you are courageous; you are kind-hearted and so much more. Where I end, you begin. You are every good thing that I am not. Together we are whole. I choose you."

Sniffles rose from the small congregation.

Lud, he should have gone first. Now not only was he dazzled by her appearance, but by her uniquely beautiful spirit. Oh, how he loved this woman.

The pastor nodded to him. "Go ahead when you're ready.

Hudson didn't need a paper to remember his vows—he'd written them in his heart. The words ordered themselves into a poem. The sort he'd once read to Sarah. He flicked a tear away.

"An anguished being, bent with grief,
A blackened heart tormenting,
Pulled from gloom, offered relief—
Redeemed, though undeserving.
But grace and beauty cleansed his stains—
Healed the wicked wretch,
Through purity and love unfeigned
His soul from hell did fetch.
Today a vow to treasure her—
A promise for all time,
How easily is love imbued
On she whose heart's divine."

Sarah buried her face in her hands, shoulders shaking. After a moment, she composed herself, then gazed into Hudson's eyes. "That was beautiful, Hudson…Lord Byron?" she asked in a hushed tone.

Hudson lifted his lips to a soft smile and shook his head. "Lord Alleyne."

A word about the author…

Jeanie Davis is an Arizona wife, mother, and grandmother who loves peach ice cream, shopping, a clean house…oh, and chocolate, of course. She has traveled extensively—from Fiji to Africa and Europe to Costa Rica—but prefers being at home creating new adventures on her computer.

Her four daughters have left her nest empty, but they return often with grandchildren who bring real fun and adventure to her life. And thankfully, Jeanie's awesome husband, Rick, loves to join in on all her escapades.

A good romance will always capture her attention; add suspense or historical ties, and she's totally hooked. She's the author of an historical fiction novel, As Ever Yours, based on the lives of her grandparents, a children's Christmas book, I Don't Know Why I Did It, a Christmas romance novella, Chrissy's Catch, and finally The Somerset Series, which includes novels: Time Twist, Time Trap, and Time Torn. Find her at: jeaniedavisauthor.com.

Jeanie is passionate about writing, and she always has a new story to delve into or an older one to revise. She began by writing poetry and music, which she still enjoys, but now novels have moved to the forefront of her avocational pursuits.

When she's not spoiling her grandchildren, Jeanie spends her free time curled up with a good book or typing away on her most recent mystery, adventure or romance.

www.ingramcontent.com/pod-product-compliance
Lightning Source LLC
Chambersburg PA
CBHW050034030726
47506CB00001B/263